since
you've
been
gone

Books by Tari Faris

RESTORING HERITAGE

You Belong with Me
Until I Met You
Since You've Been Gone

RESTORING ❋ HERITAGE · 3

since you've been gone

TARI FARIS

Revell

a division of Baker Publishing Group
Grand Rapids, Michigan

© 2021 by Tari Faris

Published by Revell
a division of Baker Publishing Group
PO Box 6287, Grand Rapids, MI 49516-6287
www.revellbooks.com

Printed in the United States of America

Library of Congress Cataloging-in-Publication Data
Names: Faris, Tari, 1975– author.
Title: Since you've been gone / Tari Faris.
Other titles: Since you have been gone
Description: Grand Rapids, Michigan : Revell, a division of Baker Publishing Group,
    [2021] | Series: Restoring Heritage ; #3
Identifiers: LCCN 2021003850 | ISBN 9780800736491 (paperback) | ISBN
    9780800740559 (casebound) | ISBN 9781493431809 (ebook)
Subjects: GSAFD: Love stories.
Classification: LCC PS3606.A689 S56 2021 | DDC 813/.6—dc23
LC record available at https://lccn.loc.gov/2021003850

Published in association with Books & Such Literary Management, 52 Mission Circle, Suite 122, PMB 170, Santa Rosa, CA 95409-5370, www.booksandsuch.com.

21 22 23 24 25 26 27   7 6 5 4 3 2 1

To my sisters,
Wendy and Janette.

Thank you for all you do to support my dream. Writing Leah and Caroline's friendship was easy because you two have made sisterhood such a blessing. Love you!

one

One person can fail only so many times. That was her theory, so after two big failures in her life, a win had to be around the next corner for Leah Williams. If only her twin saw it the same way.

Leah's heels clicked their way up the wide sidewalk toward the office building of Heritage Fruits as her sister's protests rambled through the phone.

"Yes, Caroline, I'm going to this meeting, and I'm moving back home. I've already started airing out Grandma and Grandpa's farmhouse." And boy, did that house need airing out. Caroline and Grant had taken care of the most necessary maintenance, but the inside had been left pretty much untouched. At least they'd covered the furniture with sheets, but she'd still be dusting for days.

"I just think meeting with Dale is a bad idea." Caroline's words were slow and articulated.

Her sister meant well, and Leah appreciated the concern. After all, she had heard all about the problems George Kensington's difficult brother had caused after taking over when George and his wife passed away a few years ago. But she'd had a verbal agreement with George. Dale had to honor it.

Leah squinted against the May sun as she checked her reflection in the glass door. Pinching the phone to her ear with her shoulder, she shuffled her briefcase to the other hand and retucked her white long-sleeve blouse into the back of her navy pencil skirt. The briefcase completed her "don't mess with me, I know what I'm doing" look, even if it was empty except for her sketchbook and her latest vintage-inspired dress that she'd stayed up until three in the morning sewing. She'd never been that great with numbers, but she'd spent most of the past two months poring over designs that would sell.

"Why do you even want to do this?" Caroline's words had taken on that big-sister tone. Somehow being four minutes older made Caroline believe she had all the answers. No doubt she'd be blocking Leah's path this minute if she wasn't eight months pregnant and on bed rest. "You were the one who convinced me we should close the WIFI to begin with."

"I know, but things are different now."

She'd closed the WIFI with hopes of capturing a little bit of the passion and fulfillment her brother David had written about in his letters. But being a missionary hadn't filled that nagging desire for purpose she'd been seeking for so long. She'd just been living someone else's life—again. But that wasn't something she fully understood herself, let alone would be able to explain in a two-minute phone conversation with Caroline.

"I gotta go. I'll call you later." Leah popped the briefcase open just far enough to shove her phone inside. She smoothed a wisp of her red hair back toward the severe bun that pinched her scalp. But binding her wild curls would be a small price to pay if it meant she'd walk away with a renewed lease.

She entered the building, crossed the lobby, and punched the elevator button. When the doors opened, she stepped inside, selected the fourth floor, and drew a slow, calming breath as the elevator rose to the top.

It opened to a quiet lobby and the twelve-foot ceilings that she remembered. But the sleek, frosted-glass reception desk and no-nonsense young blonde who sat behind it—not so much. What had happened to George's secretary with her warm smile and candy bowl full of peppermints?

"May I help you?" The woman looked up from her computer, but her fingers stayed positioned over the keyboard.

The bowl of peppermints had been replaced with a brass nameplate that read MARCY GOLD and the warm smile replaced with tight red lips. Leah searched her mind for any Golds she might have gone to school with but came up empty. So much for making a friendly connection.

"I have a meeting with Mr. Kensington."

"He's running late. Take a seat." Marcy pointed at one of the stiff-looking couches and returned to her typing.

Leah turned that way but paused at a large portrait of George Kensington and his family mounted on one wall. Below it was a brass plaque with the birth and death dates of George and his wife. By the look of their son Jon, it had to have been taken when he was in high school. Back when he was still all arms and legs. She almost didn't recognize the wide-shouldered point guard who now played for Valencia Basket in the EuroLeague. Her hometown of Heritage, Michigan, had practically had a parade the day one of their very own signed to play professional basketball—even if it was for a European team in a city most of them couldn't find on a map.

She and Jon had been enemies since high school, but everything had changed six months ago. Now she didn't know what they were, but seeing his portrait hanging there definitely stirred emotions she wasn't ready to deal with.

Six Months Ago

Leah couldn't be stranded in Detroit—not today. Every airline had already canceled all evening flights with the forecast of the incoming storm, but the lady at the counter had been optimistic that her flight would get out of Detroit before the worst of the blizzard hit. Then again, her flight to Grand Rapids was supposed to have boarded twenty minutes ago. She had only six hours until Olivia and Nate's wedding, and she couldn't miss it. She was a bridesmaid. Why did it have to be this year that they got a snowstorm for Thanksgiving?

"Do you think we're going to be stuck here?" A deep baritone spoke from behind Leah.

"I hope not, I need to get—" She turned toward the man but found herself looking at a wide shoulder. She tilted her head back and paused. Jonathan George Kensington the Third. The crown prince of Heritage if there'd ever been one, and her archenemy in high school. "Home."

Leah spun back to the monitor as she tugged her knitted hat down a little farther. How dare he be in her airport? Maybe it was a little egocentric to think of Detroit Metropolitan as hers, but the great thing about millions of people flying in and out of it every year was that she shouldn't have to see anyone she knew.

Especially *him* looking all good after hours of travel. His brown hair was a little long for her tastes, but his mess of curls worked. The week-old scruff only added to his good looks. Her red mop looked more like the result of an unfortunate incident with a light socket, and her face needed a good exfoliant.

He took another step closer. "Nice bag."

Leah's face flamed as she tugged her backpack to her front and out of his view. No doubt it didn't measure up to his designer standards. But she'd made it from pieces of her grandfather's old corduroys. It was one of the few items of his that she'd kept. There was no price she could put on it, but she wouldn't expect trust-fund Jon to understand that. "Do I know you?"

Maybe it was a little immature, but she was in no mood for a reunion. She glanced at the departures board as another flight's status flipped to canceled.

Jon nudged her shoulder with his. "I know you know who I am, Leah."

Typical Jon, thinking he'd be unforgettable. Never mind that he was right. She jerked her head back toward him. His large brown eyes, outlined by dark lashes she'd kill for, held a touch of amusement. She'd try to deny remembering him, but that smirk said he was onto her. "It's Caroline, actually. And you're Jonny, right?"

He released a deep laugh as he crossed his arms over his wide chest. "Nice try. Unlike most of our old high school, I could always tell you and your twin apart. Think we should go try to get a rental car while we can?"

"We? There's no *we*. I barely remember you."

She hadn't seen the guy in three years and suddenly he was acting like they were long-lost friends, but they had never been friends to begin with. Maybe they had many of the same friends, but that was not the same thing.

"You're obviously waiting for the flight to Grand Rapids. I figured since we're both trying to get to Heritage that . . ." He held up his hand and took a step back. "You know what? Never mind. Good seeing you, Leah." He walked away but stopped to nudge a teenage girl's leg. "Abby, let's go."

Abby stood and followed her brother without taking her eyes off her phone.

Leah hadn't seen Abigail Kensington in probably four years. Long gone was the brace-faced, bubbly eighth grader who wore gummy bracelets and headbands. This girl wore heavy black eyeliner, and her hair was dyed to match. Her red leather coat and threadbare jeans probably cost more than Leah's entire wardrobe.

Leah turned back as more flights changed their status to canceled. *Please oh please, Lord, I've got to get home.* God seemed to have forgotten about her, but maybe today would finally be her day for an answered prayer.

Another flight flipped to canceled. Or maybe not.

The snow continued to fall, thick now as it reached for the ground. Then the last remaining flight—her flight—changed its status to canceled. She sighed, her bag drooping from her shoulder as a bitter taste filled her mouth. Now what? Maybe she should call Caroline. But there was nothing her sister could do all the way from Heritage.

Any hope of renting a car disappeared a few minutes later as she descended the escalator. Every line that led to a car rental company had to be over fifty people long.

As soon as she stepped off the escalator, Jon blocked her path with a set of keys dangling from one finger and that annoying smirk back in place. "Need a ride?"

She nodded and waited for the inevitable "I told you so," but he just picked up her suitcase with his free hand and motioned for her to follow.

Thirty minutes later, they navigated the icy highway at a whopping thirty miles an hour. She still had five hours until the wedding, which would've been no problem on a day with clear roads, but at this rate she'd be rushing down the aisle with her carry-on still on her shoulder.

"Where are you flying home from?" Jon kept his eyes fixed on the road as he gripped the wheel with both hands.

"Costa Rica."

"Vacation?"

"No. Do you remember my brother, David? He's about three years older than you."

"Vaguely."

"He lives there and runs a program for missionary kids. I moved down there two years ago to help him out. I'm just flying home for Olivia's wedding." She dropped her phone in her purse and dialed up the temperature on her heated seat. At first she'd rolled her eyes at Jon throwing his family's money around by choosing the luxury SUV. But she had to admit, she'd feel a lot less comfortable on these icy roads in one of those compacts they'd passed in the lot.

"I was planning on going to that too. Maybe you could save me a dance."

Was it her imagination, or did he sound a little unsure for the first time? Either way, it was best to avoid answering. "I have to fly back to Costa Rica first thing Monday."

"As in the day after tomorrow?"

"I didn't really have the time to take this trip, but I couldn't miss another one of my best friends' weddings. I already missed Hannah's."

"But that was to be expected, right?"

Her head whipped toward him. "Why? Because I might have stood up and made a scene when Nate asked if anyone objected? I may have had an adolescent crush on Luke, but I think I could've handled it even without you pointing out that I wasn't good enough for him. Again."

"What? I never said that." He started to angle his head toward her but seemed to catch himself, and his attention snapped back to the road, where the falling snow obscured anything beyond fifty feet.

"You're right." Leah positioned one of the vents to point at her. "I believe your words were, 'I can't believe you think you have a chance with Luke. He's a gray T-shirt kind of guy and you're not a gray T-shirt kind of girl. You need to wake up and see what's in front of you.' Aka, 'You dress funny and you're not good enough for my friend.'"

"Whoa—that's harsh." Abby spoke up from the back seat. They were the first words she'd spoken all night. Leah had almost forgotten she was there.

"That's *not* what I meant." He glared at his sister in the rearview mirror. "Weren't you listening to music?"

"Your fighting was louder than my music. Think you two could keep it down?" She shoved her earbuds back in.

His hands gripped the wheel a little tighter now. "What happened to barely remembering me?"

"Fine. I have one memory." Or at least one that stood out more than the rest. She'd only let Caroline invite Jon to their anti-Valentine's party because she knew he'd drag Luke along. Jon had been right about one thing that night—Luke only had eyes for Hannah. And why not? Hannah was tall, gorgeous, built like a ballerina, and she dressed . . . normal. Leah, on the other hand, was of average height and average build, had wild, curly red hair, and dressed like a secondhand store had erupted on her.

Jon sighed and offered Leah a fake smile if she'd ever seen one. "How are you enjoying Costa Rica?"

"It's fine."

"Fine? I've seen a lot of pictures of Costa Rica, and *fine* is

14

not the word I'd use to describe it." The dim light outside high-lighted his profile. If it weren't for his slightly crooked nose, he probably could have a successful career as a model. But he was a little too rough for that.

"The place is amazing. The kids are amazing." She wasn't really in the mood to hash this out right now. She shrugged and prayed he'd take the hint.

"If you don't like Costa Rica, you should come visit me in Europe. There's the café in Paris that—"

"No way." She winced at the volume of her words. "Sorry. I just am not going to Europe and I'll never go to Paris."

He waited for her to go on, but he could wait the rest of the drive to Heritage, because that wasn't going to happen.

"Okay, no *Paree*. Then what don't you like about Costa Rica?"

So they were back to this. As much as she didn't want to get into it, this was an easier conversation than Paris. "I thought I'd enjoy my job in Costa Rica more. I miss Heritage. I miss running the WIFI."

"That was such a weird name for a store."

"When my grandfather opened the store in 1952, WIFI was catchy. You have to admit the abbreviation for Want It Find It made more sense before the digital age."

"True. But if you miss running it, maybe you should come home and open it again. Do you still own the building?"

"Only half of it. You own the other half."

"What?"

"Well, your dad did. Or technically, Heritage Fruits did." Jon seemed to grip the steering wheel a little bit tighter at her words, but he didn't comment, so she went on. "He didn't buy us out because he wanted us to have the option to reopen if we changed our minds. We didn't have anything in writing, but there was a verbal agreement that we could come back and reopen within five years."

"Then change your mind and go back. It's only been what, three years?"

"It didn't make it the first time." She ran her fingers across the soft leather seat. "Why do you think I could make it this time?"

"You just need a solid business model. And maybe a new name. What model did you go with last time? Or did Caroline handle that?"

"Caroline handled the books. I made other decisions—inventory, marketing, and customer service. I used the Leah model."

"What's that?"

"If you act like you know what you're doing, people believe you. It worked most of the time."

"A fake-it-till-you-make-it approach." His full laugh filled the SUV. "My uncle would love that. With him handling the company right now, you'd have to convince him to let you reopen."

"I wouldn't tell him that was the plan. I'd say, 'The WIFI was a central piece of this community that George believed in, and I believe in it too. If you give me a chance, I'll show you how dynamic it can be again.'"

"Perfect."

"Really?"

"No." He gave a slight snicker, then schooled his features. "My dad was sentimental and he may have gone for it, but Uncle Dale's a bottom-line kind of guy. If you don't have the numbers and a solid plan to back it up, he'll laugh you out of the room."

"Hey, I'm not an idiot. I also ran a successful Etsy shop before I left for Costa Rica. Besides, I think you're wrong about your uncle. He isn't all about the bottom line—that's you, apparently. From what I heard, Dale's all about whatever makes Dale look good. I'll have to appeal to his ego. Maybe I'll say, 'The WIFI was a central piece of this community, and by re-opening it, you could help the town see you aren't the ogre they all think you are.'"

"Much better. But you still may want to give that business plan a little more thought . . . and find a better word for *ogre*."

Jon laughed again, and Leah found herself settling into the sound. They'd had their problems, but maybe this grown-up Jon was someone she could enjoy getting to know.

Present Day

She had to stop poking at that memory. She hadn't heard from Jon since that weekend. Of course, she hadn't reached out either. But what do you say after something like that? "I know you were forced to be nice to me because we were trapped by the snow, but do you still want to be friends"?

That sounded as dumb now as it had every time she'd typed that text out on her phone and then deleted it. It had been nothing. And since they hadn't been friends before, there was no reason for them to be friends now.

But that conversation with Jon had reignited Leah's vision for the WIFI. She'd spent the past few months mulling over the idea until it had re-formed into a new dream, then she'd crafted that dream into the portfolio that was now tucked in her briefcase. All she needed now was her building back. And that meant this meeting had to go well. If she couldn't make this work, God was bound to give up on her for good.

A buzz filled the air, and the secretary snatched up the phone. "Yes . . . I'll send her right in." She returned the phone to the cradle and motioned to the large set of doors. "Mr. Kensington will see you now." Not even the slightest hint of a smile.

Leah stood and smoothed her skirt. Dale might be a hard-nose, but like she had told Jon, Dale had an ego and respected confidence. He wouldn't know what hit him.

She stepped into the office and nearly tripped on her heels.

Not Dale. Jon. Jonathan George Kensington the Third. All six foot four of him. His hair—still a little long—was now tamed back, and his rebellious edge had been replaced with a clean shave, black suit, and steel-gray tie. Oh. My.

"Leah?" Jon stood and came around his desk. His brows pinched as he took in her appearance.

Bringing a practically empty briefcase suddenly seemed ridiculous. Everything seemed ridiculous. The tight bun. The pencil skirt with a white blouse. The four-inch heels that had now made her toes go numb. He knew this wasn't her. And after their conversation in the car, he'd see right through any attempt to fake it.

She resisted the urge to chuck the briefcase, the heels, and the hair tie back out the door and start over. "I was expecting your uncle."

"My uncle asked me to take this appointment for him, but he didn't give me any details."

"When did you get back from Europe?"

"A couple of months ago. I finished my contract and didn't re-sign. We decided it was better to have Abby finish out her senior year here."

"Is she graduating this weekend at Heritage High?"

"Walking. She still has a few classes to take this summer before she gets her diploma." He moved back behind his desk and motioned her to one of the open chairs.

She chose the one opposite his desk and laid the briefcase on her legs.

"Let me guess, you're here because you want to reopen the WIFI?" He settled into his chair, leaned over a legal pad, and clicked a pen a few times.

"You got me." Leah released a small laugh and tucked that stupid piece of hair behind her ear again.

"I assume you came up with a killer plan I can't turn down." He held out his hand as if waiting for her to pass over something. When she didn't move, he leaned back and laced his fingers across his stomach. "You still don't have a plan?"

She searched her mind for something, anything, to make it look like she'd prepared for this meeting. Which she had. But her mind seemed to have gone on vacation.

"Leah, I want to help you. I do. But you need to give more thought to this. Unless you have a proper business plan . . ."

She *had* given thought to this—how she could update the inventory. She'd incorporate her clothing designs into the WIFI and supplement the business profits with Etsy sales. She had already received four orders for a dress she had only designed and posted yesterday. She had her sketchbook that she'd slaved over to show her planned expansion of her clothing line. She was prepared to meet with Dale. But there was no way she was showing it to Jon, who had teased her about her homemade pieces for years. She couldn't count on him to recognize their value. Not that she expected Dale to see their value either. But his opinion didn't matter to her. And whether or not she wanted it to, Jon's opinion did.

"Show me what you have." He motioned to her briefcase. When she still didn't move, he raised his eyebrow again. "Did you bring an empty briefcase?"

"No. It's just not . . ." Leah stood and prayed that her now numb toes wouldn't fail her. "You know what, I don't need you making fun of me right now."

"Leah, sit down." His voice was gentle as his dark eyes softened and held her in place, just as they had that night six months ago, right before . . .

Leah shook the thought away. "No. I need to go. But I *will* prove to you I can do this."

She marched back out the double doors, jabbed the elevator button, and pulled her heels off while she waited for it to arrive. Not the most professional exit, but this wasn't business.

This was personal.

Over the last six months, Jon had repeatedly imagined what he would say and do differently if he ever ran into Leah again. Not one of those scenarios had ended with her stomping away from him in wobbly heels.

He jotted down a few notes for his uncle, then rested his head back against the chair. This room had become his office ten years ago, long before he was ready for this job. His first day working here, he hadn't been much more than a kid—ready to start his senior year of high school with a double dose of arrogance on the side. But he'd worked as hard as any full-time employee that summer, determined to prove to his father that he had what it took. Then things changed, and when graduation rolled around, he got a scholarship to play college ball, and the room had stayed empty.

It wasn't his dad's office, which was Jon's by rights, but the only one Uncle Dale said was currently available. It was fine though. Uncle Dale had stepped in to run Heritage Fruits to allow Jon to finish his contract in Spain. Not to mention be closer to Abby while she finished boarding school in London.

But in the past two and a half years, Uncle Dale had pretty much taken over and managed to get half the board in his pocket. If Jon wasn't careful, he'd lose the entire company to his uncle.

They couldn't push him out. After all, it was only an advisory board, but what if their advice was that he give up control of the company? His dad had left it to *him*. He wanted to honor his father's memory. But his father had trusted these men, and what if they believed the best way Jon could honor his father's memory was to hand someone else the reins? He had to prove to them that he could be who they needed him to be—he could be his father.

That was also why he'd been a little hard-nosed with Leah. All it would take was a failed project for his uncle to spin it to the board that Jon was unfit to lead. No matter how much he'd wanted to give in to Leah's green eyes, he had to keep this professional. With any luck, she'd come back with a plan he couldn't say no to, because he'd like nothing more than for her to stay in town.

Six months ago, he'd let his hopes rise that maybe he'd finally get that long-awaited date with Leah Williams. Time and weather had been fickle friends, but maybe now life would finally give them a chance to fix the past.

SIX MONTHS AGO

"This is getting bad. We may have to try again in the morning." Jon's shoulders ached from navigating the snow-covered road.

"I'll miss the wedding."

"I think your friends would prefer you safe rather than in a fancy pink dress."

"It's blue."

The lit-up letters that spelled *Hyatt* in the distance caught his attention. Jon checked his mirrors and took the exit. He pumped the brakes a few times and blinked hard. Where had the road gone? Darkness and white flakes ate up the road ahead. Then, as if by a miracle, two slight divots of track appeared in the snow.

"There's a hotel." He motioned to the sign.

"I can't afford a Hyatt." Leah's voice jumped an octave higher.

His pulse sped up as the lines of the road appeared and disappeared under the drifting snow. "I'll pay."

"No, you won't."

Was she really arguing about money right now? He was just trying to keep them alive. He turned into the Hyatt and breathed a sigh of relief as the car regained traction under the veranda and came to a stop. Valet parking had never looked so good.

"I'm going to get us rooms." He left the car running and slid out, but Leah followed him.

As they crossed the lobby, her fingers gripped his sleeve. "I can't afford this."

"Don't worry about it." He walked over to the check-in desk and ignored her wide-eyed stare at the high ceilings and chandeliers. "I need two rooms."

"One. I can get my own." Leah stood with her back stiff and her wallet out. Man, the girl was stubborn.

"We only have luxury suites left, sir." The clerk's fingers clicked across the keyboard.

"That's fine." Jon reached for his wallet and passed over his

ID and credit card as the man rattled off the price per night. Jon glanced back at Leah, who had gone three shades paler. If she thought this was bad, she should see the hotel prices in London.

"Here you go, sir." The clerk passed back his cards, then set a paper for him to sign on the counter.

"Thank you. Can you tell me the setup of the suite?"

"A common area and two rooms. One room has a king-size bed and the other has two queens. Each has a private bath." The man punched something into the computer. "How many keys do you need?"

"Three." Jon shot another glance at Leah and she didn't argue.

"I'll pay you back."

"For what? I'd be getting the same room whether you were here or not. You can take the two queens with Abby." He didn't need her money, and he didn't want her feeling indebted to him.

She followed him back to the car. "Fine. But I *will* pay for dinner."

"Nope. It will be room service—charged to the room." Jon popped open the trunk. He'd have to hide the room service prices too.

"You have to let me do something." She reached for her bag, but he snagged it first.

"Fine." He handed over the keys to the valet and headed toward the elevator. "Let's do dinner while you're in Heritage before you head back to Costa Rica."

"Just the two of us?" She seemed to be struggling to swallow. "Like a date?"

"Smooth, big brother, but I still think it's going to take more than that to make up for telling her she was a loser in high school." Abby huffed as she stepped into the elevator.

23

Jon followed his sister and yanked out one of her earbuds. "I never said that." He turned to Leah. "I never said that."

Leah seemed to be struggling to hold back a smile. At least one of them found this funny. "I don't know. You're a night-on-the-town kind of guy, and I'm more of a stay-in-and-order-pizza kind of girl."

Abby replaced her earbud and seemed to have upped the volume as she reabsorbed back into her phone.

Jon lowered his voice as he leaned toward Leah's ear. "I might surprise you, if you actually took the time to get to know me and stopped assuming you had me all figured out."

He'd said the words in an attempt to continue the light-hearted banter, but whether it was the closeness within the elevator or the way her soft cotton scent reached him, his voice dipped to a husky tone he didn't recognize.

And with the way her large green eyes blinked up at him, she'd felt the shift as well. A bell chimed as the doors to the elevator opened, breaking the spell that had held them in place.

She grabbed her roller bag from where he'd set it and hurried off the elevator. "I don't think I'll have time. I was only supposed to be in Heritage forty-eight hours. Even if we get out of here first thing tomorrow, I'll have one night before I have to head back. What room number is it?"

Jon bit back his disappointment, but what had he expected? She'd been dodging his efforts to get to know her for a decade. "831."

Leah followed the signs without looking back. Jon nudged Abby in the right direction.

After a quiet dinner and a hot shower to melt away the day's stress, Jon grabbed a root beer out of the mini fridge and stretched out on the couch. He picked up the remote and started scanning the channels for the Lakers–Celtics game.

The door creaked behind him, and Leah wandered out in pj's with cupcakes all over them. Her red hair lay damp around her face, each section already beginning to form a spiral curl. "Can't sleep?"

"Not adjusted to the time change. You?" He set his pop on the table and pointed to the fridge. "Want one?"

Leah shook her head and took a seat at one end of the couch, then tucked her feet up under her. "I've been stalking my friends on Instagram." She held up her phone to display a photo of Olivia dressed in white, surrounded by her bridesmaids in light blue matching dresses.

"Sorry. Did you get ahold of them?"

"I left a message with Nate when we arrived. Do you think we'll get to Heritage at a good time tomorrow?"

The wind still blew flurries in swirling patterns outside the window. "Not looking good. But I'll do my best to get you there. I'd hate for you to miss seeing Heritage completely."

Leah leaned back, fanning her curls across the back of the couch. "When was the last time you were home?"

"My parents' funeral."

"Why haven't you come back since?"

Leah was never one to hold back, was she? He muted the TV and laced his hands behind his head. "Never seemed the right time."

"Didn't your dad leave Heritage Fruits to you?"

He had, and Jon still didn't fully understand why. He'd never be the businessman his father was, and the last thing he wanted to do was drive his father's life work into the ground. "Abby's attending boarding school in London, and I'm all she has left.

25

Playing in the EuroLeague gives me the chance to see her more often. So as long as my contract keeps getting renewed, it doesn't make much sense to come home. Uncle Dale was happy to help, but someday I'll take it over when it's the right time."

"Why are you going home now?"

"Abby had a rough semester. Her teachers thought it'd be best to take a break back home between Thanksgiving and Christmas. I took a leave of absence, and here we are. I have to be back the first of the year, and so does she. But thanks for making me look bad in front of her earlier. You know she'll never let me live that down."

"Hey, they were your words." She laughed, and he found himself wishing for an infinite number of late-night talks with Leah in his future.

"Yes, I said it. But I didn't mean it like that." He rubbed his hands across his face. With Leah he'd always fumbled over his words like a junior high boy learning to play basketball with his new man-sized feet, and six years in Europe hadn't seemed to change that.

"How else could you mean it?"

Jon picked up a small pillow from the couch next to him and twisted it, then dropped it on the floor. "Okay, first, the gray-shirt comment wasn't an insult to you, it was an insult to Luke. I love the guy, but seriously, have you met anyone who dressed more drab? Second, I was saying Luke only had eyes for Hannah, but there were other guys interested in you. You needed to look around."

"Other guys interested?" Leah seemed to choke on the words. "Not likely."

He reached for his root beer and paused. "There *were* guys interested."

"Name one." She lifted her eyebrow and tilted her head as if to dare him. When he didn't immediately respond, she dropped her feet to the floor and stood. "Exactly."

"Me."

Leah dropped with a thud back on the couch. "Don't make fun of me."

"Are you kidding?" Jon leaned forward and ran his fingers through his hair. Soon she'd be headed back to Costa Rica and he'd be back to Spain, so what was the harm? He drew a deep breath. "Yes, Leah. I had a big crush on you in high school. That's what I was really saying that day. 'Hey, wake up and notice me, the guy who likes you.'"

"You were *always* teasing me." She stood again and moved toward her room. "Like you're probably teasing me now."

Jon closed the distance in two strides and touched her arm. She could easily have pulled away, but she paused without looking back. He leaned down closer to her ear. "I'm *not* teasing you now. And I wasn't teasing you then, I was just really bad at flirting."

Leah's conflicted green eyes finally turned up and stared at him. "You weren't bad at flirting. You flirted with every girl at school."

"I thought you barely remembered me."

When she didn't move, he leaned a fraction of an inch closer, and for one second he let himself believe that Leah could be his. But then the moment fractured as her eyes dimmed and she stepped back.

"Even if I did believe you, Costa Rica is pretty far from Spain, last I checked." She retreated toward her room, looked back once with a sad smile, then ducked inside.

Right. Time never seemed to be on their side, and Leah was determined never to fully trust him.

PRESENT DAY

They had been snowed in at the hotel the next day as well, but they never neared the subject of high school again. On Monday, Jon had driven her to the airport before heading to Heritage, and he hadn't seen or heard from her since. Not until she walked into his office today. But if he had his way, it wouldn't be the last time.

The alarm on his cell chimed, and Jon stood and scooped up his stack of papers, then exited his office.

"Hannah Taylor called again, asking about the bachelor auction in July." His secretary, Marcy, held up a piece of paper.

Jon hated the idea of the bachelor auction, but Hannah was married to his best friend. And there was no way he'd be able to tell his best friend's wife no. Not to mention it was for a good cause.

He read the note over, then handed it back. "Can you call her and tell her I'm in?"

Marcy blushed as she grabbed a pen and made a note. "The ladies of Heritage will be happy to hear that."

Jon ignored the comment as he made his way to the conference room. He yanked open the heavy door, drawing every eye in the room as the debate stuttered to a halt.

He checked his watch as he moved to his spot at the table and slipped into his chair. "I thought the meeting started at ten."

"We moved it up to nine thirty. But I knew you had another meeting." His uncle waved his hand. "You didn't miss much."

Didn't miss much? The more he hung around, the more he was beginning to realize that he'd missed a lot over the past two and a half years, and if he didn't watch his back, he might end up missing everything.

He opened the agenda and scanned it. Teft Road Building Project? There was nothing on Teft Road but a few houses, JJ's Food Mart, and . . . the building where Leah wanted to reopen the WIFI.

Leah and Caroline still owned a percentage of that building. The company would have to buy them out to do anything with the space. Not to mention the verbal agreement Leah said she'd had with his late father.

Jon placed his finger on the building project line. "What's this?"

His uncle's grin widened a bit before he seemed to catch himself. "We've been approached by a chain store that would like to bring their business to town. After their interest, I put out some feelers and have received several other offers. We"—he motioned to the whole board—"feel like this would be a great opportunity for you to show your strengths as a future leader of this company. We'd like you to be the point man on it."

No doubt Uncle Dale meant show his strength by pushing Leah out and strong-arming the town into a store they didn't want. His uncle had probably pushed the meeting with Leah to Jon's agenda because he knew what she wanted, and this way he'd make Jon the bad guy.

Everything in him wanted to fight this, but one look at the men's faces and it was clear that they agreed with Uncle Dale. Which meant this was a lose-lose situation.

If he brought in this chain, Leah would never forgive him. But if he failed the board, he might lose his father's company for good.

two

Leah refused to let a little thing like money stand in the way of her dream. She climbed out of her car and approached the back door of the WIFI. The old building stood frozen in time like the day she had left—untouched by the past two and a half years. The red brick, the green paint chipping off the wooden door, even the brass plate with the address *247* that tilted slightly to the left had simply paused, waiting for her. She only had to convince the powers that be, aka Jonathan Kensington, that this *was* her time.

But seriously, if she heard the words *business model* or *marketing analysis* one more time, she might throw her coffee at him.

Leah set her latte on the concrete window ledge like she'd done a hundred times before then dug around in her purse until she located the familiar brass key but then paused. The door was the same, but that lock was definitely new. How dare he change the locks on her. She still partly owned this space.

No matter. Shifting her purse to her other arm, she surveyed the area. Not that the alley behind the WIFI was a hangout spot, but she still didn't care for a witness of this less-than-graceful move.

Leah stared down at her vintage seventies jeans and graphic tee. She hated getting them dirty, but at least she hadn't worn her newly completed rag skirt that she'd made from scraps of chiffon.

With only Oliver the stray orange cat to witness her possible humiliation, Leah ran her hand down the peeling white windowpane until she found the familiar nail and popped it free. She gave the old window a slight shove, and it swung inward with a squeak.

Her grandfather had shown her this trick back in the day. Although that had been in case she ever locked herself out, not so she could commit a felony. Was breaking and entering a felony? Surely not, if she rightfully owned part of the business.

Leah tossed her purse inside and lifted herself onto the sill. She swung her legs in and jumped down, landing hard on the floor. *Oof.* She'd always left a chair here for that very reason.

Her chest tightened at the emptiness of Caroline's office. Leah had been readying for Costa Rica the last day Caroline had locked up. She'd had a list a mile long of things to do that day, but she'd also not wanted to see it like this.

Leah swallowed back the lump in her throat, reclaimed her coffee, and secured the window before heading down the hall toward the main room. She braced herself, but the emotional onslaught didn't come. She'd expected the place to feel like home, but it was just . . . empty.

The mug tree that had held enough cups for all their friends—gone. The photos of her grandfather by the cash register—gone. The antique cash register itself—gone. All that remained was the single counter and cobwebs in every corner. And . . . well, that was new. A black box with a red light blinked at her.

Leah squinted at it and stepped closer. "What do you suppose . . . ?"

She shrugged it off and pulled a small sketch pad from her purse. It might be empty now, but Leah was ready to breathe a little life back into the WIFI. Her pencil flew across the small paper in angled lines as she laid out her plans for the revived store. She'd start with updated tables and counters for the products. Maybe she could hang her clothes over there—

"This wasn't quite what I had in mind when I said come up with a new plan."

Jon stood at the end of the hall, inches inside the back door. He'd exchanged his gray tie for a black one and his black suit for a gray one, but it fit as well as the other suit as if it had been tailored to his wide shoulders. Of course, it had been. This was Jon.

"How did you—"

"We had a few break-ins last month, so I installed cameras that are linked to my cell phone." He joined her in the main room, then pointed up at the red light.

"Your cell phone?" She glanced again at the red light. Her face warmed at the idea that there might be a camera in the office as well that had captured her entrance. "Shouldn't it be to a security system or the police?"

"Aren't you glad it's not? They might be carting you off to jail right now." Jon rubbed his hand across his jaw as he failed to hide his amusement. "Maybe I should call the police though."

"I *do* own a portion of the building, and soon I'll have a business again right here."

Jon winced at her words, and the teasing faded from his expression.

"I *will* come up with a plan. It may take a while, but—"

"You don't have a while." Jon flipped his keys on his finger a few times, then shoved them in his pocket. "The board wants me to negotiate a deal with a major chain store to take over this whole block. From Second Street to Henderson Road. We still have to decide on which company, but—"

"What?" Leah slammed her coffee down on the one remaining counter. "I own part of this building, and I won't sell."

Jon leaned back against the front window and crossed his arms. "I read over the contract that my dad had with your grandfather years ago. There's a forced buyout clause if the WIFI is no longer financially viable." He motioned to the empty room. "I think this would qualify as not financially viable."

"You can't do that." Her voice cracked, and she dropped her chin as she cleared her throat. She refused to look weak in front of Jon. She lifted her gaze to meet his. "Your dad said—"

"My dad isn't here." Jon pushed away from the window. "I'm here, and I'm trying not to lose the respect of my entire board."

"So, that's it? You made your decision, and I get no say in it at all." She picked her coffee back up and spun the paper cup in her hand as she turned her back to him. "You'll write the check and be done with it."

"I don't want this any more than you do." His voice moved closer, and its gentle timbre eased beneath her defenses, picking at that corner of what-ifs and if-onlys.

When his hand landed on her shoulder, part of her wanted to accept the comfort he offered. Cry about the unfairness of this situation and that Dale Kensington would get his way once again. Cry about the fact that she'd let her idealism drain the life out of the WIFI over two years ago and, in the process, lost the legacy her grandfather had left her. And cry about the fact that everyone seemed to be thriving in life but her. Caroline was about to become a mother, all Leah's friends had moved forward in life, and Leah was back where she'd started.

Jon gently squeezed her shoulder, but Leah stepped away from his touch and blinked away the tears. She steeled herself against the warmth he offered. She wouldn't—couldn't—open her heart up like that to him. To anyone. Her parents' marriage had taught her that love had the power to destroy a person, and Leah had vowed never to depend on a man.

Jon sighed and shoved his hands in his pockets. "I wish it could be different, but I don't see another option."

"I've got an option for you." She spun toward him and hardened her expression. "It's your company, Jon. Tell your board no."

"Sure." All emotion faded from his face. "I'll tell them that I'm going to pass on a multimillion-dollar deal because some girl I've been infatuated with for years might someday have a plan to do something with her part of the building."

Leah gasped at his confession but didn't comment.

Jon opened his mouth to say something more but seemed to think better of it. He closed his mouth and worked his jaw before glancing back toward the window. "I don't like the idea of a chain store in the middle of Heritage either, but I don't see a way around it."

"This isn't how it was supposed to go." She didn't even try to hide the emotion in her voice this time.

Jon turned away with a shrug. "I can give you a week to come up with something for me to present to the board, but other than that, I have to move forward on this."

"A week?" She'd racked her brain for the past few months and had only gotten a concept. A week more wouldn't make any difference in developing a whole plan.

He walked toward the back door and held it open. "I'd be happy to help—"

"I think you've helped quite enough." She marched toward her car. Maybe she did need help, but not from Jon Kensington. Anyone but him.

Jon slid into his car and resisted the urge to slam the door. Leah was going to drive him crazy. He'd never met someone so stubborn—except for maybe his sister. If Leah didn't kill him off, trying to raise Abby might.

He rubbed his hand over his forehead and searched his brain for ideas of where his sister could be. He'd gotten a call from the school saying Abby had been marked absent about the time the alarms on his phone went off for the WIFI. He'd been so sure it was Abby that he hadn't even bothered checking the video feed. After all, the previous break-ins had been her and her friends cutting school.

The last person he'd expected to find was his favorite fiery redhead dressed like she belonged in *That '70s Show*, complete with those low jeans that hugged her hips and a T-shirt that made him believe seventies fashion had been underappreciated in recent years. She stood there sketching away like she hadn't a care in the world. He wasn't sure he'd ever seen her so relaxed— definitely not around him. The girl was vibrant and full of life. The more time he spent with her, the more he craved her color in his gray world.

He'd have watched her a little longer if he hadn't feared she'd look up and catch him. She already thought he was a jerk. No reason to add creeper to the list.

Which was why he shouldn't have moved so close. But when

her voice began to shake, it took all his strength not to promise her that he'd make things work. He wanted to. He just didn't see how.

Heritage Fruits had branched out into real estate with his father, but it had always been more about investing in the community than the bottom dollar. And maybe that should be his priority now, but with everything that had been going on since his father's death, Jon needed to make sure the factory was being taken care of—that the workers were being taken care of. He owed that much to the families of Heritage.

His phone chimed, and he glanced at it as a text popped up from Luke.

Saw Abby heading west on Heritage Road in case you wanted to know.

West? The few friends she did have lived east of Heritage.

Alone?

Yup.

What was west? Besides the lake, the only thing west was . . . His heart lurched as he recalled the date. May 28. *Dad's birthday.* She was going to the lighthouse.

Thanks. On it.

He started his car and pulled out on Henderson, then turned west on Heritage. He was too young to be parenting a teenager. He'd still been a teenager himself nine years ago.

Over the last six months, his sister had tested him every chance she got. If he said left, she went right. If he said hurry up, she slowed down. And if he said get to school, she decided to skip her final day. Maybe he should tell her to fail the two summer classes she had to take. Then she might just ace them out of spite.

But today was different. Today would've been their dad's fifty-fifth birthday.

He pulled into the parking lot and parked next to her red Mustang. He climbed out and followed the path through the dunes to the base of the lighthouse. His eyes swept the area a few times before he spotted her tucked up along the grass line, staring out at the water.

He slipped off his shoes and socks and loosened his tie before walking over to join her.

"I'm not going to school. It's the last day. It doesn't matter anyway." Her tone wasn't defiant, just resigned—broken.

That's what they both were. Broken. The second their parents had been hit by that drunk driver three years ago, their lives had shattered, with no one there to help them pick up the pieces. Their parents had always kept the family close. Now they survived from day to day. And judging by Abby's grades and the problems at Heritage Fruits, they weren't surviving very well.

Jon dropped down next to her and stretched out his legs as he leaned back on his hands. "Do you remember how Dad always burned the last pancake on Saturday mornings? He'd scrape the batter onto the skillet and then get so busy warming up the syrup and pulling out the orange juice that he'd burn it. Every week."

Abby released a half laugh, half sob. "Yes. But he'd always eat it. Even though half the time there were too many."

"'Can't let it go to waste.'" He dropped his voice to mimic his dad's tone.

"Wow, that sounded too much like him." Abby picked up

since you've been gone

a handful of sand and let it sift through her fingers. "Do you remember how he would sing hymns in the shower on Sunday mornings?"

"So loud."

"I could always hear him through the vents. He was so off-key, and Mom would giggle from the kitchen and tell me I should appreciate his joy."

"I hated getting woken up by his singing."

"Me too. But I would kill for it now." Abby leaned forward and hugged her knees as a full sob escaped from her chest. "I miss them so much."

Jon wrapped his arm around her, pulling her to his side. "Me too, Little-Bit."

When he loosened his hold, she stretched out her legs in the sand. "Are we going to make it? I know we're set with money. But you . . . me . . . our futures. Did this mess us up indefinitely? I mean, one of my friends was ragging on his mom for grounding him the other day, and I almost punched him. At least he has a mom. But then I was thinking. It's been three years. Isn't the grief supposed to go away at some point?"

"I don't think the grief ever goes away. It just looks different. I think we'll always miss Mom and Dad. I think when I get married someday, part of my heart will grieve that they aren't there to meet my wife. Hold their grandkids. Give me advice. But there will still be lots to find joy in."

"A wife? I haven't heard you talk like that before. That wouldn't have anything to do with the woman we gave a ride to at the airport, would it?" She nudged his shoulder with hers. "I saw her at Donny's the other day."

Jon rubbed his hands together as he sifted through his words. Maybe Leah's face had popped into his mind when he said the word *wife*, but he wasn't about to mention that. "Her name's Leah. And yes, she's back, but that doesn't mean—"

"Whatever. Keep lying to yourself all you want. I can tell—"

"She's *not* interested. She's been pretty clear about that."

"Oh, she's interested. I've seen the way she looks at you." She patted him on the shoulder. "Boys really are dense sometimes."

Jon couldn't ignore the slight thrill that ran through him at her words. Could Leah be interested? Even if she was, she definitely wanted him to believe she was not, so he had no idea what to do with that.

His phone buzzed and he pulled it out. Marcy had sent him his agenda for the day. He cringed when it popped up on his screen. He'd already missed two meetings. No doubt that was why she'd sent it.

How his dad had managed to raise two kids, run a successful business, and help a floundering business in the community was beyond him. Uncle Dale had made it clear that he believed he could run Heritage Fruits better than Jon, and by the looks in the board members' eyes, they agreed.

But running the company was about more than a job and a paycheck. His father had built it from the ground up, and it was Jon's legacy. It had taken a bit to get his feet under him, but now that he was rolling, he wasn't ready to hand over the reins without a fight.

"I don't want to go to graduation tomorrow." Abby's words broke into his thoughts.

"I know it'll be hard—"

"No. Mom and Dad won't be there. These aren't the friends I spent my high school years with. I don't even know most of them. I'm not even graduating. What's the point?"

Jon swallowed hard. Maybe bringing her back home hadn't

been the right move, but staying in England hadn't been an option either. "Okay. I'll let the school know."

She rested her head on his shoulder and stared across the never-ending lake. *"Are we going to make it?"* Her words echoed in his mind.

They'd survive, but would he be able to handle the business and keep what was left of their family from falling apart? Only time would tell. Today he'd keep moving forward.

⁂

Colby Marc had heard the term *rock bottom* his whole life. He just never figured he'd hit it. He flipped through headline after headline before slamming his laptop shut. Each site had its own spin, but they all said the same thing. The guy he'd trusted most in this world until two days ago was a thief. Now half the world thought he was a thief too.

Normally he'd turn to his music when things got bad, but Dawson West had taken that from him as well. Now every time he listened to their music—or played their music—he'd be haunted by Dawson's deception. His best friend had destroyed Colby's career to the point that even God couldn't save it, then he'd cut Colby out of his life without looking back.

His phone rang, and he glanced at the unknown number without reaching for it. No doubt another reporter looking for a quote or asking him if he was a part of the scam. He had been. He just hadn't known it. After all, he'd stood up there and encouraged people to give. But he'd thought Dawson had been giving that money to the kids in Haiti, not funding the band's tour.

The phone went silent but then rang again. They were persistent, he'd give them that. He reached for his phone to shut it off, but Nate's name flashed on the screen. He hadn't heard from his seminary roommate in a few months. But if there was anyone who understood rock bottom, it was Nate.

He accepted the call and pressed the phone to his ear. "I'm guessing you heard."

"How are you doing?"

"I'm avoiding phone calls and emails, and oh, did I mention that I can't go out my front door right now? A few newspeople have camped out across the street, ready to ask who paid for my car and who paid for my house. Someone even asked who paid for my shoes the other day." Colby sank back into the couch and propped his feet up on the coffee table. "They're Vans. Sure, not the cheapest shoes out there, but they aren't high-end."

"You need to get away."

"Where?" Colby pressed his thumb and forefinger into his eyes. "If I go home, they'll follow me to my parents'. I thought about tracking down my brother, Paxton, and hanging with him for a bit, but if I left the country, some would probably question who was paying for it."

"Come to Heritage. It's a quiet place—for the most part."

Colby pushed off the couch and wandered to the kitchen. He opened the fridge and stared at the contents, but nothing looked good.

"You could stay with me. Stay with us." Nate wasn't going to let it go.

He pulled out the grapefruit juice and poured himself a glass. "Dude. I can't stay with you. You guys are still newlyweds."

"Oh, so you did get my wedding invite." Nate's words were laced with humor. "I wondered."

Colby winced. "I was on tour. What did you give me, like a six-week warning? Who gets married that fast?"

"It was four weeks. And people who don't care about a big

41

ceremony or long engagements. Besides, it worked for both of our families to do it over Thanksgiving."

Colby had downed the glass in four gulps and pulled the bottle from the fridge to fill it up again. "I'm still not barging in on newlyweds."

"Newlyweds who live in a five-bedroom parsonage. Trust me, it'll be fine. Most of the rooms are on the second floor, but there's a room on the main floor. You can have that one if you want. Private bath. It's not the Ritz, but it has the comforts of home. And space to hide away for a bit. Just come. It'll do you some good."

Colby opened his mouth to say no, but his phone beeped with another call. When he glanced at the screen, it was another unknown number. Maybe getting away would be nice. "I'll think about it."

"Don't make me drive down to Nashville and get you, because I will."

"I've been trying to get you down here."

"Maybe I'll visit when you don't have media parked outside."

Colby cringed. "Fine. I'll come on two conditions. You have to let me pay you rent, and you don't tell anyone who I am."

Nate's laughter carried over the line. "Heritage may be small, but we don't live under a rock. People here know The Redeemed and your songs. They also know who Colby Marc is. You should've seen the girls fawning over your concert poster last year. That's a great smolder you have, by the way."

"Shut up." Colby couldn't keep the laughter from his voice. Nate had a way of doing that—helping you live in the moment and forget all that was carrying you down. "If people know, then—"

"They'll know who you are, but they're good about grace and

boundaries. Trust me. They've given me a lot of grace since I've been here. And as far as the rent, I'll make you a deal. We're in need of someone to lead worship. If you lead, that'll be your rent."

His chest tightened at the idea. He'd tried to pick up his guitar yesterday, but every chord he hit had hammered the ache deeper. "I can't sing right now, and I can't play—"

"The Redeemed's songs? No, Dawson took that from you for the time being. But God has gifted you with music. Dawson can't take that from you. There's more to music than what you've written. Maybe it's time to look at all those who have gone before you. Music has been your ministry for years, so maybe it's time to let other people's music minister to you."

Could he do that? Just looking at his guitar propped in the corner poked at the bruise inside him. But staying here, trapped in his darkness alone, wasn't helping anyone either.

Colby pinched his eyes shut as he rubbed his forehead. "I'll think about it."

"I'll pray you accept."

three

Jon had always tackled problems one way—put in the time. Miss a free throw, do one hundred shots outside of practice. When his shooting percentage tanked, he put in hours upon hours in the gym until that changed. But it didn't seem to matter how much time he put in with Abby or here at the company, he always felt off his game.

He checked the app on his phone to make sure Abby had arrived at the school for her summer class, then flipped through the three proposals for the Teft Road building that his uncle had left on his desk. The first company his uncle had been pushing him toward came with the largest check, but it would likely put Janie's new bakery and JJ's Food Mart out of business. Not to mention put a strain on the new greenhouse that Austin was starting on the edge of town.

He tossed the file aside and picked up the second choice. The money was significantly less and the business didn't seem to fit with the culture of Heritage. He dropped it next to the first.

The third was a lowball offer that he'd be a fool to entertain. He guessed that the company expected him to come back with a counteroffer, but he didn't have it in him. Not one of these sat right in his gut. It was as if he were Indiana Jones standing before the mixed letters on the floor of the temple, only his dad hadn't left a journal letting him know which step was safe and which step would be his demise.

A knock at the door echoed in the room, and he welcomed the distraction. He shut the file just before Marcy entered, carrying a cardboard box.

"Your uncle had me box up a few of your father's things when he took over his office." She set the box on the corner of his desk. "I found them in the storage area yesterday and thought you might like to look through them."

"Thank you, Marcy. You're the best."

The girl offered a soft smile as her cheeks pinked, then nodded and left. Maybe he needed to hire Mable again. He had no doubt that Marcy was more efficient with the computer, but he hadn't had to worry about Mable reading into everything he said.

Jon stood and walked around the desk. He pulled off the lid of the box, trying to ignore the extra pressure in his chest. He wasn't sure if it was the fact that his uncle had been so presumptuous with his father's things and company, or if it was because so many memories were tied up in this one small box.

He pulled out the flip calendar and ran his fingers over the words *#1 Dad* written on the base. It was an ugly thing, but his dad had kept it front and center on his desk ever since Jon had given it to him for Christmas in second grade. A lump rose in Jon's throat as the date it was on registered. December 30. The day they had been killed.

Next he pulled out a lighthouse made of popsicle sticks with Abby's childlike lettering on the bottom. Her mood had grown steadily darker since Friday at the beach. He'd let himself believe that they'd finally turned the corner in their relationship that day—but no. Their small bit of peace had morphed into more anger, more yelling, and more slammed doors over the Memorial Day weekend.

He set aside the lighthouse and lifted a frame. It was a photo of his dad with Leah's grandfather from about twenty-five years back. Maybe he should show it to Leah. Not that he'd see her anytime soon. She had managed to avoid him the two times they'd crossed paths over the weekend. At Donny's she'd pretended she hadn't seen him. But her ducking behind the produce in JJ's had sent a clear message. She wanted nothing to do with him.

He still wasn't fully aware of how she'd gotten inside the WIFI. He'd checked the cameras, but she'd simply appeared in the hallway coming from the back office.

A crack ran across the glass of the framed photo. Must have happened in the move. He popped off the back, discarded the frame, and lifted the photo. There was faint writing on the back. Jon held it under the light to get a closer look.

1995—Vern Foley and I partnering to keep the WIFI going. Not all investments are about the money. Some of them are about investing in someone's dream. That's the Kensington way.

Kensington way? Maybe the George Kensington way. Uncle Dale's way was more "Get on board with my plan or I'll run over you."

His phone buzzed and he picked it up. "Yes, Marcy?"

"Leah Williams is here to see you. I told her she needed to make an appointment, but she insists—"

"Send her in."

"Very well." Marcy's clipped words carried through the phone seconds before the door opened.

Leah strode toward his desk in a long, colorful skirt and white cotton top. At least she'd abandoned the stiff skirt and heels. Not that he hadn't appreciated the look, but it wasn't Leah. She was full of life and color and had a touch of wild, just like her hair.

Jon set the photo on the edge of the desk as he motioned to the empty chair and then returned to his spot behind the desk. "Have you come back with a plan?"

Leah lifted her chin, causing those unruly red curls to sway as she held out a folder. "Yes."

He took the folder and laid it on his desk. Page by page he flipped through product ideas and sketches for the interior. She'd even sketched a new storefront. There was a glaring absence of an example of her designs even though they were on the inventory list.

"This is quite an impressive proposal for a remodel." He closed the folder and handed it back. "But it's not a business plan. I can't take that to the board and have them consider it a good investment. I need numbers. A business plan, market research, funding options, financials. It usually takes two years to make a profit, so what will you do for income until then?"

"I don't know that." Leah stood and slammed her hand down on his desk. "All I know is that I believe I can make it work."

Jon leaned his elbows on his desk and rubbed the bridge of his nose. He wanted to help her. He did. And the idea had potential, but Leah didn't seem to care about the business side of things. Maybe if she had a business partner . . . like him.

His uncle Dale would *hate* that. His gaze landed on the photo of his father and Vern again. Then again, maybe he needed to stop trying to run the business like his uncle and try to run it like his dad. Business the Kensington way. His dad had been about helping the community more than the bottom line. If he wanted to honor his father, maybe he'd start by honoring the verbal commitment his father had once made to Leah and Caroline.

He laced his fingers together across the desk, then motioned to the seat. "Please sit down, Leah."

She hesitated, then sat down on the edge of the chair as if leaning back might show some weakness.

Jon lifted the photo from the corner of his desk and held it out. "Recognize this?"

Leah took the photo with care, her finger running gently over her grandfather's face. "My grandfather had it hung over the register. They took it when your dad invested in the WIFI. It was about to go under. I think it broke your dad's heart a little the day we decided to close it. That was why he wouldn't buy back our part of the building."

"I think you're right. I think my dad would want to save the WIFI now."

She dropped the photo on the desk. "That's why you need to give me a chance."

"But your grandfather realized something that you don't."

"And what's that?"

"He realized that he needed help. And although *that's* fascinating"—he motioned to the folder—"intriguing even, it isn't a business plan."

"But—"

Jon held up his hand. "I could help you with that. We could do this together."

"What? Why would you want to do that?"

"It feels right. I want to invest in your dream, and I think it's what my father would have done." He wanted to be the son his father would be proud of, and he didn't know of a better way than seeing through what his father had started. "I think it's a good dream for you and a good dream for Heritage."

"You want to be a silent partner?" Her eyes widened as a grin stretched across her face for the first time.

Oh, he was so tempted to give in to that smile and say yes. But a silent partner wasn't what she needed. A silent partner had been why the WIFI went under before. "I want to be the business side of the business partnership."

The hope melted from her expression as she stood again. "You want to take over?"

"No." Jon stood and moved around the desk, but now he towered over her. His six-four height could really be a disadvantage sometimes. He sat on the edge of the desk, which put him more at her eye level. "It will be *our* business. You'll be the creative side and I'll be the business side."

Her eyes narrowed as she hugged the file to her chest. "Because I'm illogical."

"That isn't what I said."

Leah shook her head. "I'm not letting a Kensington come in and take over my business like your uncle has tried to do with the rest of Heritage."

"I'm *not* my uncle, and I'm not trying to take over." Jon stood up straight. "Wake up, Leah. This is your only option."

"Then I'll find another option." Leah lifted her chin, but her head didn't even come to his shoulder.

She seemed to be waiting for him to back down, but he wasn't budging on this. "Then I guess we're done."

She offered a curt nod and walked out.

Didn't she get that a partnership was the only way? No, because she couldn't seem to get past her crazy need to do it all on her own. Past how much she'd hated him in high school. And past his name, which had once upon a time meant something good in this town.

So much for the Kensington way. He had to admit, Uncle Dale's way seemed a lot simpler.

<hr/>

It had been almost two years since Madison Westmore had driven out of this town with no plans of returning—ever—but here she was. Funny how something like death changed everything. She pulled through the four-way stop at Henderson and Richard and turned into the driveway. The siding was new. Her dad must have added that after she'd left.

Being across the street from the square, he'd probably wanted to keep up with the town's restoration. No doubt he stopped at the siding though. He was all about keeping up outside appearances. Because when the outside looks nice, no one questions what happens behind closed doors.

The darkness of her past settled over her, choking out her air and crawling along her skin. She drew in a deep breath and recited the one Bible verse she'd memorized. "'He heals the brokenhearted and binds up their wounds.' Psalm 147:3."

Deep breath in. Deep breath out. Ms. Alena at the crisis center had taught her that verse. It still sounded too good to be true, but if she had even a fraction of the faith that woman had, then maybe she'd have enough faith to get through this.

Madison climbed out of the car and pushed down the nausea. She slipped a lemon drop from her pocket and popped it into her mouth. She only had to sign the papers and then drive away.

Who knew what her next stop was? But it'd be better than being in Heritage. If she didn't need the money so bad, she'd tell her dad's lawyer she wanted nothing to do with her father or his house. But she didn't have the luxury of making decisions for only herself anymore.

A black sedan pulled in behind her car. A well-dressed man with a black briefcase in hand got out. "Ms. Westmore?"

She wiped her damp palms down her jeans, suddenly wishing she'd dressed up more. But her super-slim dress pants had been the first thing she'd grown out of. "Yes."

"I'm Mr. Bates. I was assigned to your father's case. Can we talk inside?"

She'd hoped to settle this all out here and never cross that threshold again, but she couldn't very well tell him that without raising questions. She nodded and led him to her front door.

Her hand shook slightly as she unlocked the door and pushed it open. It still smelled of cigarettes and dust, and when the floor by the entryway creaked, tears welled in her eyes. Her dad was dead. Gone. And her emotions didn't know where to land. Gone was the man who had tucked her in and taught her to ride her bike. And gone was the man who had drowned his grief in a bottle of whiskey most nights until he was too drunk to stand.

Those were the good nights. When he ran out of whiskey before he passed out, Madison hid in the closet until he found her. She'd learned to hide the bruises for the most part and escape the house as much as she could, but life wasn't easy in a small town when you were the daughter of the town drunk.

She went to set her purse on the table, but the dirty coffee cups and crumbs changed her mind. She tucked it under her arm and turned back to Mr. Bates.

"Your father had no will, so as his only descendant, you'll

inherit everything. Before I tracked you down, I researched selling the property and I did get one offer, but I hesitate to encourage you to accept it." He handed her a paper, and she skimmed it over.

Talk about a lowball offer, all right. She'd done some basic market research before she'd arrived, and this was at least 30 percent lower than it should be.

Mr. Bates cleared his throat. "With all the work Hannah Taylor has done on the square and the renovations going on in the houses around here, I bet you could get double that, but it'd take a little time and hard work."

Hard work was something she'd become accustomed to over the past year. But time wasn't something she wanted to give up.

"What are my options if I don't take this offer?"

"Then the place is yours to live in or fix up and sell. This house is newer than most on the square. With some new carpet and fresh paint, you could do a lot to liven it up. I'd also recommend you find a market for your father's leather tools."

Right. Paint and carpet. That all took money. She was scraping by as it was. The leather tools would bring some money, but only if she found the right buyer.

She had a small savings, but she wasn't sure she was ready to gamble it on selling this house. What if the market turned down? What if in the end there was no better buyer? She might still have to take this lowball offer and would've squandered her bank account in the process. Maybe she should take the offer. After all, it was more money than she'd had yesterday.

That's what the old Madison would've done. She couldn't think like that anymore. She needed to get the most she could out of the place because now she had someone else to consider. But restoration would take time, and she needed to get out of town before she had to explain either of the two big changes in her life. Because neither her baby nor her faith were anyone's business but her own.

Maybe this was a time she should stop and pray before deciding. At least that sounded like something Ms. Alena would've suggested. But she didn't even know what she would be looking for in an answer if she did pray.

Ms. Alena had said that following God was easy, but maybe that was because she'd been doing it for more than forty years, not two weeks. *Lord, I'm not good at this praying thing yet. What do I do?*

She waited. Nothing. No lightning. No text on her phone.

Madison drew a slow breath and handed back the offer to Mr. Bates. "I'm not going to take that offer."

With the words came a sense of peace. She still didn't know how she'd get the house ready to sell on her own, but somehow she believed that it would all be okay.

"I think that's a wise decision." He pulled another set of papers from his case and set them on the table. "Now if you'll sign here."

Madison picked up her pen and scrawled her name across the line. That was it. With one signature her father was gone and she was a homeowner.

"I'll bring more paperwork this week to make the transfer of ownership official. Until then, Ms. Westmore." He slid the papers back in his briefcase, nodded once, then exited the way he came in.

As the door clicked shut, Madison gripped the back of the chair to steady herself. She was officially a resident of Heritage once again.

Her eyes traveled the room. Her father had been gone more

than a month, but everything still lay where he'd left it. A beer can by his chair. The day's mail discarded on the table. A sink full of dirty dishes. Her stomach lurched, and she ran for the bathroom. She'd gotten past the worst of the morning sickness, but her gag reflex was still on high alert. First order of business—a good cleaning. And she'd start with the bathroom.

It was warm for the second of June in Michigan, and Leah slowed her walk to the diner as she soaked in the sun's rays on her cheeks. She'd missed the warmth of Costa Rica the past few weeks, but she didn't regret moving back. There, she'd been living David's dream, not her own. Which was why she couldn't go into business with Jon. If she did, she'd end up living someone else's dream again.

Leah was still several yards from the diner when Hannah pushed out the door with baby Joseph in her arms and Luke not far behind. Luke leaned in and said something that made Hannah smile before dropping a kiss on her cheek. Then, after kissing Joseph's head, he walked the opposite way down the sidewalk.

Jon hadn't been wrong all those years ago. Luke only had eyes for Hannah. Leah had seen it then, but Jon's words had still stung. How different would things be if she'd realized Jon had been hitting on her and not insulting her?

Hannah paused as her eyes landed on Leah. "I heard you were back!" She rushed forward and wrapped her in a one-armed hug, making Joseph start to fuss. "Why haven't you come to see me?"

Why? Probably for the same reason this was the first time she'd agreed to have lunch with Olivia. She didn't need one more person telling her that reopening the WIFI was a useless dream.

But before she could answer, Joseph started a full-volume wail. Hannah shifted him to the other hip. "Sorry, he's overdue for a nap, and Olivia's waiting for you. But we need to catch up soon."

Leah agreed, then walked into Donny's, slid into the booth opposite Olivia, and dropped her purse on the seat next to her. "So what's this big news you have?"

Olivia leaned forward as she laced her fingers together on the tabletop. "Do you know who Colby Marc is?"

"From The Redeemed? The Colby Marc who looks like a young Robert Redford and sings like Michael Bublé?"

"So you're a fan?"

"I have every album. I don't believe what the media is saying." Leah huffed.

"Actually, it's true, but Colby wasn't involved. The lead guitarist, Dawson West, did misuse the money and is facing some serious charges."

"How do you know all that?"

"Nate and Colby were roommates in seminary the year before The Redeemed hit it big. I couldn't believe he never told me. Anyway, Colby's having a rough time with the media right now, so Nate told him to come stay with us for a bit."

"Colby Marc's going to stay in your guest room?" Leah couldn't keep the junior high giddiness from surfacing at the idea of meeting someone famous. Colby Marc!

"Yes!" Olivia squealed and gripped Leah's hand.

"That's . . . uh, wow . . . I . . ."

"Right? He's supposed to arrive in a week. And I was thinking." Olivia let go of her hand and leaned on her elbows. "He's single. You're single."

"You're not going to set me up with Colby Marc." Just the

idea of meeting him gave her stomach a whirl. An actual conversation with the guy might be beyond her.

"Come on, you two would be too cute together. And we could double. Unless there's some hottie you left in Costa Rica that you aren't telling me about."

The image of Jon flashed in her mind. Not that he was from Costa Rica, but he *was* a hottie. She shook away the thought. There was nothing between them. Maybe he'd hinted that he'd liked her back in high school, but that didn't seem to be his attitude lately.

"There's no one else." Leah lifted the menu and studied it as if she didn't have it memorized.

The bell jingled over the door as Jon walked in. Leah sank deeper in her spot, but not before he made eye contact. He nodded and walked over to the counter. Every time she'd seen him since her return, he'd been in a suit and tie, as if he was determined to remind the town he was the leader of Heritage Fruits and no longer the high school sweet talker. Not that she didn't appreciate his polished new look but today, but with his loose-fitting jeans, black T-shirt, and baseball cap, her mind traveled back to when he'd leaned toward her in the hotel. How would things be between them now if she'd let him kiss her?

"Hello." Olivia waved her hand in Leah's face. "What was that about?"

She blinked at her friend, trying to figure out how to explain her warring emotions, when Olivia spoke again.

"I thought you got past all your high school anger after he rescued you and you two played hooky from my wedding."

Anger? Right. She was angry with Jon, and it was better that Olivia thought her mind had gone that direction rather than suspect that Jon also stirred emotions very different from anger in Leah. "Okay, first of all, he didn't rescue me. Second, we didn't play hooky—we were trapped by a snowstorm. And third, this isn't about high school. He's making reopening the WIFI difficult."

Now that she'd said it out loud, she didn't have to reach far to find that anger again. She needed to stop looking at him.

"Difficult? I'd have guessed Dale would've made it impossible, so difficult sounds like at least a possibility."

"A possibility?" She dropped the menu on the table. "He wants me to go into a partnership with him."

"Like marriage." Olivia winked. "I have to say I highly recommend it."

"Very funny. He said he would handle the business aspect and I'd be the creativity and vision."

"Wow. That'd be perfect."

"Perfect?" Leah sent Olivia a look that hopefully said, *Are you nuts?* "He wants to steal my business from me."

"I think that'd be share, not steal, and let's face it. Caroline was the business side of the WIFI. You were the 'let's make it pretty and connect with customers' side."

"Are you saying I can't run a business?"

"No. I think you could, but I also think you'd hate that part. So why not take on a partner with funds who seems to enjoy it?"

"I don't trust that he wouldn't make it all about him." She fiddled with the tassel on her purse. "I went into business with him before, and that's exactly what happened."

"Wait. When?"

"In econ class when I was a sophomore and he was a senior. We had to form a business, so we decided to sell bookmarks. I created the bookmarks, and he came up with the business model." She used air quotes around the words *business model.*

Olivia waved down the waitress. "And what was his business model?"

"Use his charm to sell them." She made a face as she crossed her arms just before the waitress stopped to take their order.

After the waitress wandered away, Olivia set the menus back in the holder. "How many did he sell?"

Leah unfolded her arms and ran her hand over the new gray tabletop. "All of them, but that isn't the point."

"How's it not the point?"

"Later I found almost all of them in the trash. People were only buying them because of Jon's charisma. He wasn't pushing my art. He was pushing himself."

Olivia glanced over at Jon's back as he bantered with the girl behind the counter. "He *was* very charming in high school."

"It wasn't just that. When I showed them to Jon, he shrugged as if he didn't care and said he was just glad we were going to get an A. I'd spent hours on those bookmarks making each one unique, and to him it was about the grade. I don't want to go into business with someone who's all about the bottom line."

"That was high school. Can we agree you and I have grown up since high school?" Olivia raised her eyebrows in challenge.

"Yes."

"Then can you give Jon the same courtesy?"

Leah didn't answer. What could she say? Olivia was right and they both knew it, but there was the *other* problem. She had too many conflicting emotions when she was around Jon. Emotions she didn't have time to name. Emotions she refused to pursue. And working with him day in and day out wouldn't make that easier. Not. At. All. But she couldn't say all that, and she didn't need her friend even suspecting.

Leah shrugged as she schooled her features, but she couldn't do anything about the warmth that filled her cheeks.

"Jon," Olivia called to his back. "Come join us for a minute."

What was she doing?

Jon stared at them both a moment, then picked up his mug of coffee and slid into the booth next to Leah. When his arm brushed hers, her breath hitched, and she scooted over and tucked her arms closer to her body.

Olivia's gaze shifted from one of them to the other, but she didn't give away her thoughts. Finally she narrowed her eyes on Jon. "So, you want to go into partnership with Leah."

Jon glanced at Leah, but when she didn't comment, he set his mug down and talked directly to Olivia. "Yes. My uncle will never agree to anything less than a solid business plan. So far her approach has been . . . creative, but I think I can help her make it stronger."

Olivia tapped her nail on the table. "What will you get out of it?"

"I'll be an investor and get seventy percent of the profit."

Leah scoffed, but Olivia continued. "You have Heritage Fruits. Why do you want to do this?"

"My dad had a soft spot for the community and the WIFI. Consider it a way to complete a dream my dad was passionate about."

Olivia's brows rose, but her face concealed her opinion. "And you don't like this agreement, Leah."

"No. He's dreaming to think he would get seventy percent. I'd never give anyone more than thirty percent profit. This is my idea—my company." Leah tapped the table with each point, then gestured toward Jon. "He probably would want seventy percent of the creative decisions as well. Soon it wouldn't be my business. It would be his business, and I'd be working for him."

"That isn't true." He angled his shoulders toward her as much as he could in the narrow space. "I would give you full creative control as long as it was within the budget we will both agree upon. But I'm putting up most of the capital. Sixty percent."

Leah scooted her back against the wall to create a little more space between them. She refused to let his close proximity muddle her thoughts. "You said you'd be an investor. Sixty percent makes you the primary owner. Besides, I have some capital of my own. Forty percent."

"Forty-nine percent. That'll make you primary owner, but I get equal say in the business decisions." Jon leaned in a little closer, pinning her with his piercing brown eyes just visible in the shadow of his hat.

Leah swallowed and blinked hard. Was he trying to make her mind go blank? *Focus.* Forty-nine percent was doable. But maybe—

Olivia leaned closer, pulling Leah's attention away from Jon. "It's that or I'm guessing you can say 'so long' to the WIFI."

"Fine." She held out her hand and shook Jon's hand once.

A smile tugged at one corner of his mouth as he stood with his coffee. "Nice doing business with you ladies. I'll get those papers written up and we can meet Monday." He finished off his coffee, then placed his mug and a sizable tip on the counter.

"Hello?" Olivia waved to get Leah's attention for the second time.

Leah's cheeks warmed again. Olivia studied her as the waitress set their food in front of them. As soon as she walked away, Olivia unrolled her silverware and laid her napkin on her lap.

"Back to my earlier question. Is there some romantic interest you aren't telling me about?"

Leah pulled her glass of water closer and took a big swig, refusing to meet Olivia's gaze. She had to get this under control. "No."

"Because in case you didn't know, dating your business partner could be a bad idea."

Leah didn't answer. No kidding it was a bad idea. And working with Jon might be an even worse idea on many different levels. But she could do it if it meant getting her WIFI back. She just had to be careful.

four

Jon flipped through the papers Leah had given him, then dropped them on the desk in his home office. What had he gotten himself into? Her fragmented plan had more holes in it than Swiss cheese. The girl was reopening the WIFI with a slightly tweaked inventory and rearranged layout. But simply adding her creations to the sales floor wouldn't be enough. The WIFI may not have gone bankrupt, but he'd seen the statements and they'd been well on their way. Caroline and Leah had been smart to close when they did.

The WIFI didn't need to reopen—it needed an overhaul, starting with a new name. But what were the chances he could get Leah on board with that?

The doorbell chimed, and Jon pushed away from the desk. He rushed toward the front door, which was no short distance. He really needed to consider working from his father's den closer to the front of the house, but he wasn't ready for that.

He entered the foyer and strode across the marble tile to the double doors. By the time he opened the door, his cousin was almost to the bottom of the steps. "Seth?"

Seth hurried back up the stone steps. "Hey, Jon. It's been a while."

"No kidding. I thought you were still at . . ." Jon wasn't quite sure how to finish that sentence.

"Rehab?" Seth offered a half smile. "It's okay to say. But no, I finished that up over a year ago. I've been living at Quinn Ranch. It's the place for at-risk kids that your dad helped start."

"The one run by Caroline and Grant." Of course, because his dad had not only run a company, raised two kids, and helped the WIFI, he'd also found time to fund a ranch for troubled youth. "Well, come on in."

Seth followed him into the house and paused in the large marble entrance. "I'm not sure if your parents told you, but I lived here for a short while before rehab when things got rough at home. You were in Europe."

Jon nodded as a vague memory floated up. "I remember one of them mentioning that. How is your mom doing?"

"Her typical dysfunctional self. It's only gotten worse since your mom died. Because as much as my mom complained about her older sister, I know she loved her. We all did." His voice grew rough, and he cleared his throat. "Anyway, I stopped by because I left some stuff up in one of the guest rooms. I was wondering if I could pick it up."

"Of course." Jon motioned him toward the grand staircase that was the centerpiece of the entryway. "Are you all through at Quinn Ranch?"

"I've been clean for two years. But now that I've graduated high school, my program at the ranch is done. I start business college in a few weeks, and yesterday I signed a lease on my first place."

"Seth? Oh my goodness! You look . . . great." Abby met them

halfway down the stairs and wrapped their cousin in a giant hug, then leaned back. "I almost didn't recognize you."

Abby was right. The skinny, greasy-haired cousin who had sported dilated eyes at their last Christmas together had filled out, and his eyes were bright and clear. There was a calmness about him that Jon had never seen before.

Seth brushed hair that was still a little long out of his face. "I have your dad to thank for that. He never gave up on me."

"Dad never gave up on anyone." Abby's eyes glistened at the edges, but no tears fell. She offered Jon a half glance. "I'm going out. Don't save dinner for me."

"With who?" Jon tried to keep his voice casual, but Abby's eyes narrowed anyway.

Her tone challenged him as she hurried down the rest of the stairs. "Friends. And they'll be here soon, so I have to get ready. Don't be a stranger, Seth."

Part of him wanted to lay down the law like his father had with him. But he wasn't her father, and she was just three months from being an adult. Making her hate him wasn't going to help anything.

Jon continued the rest of the way up the stairs. "I haven't gone through all the rooms yet, but I can't promise Derek left your stuff alone. He seems to have made himself at home while I was gone."

"How *is* your entitled cousin?" Seth snickered. "I heard he enjoyed your Mustang while you were gone."

"Put twenty thousand miles on it. And there's evidence of a few rather large parties thrown here too. Not surprising that he slinked away as soon as I returned. Last I heard, he went out to California for a while with some friends, much to Dale's dismay."

"No doubt his dad wanted to groom him to take over more of Heritage. Those two were quite the destructive team." Seth turned right into the bedroom section of the house. "How's Abby doing? I couldn't help noticing a bit of tension back there."

"She's had a few bumps lately, but she seems to be doing better." Jon ran his hand through his hair as the muscles knotted in his neck. "I think we're over the worst of it, anyway."

"She may not always show it, but you being there and showing that you care means more than you'll ever know." Seth entered one of the guest rooms, walked to the closet, and pulled it open. "It's still here." He handed one box to Jon and reached for another. "It isn't valuable stuff. Just a few sentimental things that I didn't want to disappear."

They made their way back to the door and then outside to Seth's car. "If you need an internship or a job after business college, let me know," Jon said.

"Thanks." Seth popped the trunk of his car and set the box inside, then took the other from Jon's hands.

An old Camaro with faded yellow paint pulled into the circle drive too fast for Jon's comfort, its deep bass practically vibrating the driveway. A guy with bleached-blond hair and a black hoodie honked twice, then nodded at Seth and Jon. Jon took a step toward the car but stopped as Abby rushed out the front door in the ridiculously priced red leather jacket she'd convinced him to buy her in Paris.

"Bye, Seth. Visit soon." Abby waved at their cousin.

"Abby?" Jon yelled after her.

She turned back but kept walking. "Chill, I'll be back by eleven."

Then she jumped into the passenger seat, and the Camaro gunned back out onto the road, tires squealing as it went.

"I hate to tell you this, cuz," Seth said. "But if she's hanging out with Gabe Howell and his crew, you're not over the worst of it."

Great. Not only did he have to come up with how to get Leah on board with overhauling her plan, but he also had to figure out how to keep his sister from self-destructing at the same time. And he had a gut feeling that neither Leah nor Abby was going to take well to him stepping in.

But one thing he'd learned from his dad, it was not to give up on people. His dad hadn't given up on Seth, and Jon wasn't about to give up on Abby or the WIFI.

If they circled this argument one more time, Leah might throw her marker at him. She stepped around her grandmother's antique footstool, grabbed the blue legal pad out of Jon's hands, and crossed off the words *reevaluate name*, then handed it back to him. "I'm not changing the name."

"But we need something more easily understood. If this business is going to survive, then we need sales from people outside of Heritage." Jon settled onto the couch and then pulled an embroidered pillow from under his leg and tossed it aside.

Leah's grandmother had called the room cozy. Leah called it cluttered. But it did take her back to memories of her grandparents sharing evening tea by the fireplace. It was those memories that reminded her why she was doing this. And why the name couldn't change. The farmhouse hadn't changed. The name wouldn't change.

"No."

Jon leaned forward on his knees. "Advertising the WIFI is going to be more than a little confusing. People will assume it's a computer store."

She understood that. She wasn't an idiot. But letting this go was like losing the store all over again—like losing her grandparents all over again.

"But my grandfather named it that." Her voice hitched at the end, and she turned her back to him.

"I know." The couch creaked, and when he spoke again he was right behind her. "We can figure out how to honor the name somewhere in the store, but it won't work as an official name."

"I feel like I'm losing control, and this partnership just started." Leah dug her fingers into her red curls. "What are you going to want to change next—what it sells?"

Jon shifted from one foot to the other. "About that—"

"You've got to be kidding me!" Leah pulled her fingers free, no doubt leaving her hair sticking up with frizz.

"Even you want to change what it sells." Jon walked over and leaned on the mantel. "You want to sell your designs, as well as other art. Do you really see hanging them next to night-lights and yarn?"

Leah crossed her arms and stared him down. "Sounds like you have it all figured out. Maybe I should sell you my half and forget this partnership."

Jon winced and shook his head. "That's not what I want. You have good ideas—great ideas—but we're partnering on a new business together, not reopening the WIFI, and we need to start that by letting go of a name that doesn't work."

Her control was slipping away. She owned 51 percent, but she wasn't making 51 percent of the decisions. "New name, new inventory . . . Anything else?"

He grabbed his folder and started flipping through it. "I want to expand to three times the size. Plus convert the storage space up top to a second floor that's open in the center with a large central staircase."

He stopped on a page and handed it to her. Design obviously wasn't his strong suit, but the sketch wasn't so bad as to disguise the fact that the concept had promise. He had the counter in the wrong place, but the second-floor idea was spot on. This would increase the selling space by more than 300 percent. But how did he expect to fill that if he ditched the WIFI's usual inventory?

Leah handed it back. "Fine. What do you think we should sell, oh wise one?"

Jon walked across the room and examined the bookshelf. "I don't know. But not night-lights."

She stood next to him to see what had captured his interest, but his gaze seemed to bounce from one title to the next.

"I do like the idea of selling your designs." He reached up and pulled one of her high school yearbooks off the top shelf. "Maybe if I saw some of what you plan to sell, that would help. Is it something like this?"

He angled the yearbook page toward her. It was the one from his senior year. How had she forgotten her grandmother had put those there? She really should've cleaned out the bookshelf in the past few years.

Leah examined the page. She'd been wearing one of her creations. But that was when she'd just learned to sew. Back then she had more creativity than talent. "Not exactly."

He flipped a few more pages and stopped. "This one?"

"Thank you for this trip down memory lane, but no, my creations are a bit more sophisticated than when I was in high school. But you're crazy if you think I can sew enough to stock a store that large."

"No. We'd have to find inventory that complements what you have." He flipped to another page and held it up.

"We don't need to look through every page. For some reason I'm in this yearbook a lot. Most people didn't notice because they thought half of the pictures were Caroline, but she and I knew they were almost all me."

"That's what happens when the editor has a crush on you." Jon snapped the book shut and started to reshelve it.

"What? That isn't true." She grabbed the book from him, flipped the page to the yearbook staff, and paused on the picture of the editor. Jon Kensington. Her face warmed as she shut the book.

He shrugged as he took it and fit it back in its place on the shelf. "Don't look so surprised. I told you that months ago."

"I know. It . . . still seems unreal. You could have dated any girl you wanted in high school."

"Evidently not." Jon locked eyes with her, and when she didn't look away, he took a step closer. "The girl I was in love with didn't want me."

"Love? No way." She retreated a few inches. "I believe the word you used last time was *infatuated*. Which means strong feelings but short-lived."

"Did you look up the definition of *infatuated*?"

"No." She was a terrible liar, and by that twitch at his mouth, Jon knew it. "Fine, I did. I like to know exactly what people are saying."

"I like the looser definition of infatuation." He didn't touch her, but with the way his gaze burned across her face and then rested for a fraction of a second on her lips, he might as well have.

She swallowed, trying to keep emotion from her voice. "And that would be?"

"Immense attraction based on the superficial things everyone knows about you but—"

"Well, if it's only superficial, then . . ."

She shrugged and started to turn away, but his hand landed gently on her shoulder. "I wasn't done. But has the potential to turn into . . . something more as the two people get to know each other."

The intensity of his dark eyes when he'd finished talking did crazy things to her insides. Her skin tingled under his touch as if a chemical reaction were happening and molecules were changing places between his skin and hers. Every inch of her longed to step closer. But that was dangerous—too dangerous.

And that was her problem—when she was this close to Jon, it didn't feel wrong. His attention was consuming, but not in a destructive way. It empowered her. Like he believed she could be a success. When he looked at her like that, she believed it for a second too. And that right there was why she couldn't do this. If she grew to depend on his support, then she'd fail again when she found herself alone once more.

When he took another half step closer, she lost her ability to retreat or think—even breathe. She needed to remind him that this was a risky path they were walking. Not just for her but for him as well.

"Well, the board that you are so anxious to please probably wouldn't approve of this partnership if they thought this was something more." She broke eye contact. "So, it's a good thing that's in the past."

He glanced away, then straightened to his full height. "Good thing." His voice was rough as he walked a few paces away. "Are you dating someone?"

Leah's pulse picked up speed. "Why?"

"Just need to know if I should be wary of a boyfriend showing up not liking that I'm here."

"Not that it's any of your business, but no. I don't have time for a relationship right now."

He picked up a polished Petoskey stone her grandmother had kept on the shelf, tossed it in the air, and caught it. "If your stuff is different now, show me some."

"Now?" Sure, he'd see it eventually. But she wasn't sure she had the steel in her veins to go through one of his critiques tonight. She had a feeling his words now would have even more impact on her confidence than they had in high school. "It's not ready."

"Show me what you have so far."

"I told you. I want to sell more than my stuff—like these earrings." She tilted her ear to him and prayed he'd take the diversion.

"Okay." He leaned closer as he inspected the wood creations. Then again, this may have been the wrong kind of diversion.

Leah put more distance between them. "A girl in Chelsea made them. She makes a whole bunch on her laser cutter."

"So, clothes and earrings?" He tossed the rock up a few inches and caught it again. "Are you going to get stuff from a lot of artists?"

If she wasn't going to fail again, this store needed to be bigger. Her dream needed to be bigger. Partnering with other artists would help, but she also needed a more solid inventory. "Maybe. But how would we marry these personal art creations with uninspired factory spinouts?"

"Local artists and . . ."

She reached out and snagged the rock from Jon. "Michigan-themed souvenirs. T-shirts, mugs, hats all sell well on Etsy."

"I like it." Jon gazed over his drawing again and pointed to the second-floor balcony design. "What if we sold the local creations upstairs and kept the main floor for factory inventory?"

Leah narrowed her eyes at him. "Or put the art on the main floor."

"We'll figure that out later. We could call it Made in Michigan." He spread his hands out like he was displaying a sign. "Shorten it to the MIM."

"I like that theme—not the name." Leah returned the stone to the shelf. "We could also ask some of the local venders who sell at the Fourth of July festival if they want to sell stuff."

"We could find some more people at the West Shore Art Fair in Ludington." Jon sat on the couch and started scribbling notes on a clean sheet of the legal pad. "This is something I can take to the board. Now for the name." He flipped to a new page.

"Oh, the name isn't changing. I told you." She grabbed the pad and wrote *WIFI* in big letters, then circled it. "I'm not budging on that."

"But—" The alarm on his phone sounded, and he winced. "I've got to get going, but we need to talk about this further."

"I gave you the layout change and inventory change." Leah followed him to the door. "But I'm not budging on this. I'm reopening the WIFI. End of story."

Jon sighed and walked out the door. "We need an application that people can fill out to submit their inventory."

"I'll get on it. I'll also start building an inventory list from online companies we used to use for the WIFI." She leaned on the door frame as he walked toward his car. "Maybe I can even find night-lights made in Michigan."

Jon paused at the open door of his car. "No night-lights."

Leah shrugged as she gave a teasing smile. "We'll see."

Colby had never heard of Heritage, Michigan, and by the size of the place, few had. He rolled down his window to let a bit of the fresh country air in as he checked the directions one more time. Yup, he was lost. He needed to call Nate, but asking for directions in a town this size was a little humiliating. That and the fact he was probably the only guy in the country under eighty who couldn't figure out the Maps app on his phone. But he'd spent a good share of the past six years on a tour bus, letting others drive him around.

He stopped at the intersection and checked the road signs. Richard and Henderson. Neither of them Second Street. He pulled through the stop sign, then parked along the curb, climbed out of the car, and stretched his legs. He slipped on his sunglasses and pulled his hat a little lower. He didn't really need to deal with fans right now. He could see it on social media already: #ColbyMarcLost.

Across the street sat a park with a gazebo in the center, a playground on the closest corner, and an old one-room school-house straight off the set of *Little House on the Prairie* in the neighboring corner. Nate's place had to be close.

Colby walked across the street and sat on a large brass hippo whose belly lay flat against the sidewalk. He pulled out his cell phone and shot a text off to Nate.

> I'm kind of lost. But I'm in Heritage.

Give me a landmark.

> I'm sitting on the brass hippo.

That doesn't help.

How could that not help? How many big brass hippos did they have in town?

"Excuse me."

Colby winced at a woman's voice. He loved fans—he did—but there were days he wanted to be unknown.

"Excuse me." The voice was still kind but this time more urgent.

He finally looked up. The woman sat in her car with her window rolled down. Her large sunglasses hid her eyes, but the delicate features of her face testified to her beauty. Maybe being recognized wasn't so bad.

He stood and shoved his phone into his pocket. "Yes?"

"Is this your car?" She pointed to his Honda Civic.

"Yes." Maybe she was trying to work up the nerve to ask for an autograph.

"Well, it's blocking part of my driveway. I can't pull in. Would you be able to move it?"

"What?" He glanced back at his car. Sure enough, he hadn't even seen the dirt drive coming off the street.

"Can you move your car?"

"Uh, sure." He jumped into his car and pulled it forward until he'd cleared her drive by a few feet, then hopped out as she pulled in. "Sorry about that."

"It's no problem."

When she took off her sunglasses and stepped out of the car, Colby froze. She wasn't the airbrushed kind of beautiful like the women he often saw at his concerts. Although with her dark roots peeking through and the remnants of a manicure, maybe a polished look was more her MO. But there was a raw sincerity to her eyes that drew him in and made him want to know more of her story. With her large light blue eyes and slightly upturned nose, he'd describe her beauty as clean and classic.

"I would've parked on the street, but I don't want to carry the paint cans any further than I have to." When she caught him staring, she sighed and rolled her eyes as she unlocked the trunk.

No doubt this woman was used to being noticed, and by the look she just gave him, she was over it.

Nice one, Colby. Way to be your own version of a fan freak.

He rushed forward. "Let me help you."

"No, I've got it." She held up her hand.

"I don't mind." He reached for a can, but she blocked his path.

"I've got it." Her voice was firmer this time as her gaze hardened. Great, now she was shifting into stranger-danger territory. "I don't even know you."

He had to save this. There was something about her that made him want to get to know her. It wasn't only her beauty. It was the way she'd rolled her eyes at him, as if she understood people not seeing past the surface. As if no one in her life took the time to find out what made her tick. Attraction aside, she looked like a person who needed a friend as much as he did.

He held out his hand. "Colby."

She stared at his hand but didn't take it. "What do you do, Colby?"

"I'm . . . between jobs." That wasn't a lie.

She glanced at his car, which luckily backed up his "between jobs" story. It was an old hatchback that his uncle had been trying to get rid of, and when Colby had decided he wanted to go to Heritage, he needed something quick and simple that wouldn't draw attention. He'd just been glad it had made it the whole way.

Her eyes narrowed back on him. "Why are you in Heritage?"

"I'm visiting a friend."

"For how long?"

"Undecided." He shoved his hands in his pockets.

"You mean you're bumming on a friend's couch."

"Actually—"

"Save it. I don't really care." She stared at the paint, then back at him. "Are you looking for a job?"

"I could be." He didn't need the money, but something to do other than lie around at Nate's avoiding social media might be nice.

"I can't pay much, but I need to get this house painted and I don't want to paint because of the baby."

"You have a baby?" Colby peeked in the back seat of the car, but there wasn't even a car seat.

"I'm pregnant." Her words were emotionless.

He stared at her flat stomach.

"I'm only about thirteen weeks."

"Oh."

He must have still looked confused, because she added, "Sorry. Doctors talk in weeks. I'll be three months in a couple days."

He shrugged. "Cool."

She narrowed her eyes again, then spoke slower as if he still didn't understand. "So, soon I'll be fat, and since it's due the beginning of December, I'll have a baby by Christmas. So if you're here to hit on me, you can keep moving."

Wow, and he thought he could be touchy. "How much an hour for painting?"

She eyed him. "Fifty dollars a room."

Depending on the size of the room, that probably wouldn't even be minimum wage. But by the look on her face, she didn't have much more to offer. And right now he had the time. He'd offer to do it for free, but he suspected she would go back to assuming he was just hitting on her.

The lostness in her seemed to mirror his own even more than he'd originally suspected. Defensive, angry, hurt, alone . . . Dawson's face flashed in his mind. And the curiosity of who had caused her pain scratched at his brain. No, he wasn't walking away. He held out his hand again. "I can start Monday."

She finally shook his hand as a slight smile tugged at one side of her mouth. "Madison Westmore."

"Colby?" Nate's voice came from the direction of his car, and Madison yanked her hand away. "There you are. When you didn't respond to my texts, I figured I'd walk over and find you. Once I found Otis, I knew you couldn't be too far."

"Otis?"

"The hippo." He motioned across the street.

"I'll be just a second. I'm going to help this nice lady with her paint." He walked to the trunk and lifted out a gallon of paint.

"Madison?" Nate's voice held a fair amount of surprise. "When did you get back in town?"

"A few days ago." She lifted a brown sack of supplies from the trunk and walked toward the door. "Bye, Nate."

Colby lifted another can of paint in the other hand and followed her up the few steps into the house. It wasn't what he expected with her trendy style. The place was dark, with worn carpet and threadbare furniture that had a strong eighties vibe.

She led him down a hall with peeling flowered wallpaper and stopped in front of a bedroom that had been stripped of everything but the carpet. She pointed to the corner. "You can set it in there."

He carried the paint over and set it where she'd pointed, then followed her back out to the main room. "Okay, I'll see you Monday?"

"About that. I'm not sure—"

"Listen, you need help, and I have the time. Besides, I can't be all bad if I'm staying with the local pastor, right?"

She hesitated as her gaze drifted out front. "Sure." She glanced down at her stomach, then ran her hand over the nonexistent bump. "Could you not mention to Nate about the . . ."

"Not a problem. You can trust me."

He moved toward the door, but her mumbled words made him pause. "I trusted you more before I knew how you were connected to this town."

He almost turned back to question her but stopped himself. With every revelation he wanted to know more about her. And the last thing he wanted to do was give her a chance to rescind the job offer.

He hurried toward his car and followed Nate toward the house. He'd been less than a hundred yards from his destination as the crow flies, but he couldn't help being thankful that he'd gotten lost.

A woman appeared at the door. She was tall with platinum-blonde hair, not the bottle kind but the kind that came from a Scandinavian heritage. This town wasn't short on beauty, that was for certain. She extended her hand with a wide smile that lit up her blue eyes. "You must be Colby. Welcome to our home. I'm Olivia."

He set down his guitar case and shook her hand. "And you must be brave to marry that guy."

"I heard that." Nate walked up to the house.

Oliva pointed behind her. "We have the guest room ready on the first floor. That'll give you your own bathroom and a little more privacy. I'm sorry you got lost. I honestly didn't think that was possible in Heritage."

"I found him at Madison's." Nate gave his wife a look Colby couldn't quite decipher, then disappeared into the house.

"Madison? As in Madison Westmore? When did she get back?"

Colby followed Nate into the house, through the kitchen and living room, and down a short hall to a guest room. "I think it was recent. I'm going to help her do some painting next week."

Olivia's eyes rounded before she checked her reaction. "Oh. That's nice."

Nate stood in the door of the room. He crossed his arms in front of him. His wife gave him a pointed look, and he shook his head.

Olivia finally sighed and looked directly at Colby. "Just be careful with that one."

Her words may have been gentle, but her eyes shouted that she thought Madison was trouble. She didn't look like trouble to Colby. Then again, he'd thought Dawson was a stand-up guy, and it turned out that for the past two years Dawson had been lying to his face, so maybe Colby wasn't the best judge of character. But there was something about Madison that he couldn't get past.

He nodded at Olivia and set his bag on the bed. He'd be careful, but that didn't mean he'd back away. Not yet, anyway.

five

Where was Leah? Jon glanced around the meeting room, then at his phone again. She was supposed to be here ten minutes ago. They were almost through the proposal for repackaging the fruit cups. And that meant the WIFI proposal was up next. She was in charge of half the presentation.

Not that he couldn't do it. He'd been the one to write most of it, after all, but Leah was the pizzazz to his charts and numbers.

Jon rubbed his temple and glanced at his phone again. Leah knew how important it was. Which meant something was wrong. Maybe she was caught in traffic because of an accident. Maybe she was in the accident. Jon's hand tightened around his pencil as his parents' accident and the day he received the call about their death played through his mind.

Snap.

Everyone's eyes turned toward him. Jon set the broken pencil aside and reached for his water, but before he picked it up, his phone buzzed. He snatched it with enough speed to bring another round of stares. He was making quite the impression today.

He released a long breath when a text from Leah popped up.

Caroline's in labor. What do I do?

Some of the tension that had been pinching his shoulders eased. She was safe. All was well. He opened the screen and typed back a message.

Go. I got this.

R U sure?

Yes. Trust me. I'll get it done.

I trust you. U R the best! I owe you.

His fingers typed across the screen.

I look forward to collecting.

His thumb hovered over the Send button. *Business partner. Professional.* He deleted the message and sent another instead.

No worries. Let me know when the baby arrives.

She shot back a thumbs-up, and Jon set aside the phone. He ran his hand through his hair and lifted the presentation. It looked like the pizzazz was up to him. But maybe this was for the best. Leah had been right. If any of the board suspected his feelings for her ran deeper than professionally appropriate, they'd see him as that young, irresponsible kid he'd been in high school, trying to make a girl happy.

Maybe that had been partly true at the beginning, but this

was a solid idea after the research he and Leah had been able to pull together over the past week of late nights and long hours.

Of course, the long nights had made ignoring the elephant in the room harder and harder. But he and Leah had both worked side by side as if there was no attraction. No chemistry. Just business. And maybe for her it was.

He knew that getting involved with his business partner was the last thing he needed, no matter how much thoughts of her kept him awake at night. And he'd had a lot of sleepless nights lately.

Jon reached for his coffee but found it empty. He set it down with a thud as the room erupted in applause. He joined in but hadn't a clue what they were clapping for. He grabbed his pen and made a note to reread the packaging proposal.

Uncle Dale straightened the piles in front of him. "Why don't we all take a five-minute break. When we return, Jon will go over the plan for the Teft Road building." He stood and left the room.

Marcy must have seen Jon's distress over his empty mug, and she rushed over to fill it. Her eyes lingered on him a little longer than necessary as her cheeks turned pink yet again. He offered a polite smile but didn't want to encourage her. Dating someone right now might solve the tension with Leah, but he'd learned in Europe that distractions only numbed the desire for a short time. In the end, they just made him want Leah more.

The five minutes passed before Jon had even gotten around to refilling his water, but at least he had fresh coffee. The men all took their seats and stared at him, waiting. Some seemed to be waiting for him to fail—his uncle was in that category. But he could take hostility easily enough. It was the others who had his heart tightening. They weren't cheering him on to succeed as much as waiting for him to be like his father.

And those were shoes he was still trying to convince himself he could fill.

"Jon, do you have an update on the Teft Road building?" Uncle Dale tapped his pen on the table.

He had to pull it together if he had any chance of getting their support. "Yes."

His uncle pointed at the papers Jon gripped in his hand as if growing weary of waiting. "And what company have you decided on? I assume you've gotten Ms. Williams to agree to the sale."

Jon cleared his throat. "I've decided that I don't desire to lease the building."

"Excuse me?" His uncle's expression darkened. "This board has already made that decision. You simply need to fill the space. It's a straightforward responsibility. I thought you could handle that much."

His uncle's words from years back floated through his mind. *"Face it, George. Jon doesn't have what it takes to run this company."*

Maybe this was a mistake. Jon fixed his eyes on the presentation folders in his hands and pushed away the memory as another voice filled his mind. *"It's your company, Jon. Tell the board no."* Leah had made it sound so simple. Then again, she'd left him to face the wolves alone.

Jon let his gaze travel over all the board members, doubt clinging to each of their faces. They might think he was a fool, but Leah was right. He had to at least try.

"The companies we're looking at don't meet the needs or the heart of Heritage." He met his uncle's stare without flinching. "So I've decided against the board's recommendation and have pursued another option for this property."

Uncle Dale spoke up. "Now, you wait a minute—"

"No, you wait." Jon's voice had steel in it, and by the way his uncle's brows rose, he hadn't thought Jon had it in him. No doubt few stood up to *the* Dale Kensington. "This is still my company, and if you'll look at what I've proposed, then I think you might see the merit in it."

Jon opened his folder and started passing his proposal to the left. His uncle took one of the packets but didn't open it. Jon ignored the move. He was done letting Uncle Dale intimidate him. He was moving this forward, and he was going to get the board on his side.

Twenty minutes later there were many raised eyebrows and several nods of approval. Uncle Dale still sat cross-armed with a glare that could kill, but he remained quiet.

"I like this." Harold White sat forward and tapped the packet. "But the thing I can't get behind is the name. The WIFI name became quite confusing in the last few years it was open, and with this new inventory you're looking at, it no longer even makes sense."

"I agree. You need a stronger name." Bob Chapman leaned back in his chair and ran his finger along his beard. "Something clearer."

What could he say? He knew that naming it the WIFI would be an anchor to any marketing efforts, but that was the one area Leah wasn't willing to budge on. He'd brought it up several times. He'd thought she might give in yesterday, then she'd dug her heels in. But if she were here right now, she would recognize how close they were to getting what they wanted. "We have discussed other names. And Leah and I could revisit that discussion—"

"What names have you tossed around?" Harold dropped the proposal and reached for his coffee.

"I cannot make any—"

"Just tell us other names you've discussed," Bob added.

There was only one name that had been thrown out, but it hadn't been discussed. And even though it had grown on him over the past few days, saying it here felt like a betrayal to Leah.

"If you didn't even discuss other names, then maybe you aren't taking this as seriously as you want us to believe." Uncle Dale tapped at the paper with his pen, his expression flat.

"The name Made in Michigan was on the table. MIM for short." Jon cringed as the words left his mouth. "But Leah wasn't convinced—"

"I like that." Harold crossed out *WIFI* on the proposal in his hand and wrote *Made in Michigan* above it. "Catchy. Marketable."

"I can't make this decision without Leah." Jon raised his voice, but it seemed to fall on deaf ears as all the men replaced the name in their proposals.

"You didn't," his uncle said. "We did."

"Tell the board no." Leah's words echoed in his mind. But she wasn't here having to face them down.

The men all nodded and flipped through their proposals again.

Uncle Dale tossed the proposal on the table as all the men agreed to the new name. "I assume that with all the responsibility you'll be taking on with this new MIM, I'll return to taking full responsibility for the factory . . . for the time being."

Full responsibility? Jon was just starting to understand the inner workings of running the factory. Not to mention he was looking into why his uncle had instituted so many layoffs right after he took over. But maybe this wasn't a fight he needed to have right now.

"Fine. You can take over the factory operations until Labor Day. By then we should have the MIM up and operational. Leah can take over the daily operations of the MIM at that point."

His uncle moved on to the next item on the agenda, but Jon stared at the paper in front of him, where he'd crossed out "WIFI" and written in "MIM." How was he going to tell Leah?

I trust you. Her words from her last text pinched at his conscience. If she trusted him, then she'd have to trust he made the right decision.

———

Forget the WIFI. Leah had a new love in her life. She smoothed her new niece's downy red hair as she settled into the stiff hospital rocker. Two hours old and she'd already stolen Leah's heart. Leah knew she should pass the baby off to Olivia or Hannah, who were both with her, but she wasn't quite ready to. Then again, she might never be ready.

"Evangeline Leah Quinn." Leah blinked away the tears as she glanced up at her sister eating her late dinner in her hospital bed. "It's a good name."

"We'll call her Vangie." Caroline finished the last of her applesauce and pushed the tray away.

Hannah sat in the chair next to Leah and lifted Vangie's tiny hand with her finger. "You and Joseph will be the best of friends. I can feel it."

Olivia rolled her eyes. "Feel it, or are planning it? I'm surprised you two haven't set up an arranged marriage yet."

"Is that still a thing?" Caroline lifted one finger in the air. "Because I'm all for that."

"You draw up the papers, Caroline, and we'll sign." Hannah winked at her.

Leah had missed this so much when she was in Costa Rica. It was more than just friendship. It was a sisterhood of connected hearts. But with every passing day, the gap between her life and theirs seemed to grow. Part of her longed for marriage and a baby, but the idea also brought a wave of panic like nothing else.

Jon's face filled her mind. She tried to push it away, but the stubborn image wouldn't fade. So what if they had chemistry? That didn't mean he'd make a good husband or father.

"What's that look for?" Caroline studied her.

"What look?" Leah locked eyes with her sister, mentally begging her to bring it up later. Twins were supposed to have a nonverbal superconnection, right?

Caroline tilted her head. "What's up with you and Jon?"

So much for that connection. She sent her sister a glare as all the girls turned their eyes to her. Maybe she could distract them again with the baby. "Who wants a turn with Vangie?"

"Me." Hannah lifted Vangie from Leah's arms and settled her against her shoulder. "Now tell us about Jon. I mean, he was fine before, but can we all agree that Europe was good to him?"

"No joke." Olivia squeezed herself onto the end of the couch and trailed her fingers over Vangie's head. "I swear his shoulders doubled in size while he was gone."

Leah stood and walked over to the sink, keeping her back to the girls. If they saw her face right now, her next words would be less convincing. She reached for a plastic cup and filled it with cool water. "Yes, Jon's still attractive, but there's nothing to share. We're in business together. End of story." She downed the water and then glanced at her phone. Jon hadn't sent any more texts since the one telling her that the meeting went well and the board had approved moving forward.

"That means I can set you up with Colby." Olivia's voice carried across the room. "He arrived Tuesday. Feel free to stop by to borrow a cup of flour anytime."

"Like that isn't obvious." Leah leaned back against the sink. "I'm sure the last thing Colby wants is people fangirling around him."

"Oh, come on. How awesome would it be if you dated Colby Marc?" Olivia wiggled her brows at Leah.

When she didn't answer, Caroline spoke up. "Colby *is* adorable. But I'm still Team Jon. I need you to convince him to keep George's foundation supporting Quinn Ranch. Dale hasn't pulled the plug yet, but I'm always waiting."

"Caroline," Leah reprimanded.

"Okay, I'm kidding. Sort of. But I *am* Team Jon. I've always thought you two were perfect for each other."

Hannah jumped in. "I know, right? I'm totally Team Jon. The guy has had a thing for you since high school."

Leah whipped her head in Hannah's direction. "You knew?"

Hannah shrugged as her eyes darted to everyone else. "We all knew."

Leah's eyes found Caroline, but her sister just shrugged. "It was kind of obvious."

"Not to me," Leah mumbled as she picked at the cuticle on her finger. "One of you could've told me."

"And risked your wrath." Olivia huffed. "You breathed fire every time his name was brought up."

Everyone in the group seemed to silently agree.

"But maybe that's for the best. I mean, wouldn't it be more awkward now, working with him if you had a history?" Olivia pinned her with her gaze. "Which is why, if you're honestly in the friend zone with Jon, you need to consider Colby. Please let me set you up."

Her heart was definitely *not* in the friend zone when it came to Jon, but maybe that was the point. Maybe a date with Colby would keep her from falling for her business partner. Then again, that didn't sound super fair to Colby. "I need to focus on the business. I don't have time for a serious relationship anyway."

"I didn't say you need to marry the guy." Olivia, who seemed to have grown impatient waiting for her turn, claimed Vangie from Hannah's arms. "Come to dinner. Simple as that."

Before Leah could decide, the door burst open, and Janie walked in with a pink balloon and a bouquet of flowers. Her long brown hair was tied up in a bun that had become the norm since she and her husband, Thomas, bought the diner. "Sorry I couldn't get here sooner. The diner was a madhouse today."

"Well, I'm glad you came." Caroline accepted the flowers, then gave Janie a hug. "All five of us again together. It's been too long."

The last time they'd all been together had been before the WIFI closed. So much had changed since then. Back then, they'd all been single. Now Leah was the only one left.

"Libby came with me too. She's parking the car." Janie took Vangie from Olivia. "My turn."

Olivia rolled her eyes but surrendered the baby. "Are all big sisters so bossy?"

"Yes." Leah sent Caroline a teasing grin.

"Not like you listen." Caroline lifted an eyebrow, but Leah looked away. She wasn't in the mood to discuss the WIFI again.

Janie shifted Vangie to her shoulder as she began to fuss. "Well, since we're all together, it's a good time to share that

Thomas and I have completed the application process for adoption. Now we're just waiting to be picked."

Olivia clapped. "Yay! More babies."

After the hugging and cheering died down, Hannah cleared her throat as she pulled a photo from her purse and passed it to Leah. "He's not a baby, but Luke and I have started the application process to adopt Jimmy. He was the Adamses' foster kid, and he just came up for adoption. He's been at a different home for the past year over in Manistee, but we went for our initial visit last week. He was thrilled to see Luke again."

Leah studied the photo. It was of Luke, Hannah, Joseph, and a boy about age ten. The love in Jimmy's dark eyes made her ache with joy for them. She passed back the photo and did her best to keep a smile on her face. She wanted that—longed for that. But as much as she did, the idea terrified her beyond reason.

Libby opened the door and joined them. Leah didn't know her as well, but she seemed to have merged perfectly into the group while Leah was in Costa Rica. She ran the library and wasn't married, although she was dating Nate's brother, Austin.

"Speaking of news," Janie spoke up as Libby shut the door. "Libby has some."

Libby held up her hand, flashing a diamond solitaire. Leah's heart dropped. So much for not being the only one not married.

Olivia screamed, rushed across the room, and wrapped her arms around Libby. "I'm getting a new sister."

"I leave for an hour and you all decide to have a wild party." Grant walked over to Caroline and handed her a Frappuccino as he leaned over and dropped a kiss on her head. "As you ordered, my beautiful wife."

"That's why you're my favorite." Caroline reached for his hand and squeezed.

The lump in Leah's throat thickened. She dropped back down next to Olivia on the couch. "Fine. I'll let you set me up, but only this once."

Gathering with other believers was important, according to Ms. Alena, but she doubted that Ms. Alena had considered that the other believers might despise her. Madison slid into the last pew and gave silent thanks that it was empty. She set her purse on the seat next to her and turned her attention up front. The people around her all sang along to songs as if they'd been hearing them their whole life, but everything about this world felt foreign. The tune. The stained-glass windows. Even the words.

What did it even mean to compare God's love to a hurricane? Weren't those massively destructive? But everyone around her seemed to connect with the words, so she'd keep hiding back here.

After her first visit to a church, she'd determined not to go a second time. After all, she could meet with God wherever she was. But something kept drawing her back, calling her to show up. A tugging she couldn't say no to.

She'd come last week, but a different person was leading the music this week. His silky-smooth tenor carried the notes in such a gentle way that she was quite sure she could listen to him sing all day. She rose on her toes, but she still couldn't see past the tall guy in front of her. Wait. Was that Jon Kensington blocking her view? She hadn't heard he was back from Europe.

Madison closed her eyes, doing her best to push all the distractions away and let the singer's rich voice and the words flow over her.

When the song ended, everyone took their seats as if they'd

rehearsed it. Madison quickly sat, praying her delayed response hadn't stood out. It seemed like the whole service was a choreographed routine and she'd missed the memo.

Nate stepped up to the mic and motioned for someone to join him. "I'm sure many of you recognize Colby Marc, former lead singer of The Redeemed."

Nate kept talking, but Madison stopped hearing him. The man up front, the one who had a voice as rich as dark chocolate, was none other than the guy she'd hired to be her painter. If she remembered right, The Redeemed had a song hit the number one spot after it played in a movie. He wasn't the poor vagabond she'd taken him for. And she'd asked him to help paint her house for a pitiful wage. She sank lower in her seat. Colby and Nate must have had a good laugh at that one.

Even worse, Nate would've filled Colby in on her past by now. She didn't know Nate well, but his new wife, Olivia, had no love lost for Madison. They had never gotten along in high school, but the short time Madison had been engaged to Olivia's now brother-in-law, Thomas, had pretty much sealed the fact that Olivia, Janie, Hannah, Caroline, and Leah would always hate Madison. Not that she blamed them. But Thomas had married Janie like he should have. Because people like Olivia and Janie deserved happy endings, not people like Madison.

Nate's words broke back into her thoughts. "He's here taking a break, so let's show him kindness and appreciation by not sharing on social media where he's relaxing these days."

A wash of nausea had her reaching for her lemon drops again. Colby had said he'd keep her secret, but he hadn't been honest about who he was, so why would he be honest about that?

Madison slipped out of the pew and exited through the back door. Maybe church while she was in Heritage wasn't the best idea. Surely Ms. Alena would agree with her on this one. She could find a church with a service online.

She crossed the street, then paused as a pebble wedged its way into her sandal. She hobbled toward Otis, who had moved across the street from Donny's last night, and took a seat on the back of the brass hippo.

"Madison." Colby's shout filled the quiet square. When he spotted her, he started walking in her direction. Just perfect.

She got the pebble out and stood to meet him. "May I help you, Colby Marc?"

He winced at the use of his full name. "I wanted to know what time you'd like me to show up tomorrow."

"I think we both know you don't need the money, so I can hire some high school kid. Thank you for your offer though." She took a few more steps down the sidewalk, but he rushed in front of her.

"Come on. You need the help, and I . . ." He shifted from one foot to the other, then finally added, "I need something to keep me busy."

She had a feeling that wasn't what he was planning to say, but she wasn't going to fish for it. "Were you making a joke of me?"

"No." He walked back to Otis, sat down, and dropped his head in his hands before he looked up. "I didn't think about it at first. It was nice to be just Colby. Not Colby Marc, Christian music artist."

She opened her mouth to say she didn't care but stopped. Hadn't that been the very reason she'd left Heritage? Because for once in her life she wasn't Madison, the daughter of the town drunk, or Madison, the girl who dated every guy in town. She was just Madison.

Maybe that was why she'd let him carry the paint and offered him the job. Because with Colby she was starting on page one.

Maybe he needed to help her paint for reasons he didn't want to talk about. If anyone understood that, it was her.

She sat next to him on Otis. "I get that. But no more lies or half-truths."

"Deal." A lazy grin tugged at his mouth as he stared at her. His cheeks reddened before he tapped Otis's brass side. "So, this thing really moves? Nate said something about that."

"Yes." Madison let him change the subject. She wasn't ready to chase whatever thought had flicked through his mind. "He moves to anywhere on the square or across the street from the square. And before you ask, no, I don't know how."

"Weird, but kinda cool." He stood and reached out his hand. "Want to go back inside?"

"No, but you should." Madison stood as well and took another step away from the church. "You're definitely more welcome there than I am."

His brow wrinkled. "Everyone's welcome at church, Madison."

"You have a lot to learn about small towns, Colby. They may forgive, but they don't forget."

"Give them a chance. If anyone understands second chances, it's Nate."

Madison shook her head. "Tomorrow at one?"

A gentle smile filled his clean-shaven face, revealing a pair of soft dimples. "I'll be there."

"Did Nate tell you about me?"

"Not really."

Her expression must have conveyed her doubt.

"Honest. The only thing was Olivia said I should be careful."

"Sounds like wise advice. I *am* trouble."

"I don't think so." His face sobered. "I didn't tell him anything. Your secret is safe with me. And if you can still treat me like the Colby you met on Tuesday, then I can still see you as the girl I helped carry paint for. What do you say to fresh starts?"

She hesitated, then extended her hand. "To fresh starts."

"See you tomorrow." He shook her hand before jogging back toward the church.

Madison's forced smile faded as he disappeared around the corner. He seemed to have a good heart, but she knew the truth even if he didn't. Everyone eventually gave up on her. It was only a matter of time.

six

There would never be a good time for him to tell her that he'd renamed the business, but sooner was bound to be better than later. Jon slipped off his leather coat and tossed it on the seat of his Mustang as he climbed out. If it kept warming up like this, the lake would be full this weekend.

He walked up the steps and banged on the wooden screen door of Leah's old farmhouse. The inside door was open.

It had been over a week since the board meeting, but lately they had been missing each other at every turn. And without an office set up at the Teft Road building, his dropping by there to have this conversation hadn't worked.

"Come in." Leah's distant words drifted through the screen. Or had she said "Just a minute"?

Jon hesitated as he opened the door. "Hello?"

"Back here."

He secured the door, then walked toward the direction the voice had come from. "How do you know I'm not a burglar?"

"If you are a burglar, go away." A slight giggle accompanied the words. "If not, down the hall. Last room on the left."

Jon followed her directions to one of the back rooms. Leah

sat on a green shag carpet with piles of papers around her. She leaned against an antique rolltop desk with her legs stretched out. Her hair was pulled up in a ponytail, but a few curls had escaped. She wore a graphic T-shirt with a Rubik's Cube on it that he'd date from about 1984. And her jean shorts had patches circling the hem that boasted a variety of colors and words.

He leaned against the door frame and shoved his hands in his pockets. "What are you doing?"

"I put out a couple notices on local art boards about selling at our store, and these are the emails I got. I'm trying to sort them by category." She pointed to the piles one at a time. "Jewelry, pottery, glass—"

"This won't work."

Her eyes shot up in his direction. "What are you talking about?"

"We can't agree to selling something based on an email. Every person will need to fill out an application." He squatted down, picked up an email, and skimmed it over. Just what he expected—all sentiment and no numbers to back it up. "We haven't even discussed if we're charging a percentage of each item sold or charging by the space required to display their items." He waved the paper in the air. "'Dear Miss Williams, I really, really want to sell my drawings. And my art teacher says they're really good.'"

"Hey, I looked at the attachment. They are good." She yanked the paper from his hand.

"I'm sure they are, but it doesn't mean we can sell them." Jon pointed to the paper. "Has he tried to sell his drawings at a vendor event? Do they go with the theme of the store? Line drawings of Michigan lighthouses would have a better chance of selling to our target market than drawings of fantasy creatures."

"Okay, fine. I get it." She gathered all the emails into a pile. "I wish you would have run this by me before you posted them."

"I tried. But you didn't answer your phone and you weren't at your office or the WIFI building. I even went to your house, but you weren't there."

"Monday?" He dropped down next to her. "I was touring the factory, which may be why I didn't hear your call. Then I went to Chet Anderson's. Luke and I were helping him patch a section of his roof."

"I didn't know you knew Chet that well."

"He's my dad's cousin. And he and Luke have always been close since Luke's foster mom was Chet's sister."

She sighed and rested her head back on the desk. "This is what I'm talking about. You want me to okay things with you, but I can't find you. Between running around with Abby, your responsibilities at the factory, the office—"

"I get it." Jon pulled out his phone and tapped at the screen with his thumbs, then her phone chimed. "I shared my location with you. Now if you need me for something, you'll at least know where to find me."

Leah picked up her phone and stared at it before tapping her screen. His phone pinged as her location popped up on his screen. She set her phone back down without a comment and then glared at the stack of emails. "What do I do with those?"

He hated that he'd been the one to put that frown on her face. "Don't worry about it. This is an easy fix."

"Really?"

"We simply need to reply with a link to an online application where they can answer all these questions. Then we'll have them submit samples for us to establish quality control. Remember, it's our company name on the line."

Leah waved a stack of the papers in the air. "But how can we say no to some of these people?"

"It isn't personal."

"That's where you're wrong. Art is very personal." Her eyes flashed to his, and there seemed to be something more in their depth. An accusation, maybe, but he'd never said anything disparaging about her work. "The artist is putting their heart out there in every piece, and I have to be the judge of what's good enough."

He leaned back against the wall and stretched his legs out, covering half the width of the small room. Man, sometimes he felt like such a giant. "I know it'll be hard for you, Leah. But that's what it means to own a business. As the boss, I always must evaluate products, ideas, employees' performances . . ."

"I'm not sure I can look another artist in the face and tell them it isn't good enough." She closed her eyes.

"You don't have to tell them it isn't good enough." He nudged her foot with his. Probably not business partner etiquette, but it was fairly benign. "Say it isn't right for the store."

"And how will I know what's right for the store?" She tapped his toe with hers, then seemed to catch herself and pulled her knees up to her chest.

"You pick a product you believe in." Jon lifted a stack of papers and fingered through them. "But this is going to be a lot of data entry and busywork. You need to hire someone to help with that."

"Great." She pushed to her feet. "Now I have to judge whether someone will be good enough to do *that* job."

Jon stood as well. "Didn't you hire workers at the WIFI?"

"No, Caroline and I did everything. We couldn't afford to hire anyone. We did hire Grant, but I mainly pushed Caroline to do that because I thought he should marry her. And it worked, and now I have a sweet little niece out of it. But I don't think I can take that approach again."

"Probably not. Hiring someone shouldn't be hard. It isn't a technical position. Hire someone you can get along with and who's competent with computer entry. And you should probably let them know it may be only temporary. I'm not sure when we'll be able to take on a full-time staff member."

"Fine. I'll ask around. Oh, and look what I found." Leah lifted an antique metal plate that read MAINTENANCE off the desk. "My grandfather had this on his office door for years."

"His office?"

She ran her finger over the letters. "He said it reminded him that it wasn't his business—it was God's. He just maintained it for Him."

Jon lifted it from her hands. "Very cool."

"I was thinking we could put it on our office door." Her teeth tugged at her lip as her hands landed on his forearm.

It wasn't an intimate gesture. More like one friend begging a favor from another, but it still muddled his mind. Business partner or not, Leah drew him to her. In fact, the only thing keeping him in place was the inevitable rejection that seemed to be on repeat every time he showed interest.

He took a step back, letting her arm fall away. "Sure."

"Thank you, thank you! Why did you stop by?"

Right. The name. Talk about a way to ruin the moment. "Business matters we need to discuss."

"Okay, but before that, I have one more thing to show you."
She rushed toward the back door. "Come on."

Jon followed her out to an old barn and waited for his eyes
to adjust to the dim light so he could see what she was pointing
at. On the far wall, an old antique wood sign boasted WIFI
ESTABLISHED 1949 through chipped paint.

"It's the original sign. I want to use that for the front of the
store. Isn't it perfect?"

He hadn't looked forward to telling her before, but this made
it so much worse. "There's something we need to talk about."

Her eyes turned toward him, still so hopeful.

"At the meeting—"

His phone rang and he glanced at the display. *Heritage High
School.* He sighed, held up a finger to Leah, and accepted the
call. "This is Jon Kensington."

"Mr. Kensington, this is Mr. Collins, the principal of Heritage High School."

"Is Abby okay?" He dug his keys out of his pocket.

There was a long pause on the other end, then the voice returned with a touch of sympathy. "Mr. Kensington, Abby hasn't
shown up to her summer classes since the second day. I wanted
to inform you that she's missed enough classes that she'll not
receive credit even if she were to show up for all the rest."

A cold sensation spread through his limbs. If she hadn't been
at school, where had she been spending her days? "Why is this
the first I'm hearing of her absences?"

"We left several messages on the phone number you put on
file."

Abby had turned in all the paperwork, and he hadn't even
questioned it. He sighed and ran his fingers through his hair.

"It's not our policy to track people down, but because I feel for your situation and I was a good friend of your father's, I had my secretary call your secretary. Abby can still enroll in the July classes, and I believe they would still give her enough credits for the diploma. But I'd encourage you to make an appointment with the counselor. It might be good for you and your sister to talk about her options as well as . . . other things."

Jon gripped the phone tighter. Why not just say that he wasn't cutting it as a stand-in dad? "Thank you, Mr. Collins. I'll look into that."

He ended the call and shoved the phone back into his pocket. What was he doing wrong with that girl? Maybe the better question was, what was he doing right? That would be a much shorter list.

He tried to focus on Leah. "So, uh, at the meeting—"

"Jon." Leah's hand landed gently on his arm again. "Is Abby okay?"

"She's flunked out of June summer school because of absences. Which begs the question of where she's been spending her days and where she is now." He pulled up the app that tracked her phone. "According to the app she's at school, but according to the principal she's not there."

"Maybe she hides her phone on the school property and picks it up when classes let out."

Jon checked the time. "If so, she'll be showing up in the next fifteen minutes to retrieve it."

"Go. Whatever you wanted to talk to me about, it can wait." She waved her phone in the air. "You know where to find me."

She was right. He needed to tell her, and soon, but that needed to be more than a two-minute conversation. He took a step toward his car. "Oh, can you pick up the revised blueprints Monday morning and meet me at the storefront?"

"Consider it done."

Now he had to go figure out where Abby was. He'd gotten detention once in high school for skipping class, and his father had made him spend the week doing janitorial work at the factory. But that had been his dad. Jon didn't know what the rules were for a brother.

Colby dipped his paintbrush in the light gray paint and ran it along the wall right next to the ceiling, taking his time to cut it in. His grandfather had made his living painting houses many years ago, and he'd been taught at a young age how to hold a brush to get the clean line at the edge.

A familiar tune floated down the hallway, and Colby soaked in the sound. He'd never gone so long without music in his everyday life, but his normal go-to bands didn't bring the peace they once had. Instead he saw Dawson's face. He tainted every memory that Colby had of music, and he didn't know if he could ever hear it the same way again.

But this song wasn't one he recognized, at least not this arrangement. There was an alto harmony that he'd not heard before. It gave new life to the song and tugged at his soul. He set down his brush and followed the sound to an old stereo at the end of the hall. But that wasn't where the harmony was coming from. He followed the voice around the corner and stopped in the kitchen.

Madison was cleaning out a cupboard with her back to him, and she was singing.

He leaned against the counter. "Wow."

She let out a little scream as she spun toward him, dropping the rag. "Don't scare me like that. Are you done for the day?"

"No, I came to find out where the music was coming from. You're really good."

Madison picked up her cloth again and resumed wiping out the cupboard. "Don't make fun of me."

"I'm serious." He poured himself a glass of water, then returned to leaning on the counter. "Did you ever sing professionally?"

"You're joking, right?"

"No. You had to at least have sung in choir."

"My freshman year." She dunked her rag in a bucket of water. "But after my father showed up at the spring fundraiser intoxicated, I dropped out. After that, I stuck to extracurriculars that didn't require parent involvement."

A new ache filled his chest. "That must have been rough."

She shrugged as she wrung out the dirty cloth and ran it one more time over the shelf. "It's in the past. Although small towns don't always let you forget your past."

"Is that why you're anxious to leave this place?"

She ran her hand over her barely perceivable stomach. "I lived under the shadow of my father's mistakes most of my growing-up years. I want better for her."

"You know it's a girl?"

"I found out at my last appointment. You're the first person I've told."

"Me?"

"Who else would I tell?"

Something about the question hit Colby square in the chest. If he had news like that, he could think of more than a hundred people he'd want to tell. And she'd only told him. A guy she'd met less than two weeks ago. "Don't you have friends from where you were living before here?"

"I wouldn't call them friends. They invited me to parties, but we never shared personal stuff."

"You could make friends here."

Madison released a humorless laugh. "People here only see me one way. That's why after I sell the house, I'll go someplace to get a new start. You of all people should understand wanting to go somewhere no one knows you."

He took a long gulp of water before setting it aside. He understood new starts, but he didn't understand being so alone. Nate had been one of many to reach out to him. If Colby was the closest thing Madison had to a friend right now, then maybe he needed to start showing her that he valued their friendship. And part of friendship was sharing those pieces of yourself that you hid from most people.

"It's kind of crazy," Colby said. "In some ways, I hate music right now, and in other ways I still long for it. It's a part of me, and I can't seem to let go of it. But every time I sing one of The Redeemed's songs, I get so angry. It may not have seemed like it, but I really struggled on Sunday."

Madison stared at him, and he ducked his head. Maybe admitting he hadn't been as into the worship as he was supposed to be wasn't the best place to start. Then again, Madison seemed like someone who'd understand trying to hold up an image.

"When's the last time you enjoyed a song?" Her gentle voice broke the silence as she opened the next cupboard and set to scrubbing it.

"About five minutes ago."

When she glanced at him over her shoulder with a lifted eyebrow, he rushed on. "Okay, I know that sounds like a pickup line, but it isn't. You have an amazing voice. But it's more than that. I could feel a calmness in your singing that I haven't heard in a long time."

"Well, I guess you need to remember that moment next Sunday . . . but without me."

"Or you could sing with me."

"In church?" She shook her head. "I can see it now. The only ones who wouldn't leave would be the ones frozen in place out of shock."

"First of all, you aren't giving people in this town enough credit." He leaned against the table and crossed his arms. "Second, that's not what I was talking about. I just meant I could bring my guitar over here and we'd jam."

Some of her long blonde hair fell in her face, and she brushed it away without even looking up. "Jam?"

"I play the guitar and we sing together. I think our voices would blend well." When she stared at him again, he shook his head. "Again, not a pickup line. I'm only talking about singing. Honest."

She rinsed her rag again, her face giving nothing away. "I'll think about it, but I may not be around when you paint next week. I need to find a job if I'm going to have enough money to finish this remodel. Although finding one close enough is proving harder than I thought."

"What type of job are you looking for?"

"I don't want to be near food." She rubbed her hand over her stomach again. "I'm still not over all the nausea. I also can't do heavy lifting, and most people don't want to take on a temporary employee who'll go on maternity leave in four and a half months."

His phone buzzed with an incoming text, and he read the display.

Nate
Dinner's at six sharp. Don't forget we have a
guest coming, so don't be late.

He put the phone back in his pocket. "I need to go clean up the paint. Nate and Olivia have a dinner guest coming, so I can't be late."

"Dinner guest? Sounds rather formal for Heritage." Her voice followed him down the hall.

He put the lid on the can of paint, then carried the brush to the kitchen sink.

She scooted to the side so he could get to the sink. "Did they say who?"

Colby stuck the brush under the running water, his shoulder brushing hers as she continued to clean. He tried to shut out how every one of his five senses were way too aware of each innocent contact, but it didn't work. "I think her name is Leah."

Madison paused. "They're setting you up. You know that, right?"

"What?"

Her movement had put a few more inches between them, but now that she faced him, it took all Colby's strength not to focus on how close she stood. The more time he spent with Madison, the less he saw her as just a friend.

He scrubbed at the brush a little harder. "Leah's a friend of Olivia's."

"Boys can be so dense." Madison set to scrubbing again, her motions a little more aggressive than before. "Leah is the last of the Conjoined Five left single."

"The what?"

"The Conjoined Five. It's what I always called them. Growing up, it was always Hannah, Janie, Olivia, Caroline, and Leah. They did everything together—thus the conjoined. Anyway, Leah's the only one left in the group not married, so my guess is that they're trying to remedy that with you." She gave him a once-over. It wasn't a warm, appreciative glance but rather almost a glare. "And you're exactly the type of guy they go for."

"What's that supposed to mean?" He shut off the water and shook the brush in the sink.

"It's not an insult." She tossed her rag in the bucket. "You're good-looking, involved in the church, and if you have a wounded past, I'm sure it's a bonus point for them."

Was she jealous? If so, maybe he wasn't the only one affected by their nearness.

He faced her head-on, waiting until she made eye contact. "But you only go for the ugly guys who are heathens and had a perfect childhood?"

"You got the heathen part right." She sent him a pointed look as she tapped her belly. "But since we see where that landed me, I've sworn off dating."

"Is that so?" He narrowed the space between them to a few inches. "Well, that's a shame."

"What do you mean?" Her eyes widened with fear.

That wasn't the emotion he was going for. He leaned back against the sink. One false move and he had no doubt she'd find someone else to paint the walls for her. "I mean it's a shame if they're setting me up, because I'm not looking for a date right now."

Madison laughed, but it seemed forced, as if she didn't know if she believed him. "You'll like her. She's cute and—in my opinion—the most original and interesting of the Conjoined

Five. Not to mention she has loved Jesus her whole life, so she's perfect for you."

He crossed his arms again. "You're hilarious. But I'm telling you I'm not looking to be set up. And I think Nate knows better than that."

Why had she ever agreed to this setup? Leah pushed her mangled lasagna around her plate and shot a look at the oversized wooden clock on the wall. According to the pale gray hands, she'd arrived only twenty minutes ago—yet she could have sworn it'd been longer.

She offered yet another awkward smile to Colby. Maybe she should ask him about his music. Then again, Olivia said that was a sensitive subject these days. "Are you enjoying Heritage?"

He paused between bites and wiped his mouth with his napkin. "Yup. It's cool. I mean, how many towns have a moving hippo?"

"Right." She nodded and toyed with her food again. "Have you met any new friends?"

Colby's eyes flicked to Nate, then back. "A few."

Her phone vibrated in her purse on the counter, and she resisted the urge to stand and grab it—both for the escape from this table and just in case it was Jon. She didn't expect him to call her and update her on what had happened with Abby, but she couldn't keep the curiosity from getting to her.

But they were already walking a fine line with their relationship. Most business partners didn't share their phone location with each other. They also didn't look at each other the way Jon had looked at her or stir those dangerous feelings he had stirred in her.

"Leah?" Olivia nudged her foot under the table, snapping her back to the present.

She blinked and found every eye on her. Maybe she'd missed something.

"How's reopening the WIFI going?" Nate asked the question slowly as if he was repeating it—probably was.

What was wrong with her? She loved Olivia's cooking, and a date with Colby Marc would have been a dream come true at one point in her life. He was funny, he had a great heart, and his easygoing smile was even more attractive than the polished brooding gaze from the poster. Not to mention he'd shown up to dinner in a retro Petra T-shirt that highlighted his athletic build. What more could she want?

Jon's face popped back into her mind, but she shoved it away.

Leah drew a slow breath and plastered what she hoped was a pleasant look back on her face. "Slow, but we're making progress. Do you know anyone looking for a job? I need to hire someone for data entry, but it's only a temporary position, so I'm having problems finding anyone who's both qualified and willing to take on something short term."

"Not that I can think of. But we can ask around." Olivia shrugged, then looked at her husband.

Nate moved like Olivia had also nudged him under the table. "Right, I'll ask around."

By the look on Olivia's face, she was hoping he'd carry the conversation a little further. But he just dug back into his lasagna, seemingly oblivious to the tension.

"Are you opening a computer store?" Colby bit into a breadstick, then glanced at his watch.

"No, it will carry a variety of arts made right here in Michigan."

"That sounds cool." Colby frowned, then cocked his head. "Then why are you calling it the WIFI?"

"It was a name my grandfather came up with that stood for Want It Find It because it used to be a general store that carried a hodgepodge of items."

"I can't believe Jon agreed to keeping that name." Olivia lifted an eyebrow. "I mean, since 'WIFI' means something else now. That and it no longer is going to carry the same inventory."

Leah pressed her lips together to keep from going off again. But they couldn't know she'd gone around this circle more than once with Jon. "I think the locals will enjoy the nostalgia of the name."

"Can a business like that survive based on local sales? It seems like you might need a name that has a further reach." Colby cut another piece of his lasagna and popped it into his mouth.

"It isn't changing."

Everyone paused at her tone. Awesome. She wasn't trying to argue, but she was tired of this subject. "Sorry. Jon and I don't agree on this. But it's important to me."

Olivia and Nate exchanged a look, and Leah didn't have to be a mind reader to know this whole night was falling apart—fast. She wasn't being fair to Olivia or Colby, but her heart just wasn't in this.

All because of stupid Jon. The more time she spent with him, the more time she wanted to spend with him. And the more time she wanted to spend with him, the more her head screamed at her to run. She was seriously messed up. One look around the table and it was clear no one would argue with that assessment.

Olivia's hand landed on Leah's shoulder. "Why don't Nate and I clean up and you two can go visit on the porch. Nate hung a swing out there the other day, and it seems like the perfect night for someone to try it out."

Leah was about to let everyone out of this horrible night by saying she had to go when Colby stood, thanked Olivia for dinner, and held the door open for Leah. "Shall we?"

Sure, why not drag the night out a little longer? Leah carried her plate to the sink. "If you're sure you don't need help."

"I'm sure." Olivia sent her a pointed look. "Nate loves dishes."

"Uh . . . yup." Nate stood and started gathering plates.

Leah followed Colby out the door, and they took opposite ends of the swing as she finger-combed her curls from her face. "This whole night is my fault. I'm sorry."

Colby set the swing into motion. "You couldn't know any more than I did what they'd planned."

Leah pulled her sweater tighter around her. "Actually . . ."

"I see."

"Olivia has been begging me to let her set us up." Leah rested her head back against the swing. "Then my sister had a baby and Libby announced she was engaged . . . What can I say? I caved."

"You have to love friends trying to cure you of singleness."

Leah ran her hand along the smooth wood of the swing. The pine was still pale and held the scent of fresh lumber. "They mean well. And you're an amazing guy. I mean, any girl would be so lucky to date you. It's just—"

"Wait, are you giving me the 'It's not you, it's me' speech?" Colby's eyebrows shot up, and then he released a deep laugh. "I'll admit it has been a while since I heard that one."

She joined in his laughter and shook her head. "No, really. It's not me either, it's someone else."

Colby paused the swing. "Let me guess. Someone Olivia doesn't know about."

"It's complicated."

He lifted his legs and the swing drifted forward again. "Of course it is, or you'd be with him tonight."

"We work together, and it's not wise to mix the two." That was only a small part of the reason, but it was all she was going to talk about with a near stranger.

"Ahh. The one you're reopening the WIFI with? I guess that makes sense."

"Right?"

"No."

"What?"

"Let's be honest, how often do you meet someone who catches your interest and you catch theirs in return? I mean, look at us. Olivia setting us up makes sense. We both prioritize our faith, I think you're good-looking, and I've been told I'm not terrible to look at."

"Not to mention you're humble." Leah nudged his arm.

"Naturally. I'm just saying that even what seems like a good match lacks . . ."

Leah's mind flashed back to every time Jon stood close to her. "Chemistry?"

"Exactly. If you have that with someone, don't ignore it because it's inconvenient at the time. You can't keep every relationship in a neat little box."

Colby's words hit her in the sternum. But what if Jon was safer in a box? The emotions he stirred in her made her feel out of control.

"It is more than the job thing, isn't it?"

She needed to get better at hiding her emotions. She fixed her eyes on the wood planks of the porch. "Yes, it's more than the job thing."

"Does he like you?"

"Yes. Maybe. I don't know. He did at one time."

"So what made you say no to a date with him and yes to a date with me?"

A sickening sensation filled her chest at the question. Why had she? Because Colby was safe. Because no matter how great he was, she wasn't going to fall in love with him. Maybe she should feel guilty about that. But it was pretty clear he wasn't any more invested in this blind date than she was. "I'm sorry, Colby."

Colby let his head fall back. "Don't be. I'm glad we did this. I don't have a whole lot of friends in Heritage, so it's nice to have one more. But I am definitely telling Nate and Olivia no more setups."

"I'm not sure they will try again after tonight." Leah laughed and shook her head. "Dinner was . . ."

"Awkward?"

"That was my fault."

"Not all your fault."

"Right, because you were the one thinking of someone else during dinner." When his face reddened slightly, she sat up straighter. "Oh, I was kidding, but there is someone, isn't there?"

"I'm taking it slow."

"So slow that Olivia and Nate don't know about it?"

"They know. Well, sort of. But I'm not sure they approve."

"Now I'm intrigued."

"I'll tell you, but you have to hear me out and consider giving her that temp job you mentioned in there."

"Okay, deal, because now I really want to know."

"Madison Westmore."

Leah faced forward and took care not to show any expression. "Oh."

He pushed the swing a little harder. "I guess you're in Nate and Olivia's camp."

"I'm sorry. But you have to realize that Olivia and I have a history with Madison, first in high school and then a couple years ago." She ran her hands down her jeans a few times, then tucked them close to her body. "But I promised to hear you out. Maybe she's changed."

"That's more optimism than I got out of Olivia."

"I can imagine. Olivia probably feels giving Madison a chance is being disloyal to her sister Janie. Janie is married to Thomas, and Madison was engaged to Thomas for a short time. I wasn't here then, but I do remember Olivia writing me that she thought Madison was manipulating Thomas. I'm sure she's just worried about you."

"Will you give Madison that job?"

Leah hesitated, her foot pausing the swing. It was one thing to let Colby make his own choice and another to put her faith in Madison. Because in truth, just the sound of Madison's name caused a bit of anger to rise to the surface. She might not have been around for the whole Thomas thing, but Madison Westmore had been horrible to her in high school. She and her minions could never let Leah pass without making fun of her clothes.

Colby turned toward her, pulling his knee up to the space between them. He grabbed her hand in both of his. "Please, I promise she'll do a good job. As a favor to me."

Her head kept screaming she was crazy, but something in her gut told her to listen to him. "Do you think she'll be okay working from home?"

"Absolutely."

"Tell her I'll bring a laptop to her place Monday." She really hoped she didn't regret this decision.

He gave her hand one last squeeze, then dropped it. "Thank you."

"Leah?" Jon's voice reached her from the sidewalk.

Leah lifted her gaze as Jon stepped out of the darkness and paused by the bottom step of the porch, his eyes traveling from Leah to Colby and back.

Colby stood and walked down the steps. "I don't think we've met yet. I'm Colby."

"Jon Kensington. I saw you in church on Sunday. You've got quite the talent." Jon shook his hand, then turned to Leah, who hadn't moved. "I was coming to finish a conversation about . . . work. I didn't realize . . . there would be people other than Olivia and Nate here."

Leah walked to the edge of the porch, searching for something to erase the tension. "Colby's staying with Nate and Olivia." That wasn't it.

"How convenient." Jon shoved his hands in his pockets and stared at Colby.

She hated to ditch Colby, but from their conversation she knew he'd understand. "We can talk now."

"You know what?" Jon smiled, but it wasn't the easygoing grin she'd come to know. "You guys finish whatever this is, and I'll catch you at the storefront Monday."

"I'll be there with the blueprints." Leah lifted her voice, but Jon was already retreating. Before she could even think if she should say more, he disappeared into the dark.

Colby walked back up the steps and claimed his spot on the swing. "Let me guess. That was Mr. Mystery."

"Yup." Leah sat down again and pulled her knees up to her chest.

"Well, I can promise you this, with the way he looked at you and the way he looked at me, he likes you. Now you have something to decide."

"What's that?"

"What do you want, Leah?"

That was the problem. Right now her head and her heart wanted very different things, and she didn't know which one to listen to.

seven

Jon should be thrilled. Heritage Fruits' new packaging had passed the test group with great success. The architect for the MIM had come in under budget. And Abby was twenty feet from him, so he knew she wasn't off getting into more trouble.

He flipped through his agenda and crossed another item off his list, then made a note and checked his watch. Everything was on track—except for Leah. She was supposed to have been here ten minutes ago.

He'd avoided her since Friday night. Not that it was difficult, since she hadn't seemed too anxious to talk to him yesterday at church either. He never should have used the app to find her on Friday. He wouldn't have if he'd had any idea she'd been on a date. He'd seen the icon at Nate and Olivia's and hadn't thought much of it.

"When are we leaving?" Abby leaned against the wall.

"As soon as Leah gets here with the blueprints."

"Kill me now." She pulled out her phone and started tapping away at it.

"Nope." Jon walked over, pulled the phone from her hand,

and gave her the push broom. "Here's something for you to do."

She didn't comment, just sent him the familiar glare, then took the broom and began a half-hearted attempt at sweeping. She hadn't seemed surprised or repentant when he found her retrieving her phone from its hideout at the school. After a little more pressing, she admitted she'd been hanging out with that Gabe kid with the yellow Camaro.

Jon had taken the keys to her car and grounded her for a month, and since he couldn't trust that she'd do what he said, the grounding meant she followed him around, doing whatever chore he could find. He wasn't sure how he'd missed taking her phone. That was parenting basics, but then again, he wasn't sure he'd pass the most remedial parenting class right now.

Abby's sweeping grew more pathetic by the second, but it didn't matter. This was all set to be torn apart Thursday, assuming Leah ever got here with the blueprints. He checked the time again. He pulled up the app to check her location but stopped. If she was with Colby right now, he didn't want to know.

Jon's own schedule was crammed so full that he could barely find time to breathe, let alone time for a date, and he'd foolishly assumed the same would be true for Leah. Evidently, he'd been wrong. She had time to hold hands with Colby on a porch swing.

The pencil in his hand snapped. What was it with him and pencils?

"Something vexes thee?" Abby quoted the familiar line from one of their favorite classic movies as she jabbed the broom at the floor.

"I'm fine." Other than a hefty dose of indigestion.

"Obviously." She huffed but continued her work.

Okay, maybe he wasn't fine, but he didn't want to talk relationship drama with his baby sister. Then again, maybe she had magical insight into the inner workings of the female mind.

"Why would a girl say she doesn't have time for a relationship, then go out with another guy?"

Abby paused her sweeping and stared up at him. "I'm assuming you're looking for something more than the obvious answer."

"Which is?"

"She's not into you and she likes the other guy."

The constant aching in Jon's gut twisted a bit further.

"Or it could be a misunderstanding," Abby rushed to add. No doubt she figured the happier he was, the easier the chores he'd come up with for the day would be. She wasn't wrong. "I mean, you're my brother, but I hear the gossip. You're one of the most eligible bachelors in town. You're good-looking, you own your own company, you were a professional athlete. She'd be crazy to pick someone else."

Okay, now she was laying it on a bit thick, but he'd give her props for trying.

She leaned against the counter. "Who's this other guy anyway? I'm sure he has nothing on you."

"Colby Marc."

Her jaw dropped. "Never mind. You don't stand a chance."

He pointed at the broom. "Finish sweeping."

Not that she was saying anything he didn't know.

He rubbed at that spot in his gut. "Maybe I'll swing by the house to get some antacids."

Abby stood up a little straighter. "Perfect, you can drop me there."

"Not a chance. You are going with me to the office."

"Great, what will I have to do there?"

"Whatever I say. If you don't want to do dumb jobs, then don't make me babysit you at seventeen."

Abby's eyes narrowed as she pressed her lips into a thin line and leaned on the broom, giving up any pretense of sweeping the floor.

The back door slammed just before Leah appeared in the hall. "Sorry I'm late, but I brought you coffee. Fresh from Donny's."

Jon shoved his folder under his arm and took the coffee. He sent Abby a look that hopefully conveyed that he expected her to keep her mouth shut regarding their conversation. "Thanks." He took a sip and paused. Since when did she buy coffee?

"I would've brought you one too, Abby. But I didn't know you'd be here." Leah lifted her brows at Jon.

What was he in trouble for? Was he supposed to tell her the drama of his family? She hadn't thought to mention she had a date. "Did you have fun at dinner Friday night?"

Leah jumped at his tone, her eyes slightly larger than they had been. "Yes."

His sister, who was across the room behind Leah, smacked herself in the head as she mouthed, *Seriously.*

He hadn't meant to sound so accusing. He set his coffee aside, leaned against the counter, and relaxed his shoulders. Taking care with his tone, he tried again. "Colby seems nice."

Abby snickered as she leaned the broom against the wall. "I'll be in the car."

"He *is* nice." Leah laid the blueprints in front of Jon, then moved around the counter and booted up the computer.

Could the girl be more vague with her answers? He slid the

blueprints out of the cylinder and unrolled them across the counter, checking over the latest changes. "You two seemed to have a lot to talk about."

"We did."

"Like . . . ?"

Her hands stilled on the keyboard. "Stuff."

"Music? Our store?" He needed to mind his own business, so why couldn't he let this go? Did he really want to know what they had talked about?

Yes.

"We didn't talk about his music. We did talk about this place, I guess."

"What did he have to say about it?" He rerolled the blueprints and started sliding them back in the tube.

"For one thing, he said naming it the WIFI was a mistake."

Jon paused with the papers halfway in the tube. He still hadn't told her about that change. Then her words hit him full force. "Wait. What?" Was she saying that she was now reconsidering the name because some good-looking musician suggested it?

"He said that it'd be confusing and less marketable. It makes sense, but—"

"Seriously? Colby says it and suddenly it makes sense?" Jon shoved the prints in the rest of the way and snapped the cap on. "I've been saying that the whole time, but you wouldn't listen. But what do I know? I only have a degree in business. Better go with the famous musician. I know my uncle doesn't believe in me, but I at least thought you did." He scooped up his coffee, leaned his shoulder into the door, and shoved it open.

"Jon."

"I've got to go. We can talk later." He stepped out on the sidewalk and turned toward his car.

The door flew open behind him. "Jon."

He spun to face her. Her teeth tugged at her lip as if she needed to confess something, but he didn't really want to hear her confess her newfound love for the local celebrity.

"What?" The word came out more pained than he meant it to. When she didn't respond, he drew a slow breath and softened his voice. "What do you want, Leah?"

The fight in her seemed to drain away at the question. She stepped back and reached for the door. "I'm meeting with someone today about the data entry position."

He gave her a curt nod, then turned back to his car. What did Leah want? Not him, and that was all he needed to know.

The last thing Madison wanted to do this morning was beg for a job from Leah Williams, but the moment she'd become a mother, she no longer had the luxury of doing what was easy. She wiped down the counters in the kitchen and then cleared the table. She scanned the entryway, but there wasn't much she could do to make that look better. She'd already removed her dad's old boots and the trash he'd left piled by the door, but both had left stains on the light blue carpet that weren't going anywhere soon.

Those stains, along with another couple dozen that spread throughout the house and the lingering scent of smoke that would never come out, put new carpet at the top of the list as soon as Colby finished painting. But everything needed money, and that was why she needed this job.

Colby wandered out of a back room in a well-worn pair of

jeans and an old Redeemed T-shirt with a fair amount of paint across the front. The way the gray paint smeared across his band's name didn't appear accidental. After all, other than the paint rag hanging out of his pocket and a few dots of paint on his hands, there was little evidence that he'd spent the morning painting at all. "Would you stop fussing? I told you. Leah's cool."

"And I told you that you don't understand the workings of a small town." Madison rinsed the rag and hung it in the sink. "I'm sure the Leah you know is a delightful person. But I have to make a good impression on the Leah I wasn't very nice to in high school. The Leah that is friends with people that don't like me, and for good reason. The Leah that if she knew I was pregnant would know that everything she believed about me in the past is true."

Colby gripped her gently by the arms. "The Leah that if you let get to know you—really know you—will adore you as much as . . ."

Madison's heart beat against her chest as her breathing grew difficult. "As much as?"

Colby cleared his throat as he released her arms and moved back, but his look remained intense. "As much as everyone else who's gotten to know you."

As much as you do?

"Aren't you the one who said she had a soft spot for tragic pasts?" he asked.

"The tragic past is only a bonus for sexy heroes. I'm still the former mean girl." She tried to lighten the mood with a joke, but based on the way Colby's eyes lingered on her, it hadn't worked.

"You think I'm sexy?" His voice was deeper, and the timbre of it sent a trail of awareness down her spine.

Of course she thought he was sexy. She wasn't blind. But she hadn't planned on admitting as much out loud.

A heavy knock echoed through the house, causing her to jump. Colby walked back to where he'd left the roller without another comment.

Madison squared her shoulders and lifted her chin as she pulled open the old wooden door. Leah wore a skirt made of multiple patterns and a white baby-doll shirt. It was a unique mix but cute. No doubt any comment Madison made about it would be taken the wrong way, so she just stepped back and held the door wider. "Hi, Leah. Thank you for this opportunity."

Leah set a briefcase bag on the table before offering a fake smile if Madison had ever seen one. "Colby insisted you were perfect for the job."

"Hi, Leah." Colby's voice carried from the living room.

"Colby." She turned toward him, her face morphing into a look of genuine happiness. "I didn't know you'd be here."

"Just painting." He held up the roller, then dipped it back in the pan. But not before he shot a look at Madison that seemed to say, *See, what did I tell you?*

Colby meant well, he just didn't get it. Sure, Leah's words said she was giving Madison a chance, but her eyes as she watched their little exchange said, *I'm doing this as a favor to Colby. Hurt him and you'll have me to deal with.*

Everything in Madison wanted to turn on her heels and run. From this house. From this job. Most of all from this town. But she needed this job, and Colby had stuck his neck out for her. "I hear you're looking for someone for data entry."

Leah pulled a laptop out of the bag and booted it up. "Yes. Do you have any computer experience?"

"I was a receptionist for a dentist while I was living in Chicago last year. I dealt with records management."

Leah nodded as if slightly impressed and then pulled a manual out of the bag. "This is the software we'll be using. I've already loaded it onto the computer. This folder has all your log-in and access codes, and that folder has the applications I want you to start with. Why don't you take a few days to get comfortable with this and then we can meet again?"

"Great."

"Great." Leah held out yet another file. "This details your work hours, hourly wage, and forms like your W-2 so you can get paid. Colby told you it was temporary, right?"

"Yes. That's perfect because I plan to move when I sell the house."

Leah studied her a moment, then nodded and picked up her purse. "I have to get going, but Wednesday I'll be at the WIFI, and my cell number is in there if you have any questions. Bye, Colby."

"Bye!" he yelled from the other room before the door shut behind Leah.

Madison dropped into one of the wood chairs at the table. The whole interaction had truly exhausted her. But she had a job, which meant she was closer to having the money to fix up this place and sell it. And one step closer to getting out of Heritage and avoiding more interactions like that in the future.

Colby's hand landed on her shoulder and offered a comforting squeeze. "See? Easy."

Colby didn't get it, and he never would. Just one of the many reasons things could never work between them.

Leah unhooked the power cord from her laptop and dropped it in a cardboard box. How she had accumulated so much at the storefront in such a short amount of time, she'd never know. But since demolition was set to start tomorrow, she had to get it all cleared out.

Jon had offered her an office at Heritage Fruits during construction, but the idea of working a few doors away from him all day was unsettling. They hadn't really talked since their last argument. She still wasn't sure what had set him off, and now he probably thought she was considering changing the name of the WIFI. She needed to clarify that, but his words "What do you want, Leah?" had paralyzed her.

That and her non-date with Colby, whose words had been rolling around in her mind as well. *"You can't keep every relationship in a neat little box."* But boxes were good. Necessary. And when Jon had tried to jump out of the friendship box, she'd quickly wrapped him in a "professional relationship" box. But now even that didn't seem to be enough to contain him. And she couldn't seem to answer the question of what she wanted.

She'd dated a few guys in college, but nothing serious. She'd always picked guys who didn't have the potential to become serious, because why would she open her heart to someone who had the power to break it?

And that was exactly what Jon had the power to do. Because with Jon, it wasn't just attraction. He went toe to toe with her and yet still made her feel empowered rather than run over. Around him, she was stronger and more alive. And the idea that someone could stir all those sensations in her terrified her, because if she leaned into that strength, it'd destroy her when it was gone. She'd seen it firsthand.

The door swung open as Janie walked in, bringing in a summer breeze thick with humidity. The Fourth of July was less than two weeks away, and the heat needed to break before then, or they were in for one hot Heritage Festival.

Janie stopped in front of Leah and held up a white pastry bag. "I thought you should have a scone in honor of the last day for this counter. After all, this counter has witnessed hours of girl talk over scones."

"You're an angel." Leah gave her friend a big hug and accepted the gift. Unfolding the bag, she peeked inside and drew in the scent of cinnamon and sugar, making her stomach growl.

"Have you considered who you're going to hire to paint the outside?" Janie asked.

"No. Why, you know someone?"

"Kade Paxton. He graduated with Gideon two years ago. He could do something amazing with it."

"Doesn't he work at Dan's Garage?"

"Yes, but it turns out he's an amazing artist too."

"Okay, I'll give him a call." Leah made a note on a piece of paper and picked up the bag, but Janie made no effort to move. "Was there something else?"

"Speaking of people you're hiring . . ."

Leah paused with the scone halfway out of the bag. "I guess you heard I hired Madison. I'm sorry. Colby asked me to hire her and—"

"I'm glad you did." Janie stood up straighter a moment before leaning a little closer. "And I hope you two will become friends."

Leah's lips twisted. "You do?"

"Madison needs friends, and with our history I'm not sure she would accept my friendship. Not to mention it'd be . . . awkward for both of us." When Leah didn't respond, Janie rushed on. "Thomas and I have talked about . . . everything. And though he admits it was a mistake to date her, he also has shared a lot about her that makes me wish I would've been nicer to her in high school."

Were they both talking about Madison Westmore? "She was horrible to us."

"I know. But maybe we didn't make it that easy on her either. I'm not going to share all the stuff that Thomas told me, but let's just say . . . I wish I would've taken time to get to know her better. I'm not sure it would've made a difference back then, but I'm glad you have that chance now. Because I think she's changed. I think we've all changed."

No, *they* had all changed. Four out of the five who made up their original group were married, but who hadn't changed? Leah. Leah was back where she started. Leah was still holding Jon at arm's length. Leah was the one who couldn't seem to let go of the past. The past with Madison. The past with Jon. The past with her father.

Another blast of humidity filled the room as the door swung inward. Madison strode in and then paused her steps, her gaze hopping between Leah and Janie. She clutched a stack of papers to her chest tight enough to wrinkle the edges and retreated a half step. "I can come back."

"No." Janie held up her hand. "I've got to go anyway. I brought scones for you two to share."

"Really?" Madison's brow wrinkled.

Janie nodded and moved toward the door before looking at Madison. "I'm glad you're back."

Madison's mouth dropped open slightly, and her gaze followed Janie outside. "What just happened?"

"I'm not sure myself." Leah lifted the paper bag. "But Janie's an amazing person who brought us scones to share. Come on. You won't want to miss these."

"O-kay." Madison set the papers on the counter and stood opposite Leah with her back perfectly stiff.

Leah pulled out a scone and set it on a napkin in front of Madison. "Did you get the software figured out?"

"Yes, it's up and running, but I have a few questions about some submissions." Madison tapped her finger on the stack of papers.

"Okay. Fire away." Leah placed a scone in front of herself. Maybe Madison *had* changed, but she was still the girl who had been mean to Leah in high school and who had caused Janie so much hurt two years ago. But if Janie thought it was time to let that go, what right did Leah have to hold on to it?

Madison held up two pieces of paper. "This artist is only sixteen and this one is only fourteen. Do you want anyone under eighteen to submit a parental signature?"

Leah took the papers and studied them. "That makes sense. I'm not sure—"

"I already researched it and have come up with three potential revisions on the form to accommodate underage sellers. I'll email them to you and you can let me know which you like best. Then I'll contact them." She paused, then rushed on. "That is, if you want me to."

"That's actually perfect. Thank you."

Madison's face lit up at the affirmation, and for a brief second Leah got a glimpse behind the thick wall Madison had built around herself. Maybe the first step in letting go of the past was moving forward.

Leah pushed the napkin closer to Madison. "Now, let's eat."

Madison hesitated but finally broke off a small piece of scone. "Thank you."

Leah picked at her own pastry as the silence stretched out. Why was building a bridge so doggone hard? "How are you and Colby doing?"

Madison picked at her scone again. "I know you're afraid I'll hurt him. But trust me when I say that's exactly what I'm trying not to do. I've told him nothing can happen between us. But he's so . . ."

"Persistent."

"Yes. Persistent and kind and gentle and stubborn." Madison huffed, then seemed to catch herself. Her eyes darted back to Leah.

"Definitely stubborn. He wouldn't let up until I'd given you this job." Leah popped another bite into her mouth.

"Sorry about that."

"I'm not. You're obviously good at it." She pointed to the papers. "And I'm not sure I would've . . ."

"Given me a chance otherwise?"

Leah picked at her nail. "I was going to say, 'thought of a minor waiver,' but you're right. I *am* sorry about that too. It's just . . ."

"No." Madison held up her hand. "I'm sorry for the way I treated you in high school. I wasn't a happy person after my mom died, but that's no excuse."

"What happened to your mom?"

"Breast cancer when I was ten. Then it was only me and my dad."

Leah broke off another piece of her pastry. "Looking back, I'm not sure why we weren't friends. I mean, we had that in common. My mom died when I was thirteen and I only had my grandparents."

Madison pressed her lips together a moment. "I know you're

trying to connect and be nice like Colby asked you, but please don't suggest our childhoods were anything alike."

Leah stared at her. She'd obviously hit a nerve. So much for moving forward.

Madison walked back toward the door but paused halfway there and turned back. "You were left with two grandparents who loved you and were respected in the community. I was left to be raised by the town drunk. I'm not sure the two really compare." She took another step toward the door.

"Wait. I'm sorry. I guess I never really knew much about your dad."

Madison locked eyes with her and seemed to be weighing her sincerity. Finally she nodded and returned to the counter. The fight seemed to have drained out of her. "I didn't mean to bite your head off, it's just, I would've given anything for your life. My biggest goal in school was to graduate without CPS being called. I started wearing makeup at a young age to cover the bruises—"

"Bruises?" Bile rose in Leah's mouth.

"My dad wasn't a happy drunk. Others saw my efforts with makeup as . . ."

"You wanting attention from boys." Leah's stomach twisted. That was exactly what she'd thought—what they'd all thought. And the grown-up look mixed with Madison's natural beauty and flawless figure had quickly made her the queen of the school and extremely popular among the boys. Leah forced herself to meet Madison's eyes. "And the boys thought you wanted their attention too."

Madison shrugged. "I was a broken girl who learned early on that people were nice to you when they could get something out of you. Popularity. Affection. People gave to get. So I hid behind a persona that got me what I wanted. What I thought I wanted."

Janie was right. There was so much they hadn't known. "And now?"

"I don't know. Right now I'm trying to learn who Madison Westmore really is."

"What about Colby?" As much as Leah was fond of Madison turning over a new leaf, she didn't want Colby to get run over in the process.

Tears filled Madison's eyes. "Colby's the first person who's made me believe that the real Madison Westmore might be someone worth knowing." She dusted the crumbs off her hands into the trash, then tossed in the napkin. "There's probably something I should tell you—"

Leah's phone rang and she glanced down. Jon. The look of torn allegiance must have shown on her face, because Madison waved her off. "I need to get going anyway. We can talk more later."

"I would enjoy that." And she would. Madison wasn't at all who she'd thought. The more layers she pulled back, the more Leah believed that Colby was onto something. Madison was definitely someone worth knowing.

Leah answered the call as the door swung shut behind Madison. "Hey, Jon, what's up? Are we still set for construction to start tomorrow?"

"Yes, but I need a favor that falls slightly outside the business partner box."

"Outside the box?" Leah's voice cracked on the last word, and she cleared her throat. "What would that be?"

"Abby's grounded to my side until the next session of summer school starts. But Friday I have a meeting she can't be in. Can she spend the day with you?"

"Of course." Not quite the out-of-the-box favor that had popped into Leah's mind, but a safe one. And one she could handle.

eight

If Jon had asked Leah to supervise Abby earlier in the week, then maybe she could've at least passed off some of the data entry to her, but as it was, Leah was at a loss for what to do with the seventeen-year-old. She made a few more marks on the new shirt she was designing in her sketchbook, then glanced between Abby slumped on the couch and the floor she'd attempted to sweep. Nah, *attempted* was a strong word. The floor that Abby had sort of moved a broom around on briefly.

How did one babysit a teenager? She understood Jon's reluctance to leave her alone, but she doubted hovering over the girl was the best solution.

Part of her wanted to shake Abby and tell her to grow up and stop making Jon's life so difficult, but the rest of her understood what was going on under that tough shell a little too well.

Madison was right. Leah had been lucky to have loving grandparents to fall back on. Madison hadn't been so lucky. Did Abby have anyone besides Jon?

Leah hadn't made it easy on her grandma, unlike Caroline, who had been the model granddaughter from the start. But her grandma hadn't given up on her. She had offered the perfect balance of tough love and grace.

When Leah had been at her worst, her grandma hadn't yelled at her. She hadn't even been one to punish. She'd just been there during Leah's grief, and maybe that was what Abby needed too.

Leah set her sketchbook aside and stood. "Come in the kitchen. We're making cookies."

"I don't want cookies." The words came back stiff.

"I didn't ask if you wanted to eat cookies. I said get in the kitchen. Not everything is about you, Abby. We're making them for my uncle Henry, Nate and Austin's dad, who lives in a care home." Leah's heart beat double time as she tried to keep her tough exterior. If she'd gauged Abby wrong, this could all blow up in her face, and then what would she tell Jon?

When Abby still hadn't moved, Leah gave it one more go. "Abby, please come to the kitchen."

Abby sent her an icy glare but rose from the couch and walked into the kitchen.

Yup. She'd been that girl. And as much as Abby wanted everyone to believe she had it figured out, Leah knew the truth. She was just a little girl missing her mother.

Leah swallowed past the lump and set the cookie recipe on the counter. Abby stared at it but didn't say anything. She didn't say anything as Leah pulled out the ingredients. She didn't say anything as they measured out everything. And she still hadn't said anything when they placed the first batch of cookies in the oven.

"Who taught you how to make cookies?" Abby's voice finally cut through the quiet kitchen as she scooped the batter onto the next baking stone.

"My grandmother. My grandfather made sure we knew how to shoot, fix a leaky sink, and change a tire, but it was my grandmother that made sure we knew how to make an amazing batch of cookies and cook at least ten meals." Leah closed the flour and sugar and put them back in the cupboard. "They hadn't planned to be raising kids again at seventy-five, but they knew life didn't always go as planned."

"What happened to your parents?" Abby's hand shook slightly as she scooped out the next cookie.

"My dad disappeared from the picture the summer I was thirteen, and we never heard from him again. My mother got ill shortly after that and died before Christmas."

Abby paused with the scoop hovering over the baking stone. "You didn't hear from your dad even after your mom died?"

"Nope." Leah returned the spices to the cupboard. "He's never even contacted his family. My dad and Nate and Austin's dad are brothers, and as far as I know there was never any contact there either."

"What a jerk." Abby plopped another cookie on the stone.

Leah's hand tightened on the wooden spoon as she carried it to the old farm sink. *Jerk* was one of the kinder names she'd had for her dad over the years.

"I used to make cookies with my mom." Abby's voice lowered to a whisper as she dropped the final cookie on the stone. "We were supposed to make them the day before the accident, but I talked her into ordering pizza and having a movie night instead. I've wondered what we would've talked about that night if we'd made cookies. But we did have a good time watching the movie. I can still hear her laugh. I wouldn't trade that movie night for anything . . . I just wanted both. I wanted more. You know?"

"I know."

The timer buzzed, and Leah pulled the hot cookies from the oven and replaced them with another full stone. The silence hovered in the room as she moved the cookies to the cooling rack. She bit into one of the large ones, then held another out to Abby.

"Aren't you going to say something like it's God's will and we can't argue with that?"

Leah whipped her head toward Abby. "Sweet girl, it wasn't God's will that your parents were killed. Death and sin are not a part of God's desire for us."

"Then why did He allow it to happen?" She hiccuped as a tear trailed down her face. "He could've saved them."

Leah wrapped her arms around Abby's shoulders. "I don't know why your parents died. I don't know why my mom got sick. I don't know why my cousins have to watch their dad go through the ugly disease of Alzheimer's. But I know all of this breaks God's heart too. And I know He's still at work in our lives. There are things we may never fully understand until heaven, but I want you to know you're not alone in this. You aren't alone in your pain. And you aren't alone in life."

"You mean God?"

"God. Jon. Me. We are all here for you, and no matter what happens with your brother and me, you can depend on me."

Abby lifted an eyebrow as she studied Leah. "So, something might happen between you and my brother?"

Had she said that? Leah grabbed a cookie and shoved it in her mouth.

Abby leaned on the counter and reached for another cookie. "Are you into my brother or not?"

Leah coughed against the cookie that she'd partially swallowed and reached for a glass of water. How had they gotten on this subject?

"I mean, I get it if you're not into him. Colby's hot and all, but—"

"Hold on." Leah took another drink of water as she held up her finger. "I'm not into Colby. We're just friends."

"That's not the impression my brother has." Abby downed the rest of her cookie, then dusted off her hands.

"He only saw us talking."

She shrugged. "All I know is that he's fairly sure you two are getting together and he's been miserable to live with for a week now. If you're not getting together with Colby, would you mind letting Jon know so he isn't such a grump?"

The idea of Jon being jealous did strange things to her heart. It wasn't that she wanted to make him jealous, but the idea that his feelings were strong enough to . . .

"What's that look for?" Abby's voice cut through her thoughts.

"What?" Leah pulled her grandmother's antique pink mixing bowl into the sink and added some soap.

"You *do* like him."

"I . . . uh . . . no."

"Well, that was convincing."

Leah pressed her lips together. How had this kid squeezed out a confession she hadn't even admitted to her twin sister?

"Even if you aren't ready to confess your love, could you at least call him up and say, 'I thought I'd let you know that Colby and I are only friends'?" Abby leaned forward, her eyes teasing. "Or maybe, 'Colby and I are only friends, because I want to date you'? That would put Jon in a great mood, and when he's in a good mood—"

"I never said—"

"Of course. I totally believe you." Abby gathered up the dirty measuring cups and spoons and carried them to the sink. "I know you like him and he likes you. What's the problem?"

"We're business partners." Leah's face warmed. "And if we try and fail... I mean, talk about an awkward working relationship."

"Do you always go into a relationship expecting it to fail?"

Yes.

Leah bit back the word as she dismissed the question with her hand. "Jon and I never seem to be on the same page at the same time. I can't help but wonder that if this thing between him and me was meant to be, it wouldn't be this hard. We're like two ships never in port at the same time."

That wasn't the whole issue, but it was the only one she could talk about.

"Well, I don't know much about relationships, but from what I remember my mom saying, even the good ones take work. All I'm saying is that he really likes you. Give him a shot."

"You love your brother, don't you?"

"Of course I do. I don't mean to be so difficult." Abby leaned back against the counter and wiped her hands on a towel. "I know Jon's trying. And I know he gave up his basketball career to bring me home, but I still get so mad at him and I don't know why."

"Do you really not know why, or do you just not want to talk about it?"

"Okay, fine, I'm mad at him for laying down all these rules for me when I know he did things he shouldn't have in high school. I'm mad because he had parents at my age and I don't. I'm mad because he's not my mom and dad." Abby let her head fall back as another tear trailed down her face.

"He knows all that. But he loves you and wants what's best for you. Talk to him. And if you'd stop fighting him, I think you'd find he misses your parents too. He feels as lost without them as you do. And flunking out of high school won't help anyone."

Abby wiped the tear with the back of her hand as she cleared her throat. "When I go to school, I get so terrified about what to do next year. College was supposed to be a decision I made with my parents."

"Talk to Jon. Talk to me. Just don't hide away."

"You'd really help me look at colleges?"

"Of course. I've been where you are."

"And your grandparents helped you?"

"My grandparents and my twin sister and my older brother, David, who was bossy."

"Older brothers are so bossy." Abby laughed as she wiped another tear away.

"Yes, but over time I realized that David didn't want to control me. He was just trying to hold the family together." Leah swallowed back a lump as memories of serving with him in Costa Rica filled her mind. She needed to call him again soon. "I think Jon's trying to do the same thing."

"You say that, but he has me on house arrest with you."

"If you promise me that you won't skip summer school again and start communicating with him more, even if it means arguing with him more, I can probably get your sentence reduced. Silence is hard on him."

"Fine." Abby studied her for a moment. "As long as you agree to tell him how you feel."

"What? Not the same thing."

Abby shrugged. "Silence is hard on him."

"Fine." Leah huffed as she gathered the mixing bowls and carried them to the sink. "Next time I see him I'll mention

141

that Colby and I are only friends." But since he seemed to be avoiding her, she had some time.

"Deal." Abby extended her hand and Leah shook it. "Do you want to show me one of those meals you learned how to make? Jon's good at a lot of things, but cooking isn't one of them."

"When do you need to be home?"

"I'll text Jon, but I think he has dinner plans."

"Oh." Dinner plans on a Friday night? Maybe he wasn't as concerned about her and Colby as Abby thought.

Her disappointment must have shown, because Abby's face lit up. "I knew you liked him."

Leah didn't comment as she reached for her grandmother's recipe box. There was no point in arguing.

The last thing he'd expected today was to get a text from Abby inviting him to dinner with her and Leah. Especially since he'd thought he still had her phone. But Abby's enthusiasm about some meal she was making didn't leave room for him to turn down the invitation, even if it did mean he'd have to find out if Leah and Colby had a second date or not.

Jon climbed out of his car and pulled the flowers from the passenger seat. They weren't much, but they were the best JJ's had to offer, and he hated to show up to dinner empty-handed even if it wasn't a date.

He approached the side door and knocked twice, rattling the wooden screen door.

The hinges squeaked as his sister flung it open. "Right on time. Ooh, flowers. Nice touch."

What was she babbling about? He walked in and scanned the room. "Where's Leah?"

"Changing because she spilled something on her shirt. Which was perfect." She yanked the flowers from his hand and walked over to the sink.

He shed his coat and hung it by the door. "It's perfect that she stained her shirt?"

Abby sighed and held up her hand. "Please don't interrupt. I only have a minute before Luke gets here. Grab that vase." She pointed to the top shelf in the cupboard.

"Who's Luke?" He reached up, grabbed the vase, and held it out.

"Uh, your best friend from high school." Abby cut the stems of the flowers, then added them to the vase with water.

Oh, that Luke. At least it wasn't another guy from her school. "Why do you have your phone anyway?"

"Not important." She waved him off, then carried the flowers to the table. "Leah taught me to make Greek pasta." She lifted the lid of the pot, revealing a colorful array of noodles, peppers, sun-dried tomatoes, and feta cheese.

His stomach rumbled as the spicy scent wafted toward him. "It looks great. Why are there only two plates?"

She rolled her eyes. "I've done all I can. The rest is up to you."

"Sorry, what?" he said. A car honked from the driveway. "Abby, what did you do? And you can't go anywhere. You're still grounded."

"True, but since you let me hang with Leah for the day, I figured your friends were on a preapproved list." Abby grabbed her purse and black jacket from the hook by the door. "That reminds me. Did I leave my red leather jacket in your Mustang? I can't find it anywhere."

"What? No. Who's that?" He pointed to the driveway.

"Catch up, Jon." Abby pulled open the back door and rushed

out. "I'm babysitting for Luke and Hannah tonight to give you and Leah some *time*."

"Abigail Joy . . ." Jon followed her out and paused at the sight of the minivan sitting in the driveway.

The driver's side window rolled down, and Luke stuck his head out. "I was so glad Abby texted to ask if we needed a sitter tonight. Hannah needs a night out."

When Jon glanced back at Abby, she shrugged. "Have fun, and tell Leah I said the ships are in the harbor and a deal is a deal."

Before Jon could question her further, she hopped into the passenger side and Luke backed onto the road.

Abby had set them up, but the question was, was Leah in on it?

He returned to the house and shut the door just as Leah emerged from the hall in a flowing blue skirt, a sleeveless floral top, and her red curls a little more wild than normal. Her eyes widened as they landed on him. "Jon, what are you doing here?"

That answered that question. This wasn't going to be awkward to explain at all.

"Uh . . ." He pointed to the table, then back at the door. "Abby went to babysit."

"She what? I thought—" She dropped her hands on her hips. "Did she say anything else?"

"Something about two ships and a deal is a deal."

Leah's face turned deep red. But he couldn't gauge if it was embarrassment or anger. "I'm sorry. This is my fault."

He had no idea what she meant by that, and from her look she wasn't going to explain anytime soon.

"Maybe we should eat." Leah took her seat at the table and dished up the food.

Silence stretched through most of the meal until Leah finally spoke up. "Thank you for keeping your father's foundation going. Grant and Caroline were worried about Quinn Ranch for a while."

"Tell them they don't need to worry about that. That foundation was my father's heart and soul. Their funding is secure. And I've seen the good it does for kids like my cousin Seth."

She nodded, then returned to silence.

He had to do something to rescue this disaster of a date. Was it a date?

Leah stood and started clearing the dishes, and Jon jumped up to help her. "I think the last time I had dinner here was when you had that anti-Valentine's party my senior year. We had that Mario Kart tournament."

A slight smile transformed her face. "Which I won."

"You mean you cheated."

"Did not. You want to go again? Because we still have it in the living room."

"You still have a Wii that works?"

"Of course. You don't?"

"I think I've updated my gaming system about five times since my Wii."

"Your loss."

"After we get this cleaned up, you're on." Jon held his breath. Was it being too presumptive to invite himself to stay longer?

Leah didn't comment as she carried her plate to the sink.

"That was also the night—"

"That you told me Luke wasn't interested." Leah took the plate from his hands. "I remember."

"Sorry."

"You weren't really telling me anything I didn't know, but

that didn't make it sting less." She rinsed both plates and added them to the dishwasher.

"I never really understood your crush on him. I mean, he's a great guy and all, but you two were so different."

"I think a part of me liked him because he was safe to like. If he didn't like me back, then he couldn't break my heart, right? But I think I also liked how calm he was. He did his own thing. He seemed at ease with being himself. And that was who I wanted to be." She carried the empty pasta dish to the sink and filled it with water. "He never tried to go with the flow or bow to the crowd."

"You mean unlike me." Was that what she really thought of him?

"Jon, you led the crowd in high school. You got Converses one Christmas, and everyone had them by Valentine's Day." She snagged the towel from the counter and dried her hands. "Almost every girl painted your number on their face for basketball games—"

"You didn't."

"No." Her movements had stilled with his words. "I didn't think you needed one more groupie. Honestly, I didn't think you noticed."

"I noticed." He lifted the towel from her hands and set it aside. "Did you know I never gave my jersey to any girl to wear at the game?"

"I figured you didn't want to limit your attention to one." Her voice was softer now and held a touch of grit.

"No." His hands found hers, and he ran his fingers along her palm. "The one that had my attention didn't want it."

"I didn't know." The words came out just above a whisper.

"If you'd known, would it have made a difference?"

146

"Of course not." She cleared her throat, put a little distance between them, and sent him an impish grin. "I mean, I don't think I could ever love anyone enough to wear their jersey."

"What's wrong with a jersey? It's classic girlfriend attire."

"Maybe for girlfriends that don't care about the way they look."

"It's hot." He stepped closer again.

She lifted one eyebrow. "No. There is no way to make a jersey look pretty or sexy."

"Whatever." They were not going to agree on this. "What about being my girlfriend? Would it have made a difference if you'd known how I felt?"

She gave a soft shake of her head. "I think I hated you partly to keep myself from liking you. Because unlike with Luke, I had little doubt you could break my heart."

He took a half step closer as he trailed his hands along her arms and up to her shoulders. "Are you still afraid I could break your heart?"

"Yes." The words came out breathless, and her eyes closed as he drew his finger along her jaw, then traced *#14* on her cheek.

"Did you ever consider that you could break mine? I mean, when I saw Colby holding your hand, I—"

"We're only friends." Leah's eyes flickered open. He must not have looked convinced, because she rushed on. "Honest. He likes Madison, and I told him that I liked—" Her eyes widened before she swallowed hard.

His hand traveled from her cheek to behind her ear to the back of her neck. "You like . . . ?"

"Uhh . . ." She placed a hand on his chest with enough hesitation that he still wasn't convinced she wouldn't bolt at any second. "You?"

"Is that a question? Because if it is, I'd vote yes."

Her teeth bit her lip as she fought against a smile.

And that was all Jon could take. With the slightest tug, he pulled her closer until his lips brushed across hers. Just the faintest touch. He leaned slightly away, trying to gauge her reaction, but her hands gripped the front of his shirt and pulled him closer.

That was all the encouragement he needed. His hand slipped around her shoulders and down her back. Over the years he'd kissed a girl or two, but those had meant little beyond a distraction. But this . . . this was a kiss he wouldn't soon recover from. With every passing second, she reached into his soul and carved out a piece that would always be hers. And when her body molded to his, he would've committed to never leaving her side again. As if deep down he'd always known she was his, and as she responded to him, he could see not just this moment with her but all his moments—his dreams, his hopes, his entire future—entwined with hers.

When she leaned back, he released the grip he had on her. Her lips were a bit swollen and red, but the laughter in her eyes made him want to go for round two.

He brushed her hair back from her face. "Can I assume this means you'll bid on me at the auction?"

A touch of the hesitation returned to her eyes. "As much as I want to, I don't think I can afford you."

"You have to bid on me now that you're my girl." Jon read his mistake in her eyes the instant the words left his mouth. The words *my girl* had shifted her from in-love Leah to analytical, redefining Leah.

Don't retreat.

He needed to keep it light. No doubt an old-fashioned DTR

wouldn't be in his favor right now. "You bid as high as you need to. I'll fund any amount you put in." He ran his hand up her arm, desperately trying to keep that connection, and took it as a good sign when she didn't flinch away.

"Look at you, Mr. Moneybags. You're the big-ticket item. You or Colby will probably bring in the highest bid."

"Well, to tell you the truth, I wouldn't mind breaking Luke's record from a couple years back." His phone buzzed, and he glanced at the text from Abby.

Update? Did it work?

When his gaze found Leah again, she was biting her lip. And not in the teasing, kiss-me sort of way. "Jon . . . maybe . . ."

He waved the phone in the air and then slid it back into his pocket. "Can I take a rain check on that Mario Kart? I've got to get going."

He could ignore Abby, but he couldn't keep Leah from running. And if he stayed to hear her out, he had a feeling it might end with an excuse for why things between them wouldn't work.

When she nodded, he leaned down and placed a quick kiss on her lips. He'd been honest that she had the power to break his heart. And the girl was as skittish as a rabbit. Right now, his best move was not to push and let her get used to the idea.

Colby had meant it when he told Madison he wasn't hitting on her, but it definitely wasn't because he wasn't interested. He just didn't think he stood a chance. He ran the roller under the stream of water again as more paint dripped out. How did paint always seem to multiply when it came time to rinse the rollers?

"You're here late tonight." Madison leaned into the garage, a kitchen towel slung over her shoulder.

"I wanted to get that back-corner room finished." He held up the wet roller. "All done with the accent blue."

"Wow. You'll be done in no time."

"Just the gray left. So only the living room, dining room, and kitchen. Oh, and did you decide on the bathroom yet?"

"Okay, okay. I get it. You're not almost done." She glanced at her watch, then toyed with the ends of the towel. "It's late and I have dinner ready. I mean, it's nothing fancy, just some frozen pizzas, but if you want some . . . Of course, you probably have plans with Nate and—"

"Maddie."

Her eyes rounded. He'd never used the nickname before, and he'd never heard anyone refer to her as anything other than Madison. But now that it was out, he liked it. It suited her.

He dried his hands and hung his towel back up. "Do you mind if I call you Maddie?"

She swallowed and shook her head.

"Good." He reached up and tucked a piece of hair behind her ear. "I'd love some frozen pizza."

Her cheeks flushed slightly as she took a few steps back. "Good. It will be ready in about five minutes."

He flipped off the light and shut the door to the garage but then paused. There was another door to the left of the garage. "What's in here?"

"My dad's shop. You can go in. Someone needs to."

The creak as he opened the door testified that it hadn't moved in a while. The scent of leather hit him square in the face as he ran his hand along the wall until he found a switch. He flipped it on, bathing the place with fluorescent light. He hadn't known what to expect when she'd said *shop*, but this was definitely not it. Probably close to a hundred leather boots lined the far wall. A saddle sat on some sort of stand in the middle. There were a lot of unfinished projects here and there, but the room was clean and orderly.

He ran his hand along the soft skin of the saddle. The detail of the etching was impeccable.

"My father was good at one thing. Leather craft."

Colby spun at Madison's voice. She stood in the doorway with her arms crossed over her chest, her expression far away as her eyes stayed fixed on the saddle.

"That's how he paid to keep us in this house, even after Mom was gone and he was drunk half the time. He'd find a way to be sober long enough to put out some of the most amazing things. I still need to find a buyer for the tools and for the boots and other projects that are complete."

"Did you work with him as a kid?"

His question seemed to snap her back from wherever her mind had drifted. She pointed to a shelf behind him, where a pair of small boots sat all by itself. "It was the one time when I was little that I knew I didn't have to be afraid of him. When he was in this room, he became a new man."

He picked up the children's boots for maybe a ten- or eleven-year-old. He brushed off a layer of dust to reveal MADDIE.

"He helped me make them. I think that was one of the last projects we did together. At least one that I finished." She glanced at the worktable to her left where a few pieces of leather had been cut and stamped. Two pieces had been abandoned partway through being stitched together. The layer of dust there was thicker than anywhere else in the shop.

"Why did you stop working with him?"

"It was the anniversary of my mom's death, and he was hurting. I was hurting. I was twelve and I mouthed off to him. He knocked me clear across the room. It was the first time I had to call in sick to school because of the bruise he left."

"The first time?" The reality of that statement gutted Colby in a way he hadn't known was possible.

"Most of the time I could cover the bruises with makeup. But there were a few times . . ." Her voice trailed off.

Colby's fist clenched. He'd never been a violent man, but if her father were standing here now, Colby wasn't sure he'd have been able to keep himself from doing some serious damage to the man.

Madison cleared her throat. "Anyway, he apologized, but we avoided each other as much as possible after that. I've never been back in here since. The closest I came was this far to tell him dinner was on the stove when he was ready."

Colby closed the distance to her and wrapped her in his arms. She tensed at first, but when he continued to hold her, she slowly relaxed into him.

"I hadn't planned on dumping so much of my past on you," she said.

"I'm glad you did."

"Why?" She pushed away, wiped at the corners of her eyes, and walked toward the kitchen.

Colby flicked off the light and pulled the door shut. "Why? If you haven't picked up on it yet, I want to know everything about you. I like you. A lot."

Her eyes widened, and she stood frozen until the timer went off. She grabbed a hot pad. "Well, you shouldn't."

"And why's that?"

"Because I'm not the girl for you."

"Oh, really? And who *is* the girl for me?"

"Leah. Or, well, pretty much anyone would be a better choice than me." Madison dropped the pizza on the stove top with a clang and tossed down the hot pad.

"Too bad. I like you. I was thinking we should go out on—"

She rushed forward and covered his mouth with her hands. "Don't even say that."

Colby gently removed her hands. "Why not?"

"Because I . . . don't feel the same way."

Something jerked inside Colby. "Oh."

"I should've told you sooner. But I don't see you like that. I only see you as a friend." She broke eye contact, and the wall went back up between them.

"I see." Colby stepped back as if she'd smacked him. Here he was falling for her, and she only saw him as a friend.

"I guess you probably want to go." She lifted a paper plate from the table. "I can make you a plate to take with you."

Right. Because the people in Madison's life had left as soon as they stopped getting what they wanted from her. But that wasn't him, and it was time for her to learn that not everyone was like that.

Colby shook his head as he took the plate and dropped a slice of pizza on it. "No, I'll stay for dinner."

"Why?"

Colby paused with the slice halfway to his mouth. "Uh, didn't you invite me to stay for dinner?"

"Yes, but—"

"Then I'm looking forward to eating dinner with my friend Maddie."

Her eyes hardened. "I'm not changing my mind. I'll never date you."

"Good to know." He lifted his pizza and offered a smile even though the words were a punch to the gut. "And I'm not changing my mind about being your friend, no matter what you say to me. We all need a friend, Maddie. Why don't you let me be yours?"

Madison placed a piece of pizza on a plate, then took a seat.

Colby didn't know if they'd ever get beyond friendship, but he was still trusting that God had dropped them in each other's life for a reason. He wasn't jumping ship just because it might look different than he'd imagined.

nine

She'd done it. She'd opened the proverbial box, and Jon had leapt out.

Leah paced the sidewalk across from the WIFI, then sat on Otis's back as she checked the time. She was set to meet with Kade Paxton about painting the storefront today, but he was running late.

Which gave her more time to think about Jon.

Think about the kiss.

Think about the way his arms had made her feel so small and so protected.

Think about the way his lips had taken control and yet she hadn't felt out of control. Rather, the kiss had ignited a fire in her that had made her want to do nothing else for the evening besides explore his lips, his arms, his shoulders.

She might have done that very thing if it hadn't been for the words that were an ice bucket of reality. *My girl. My girl. My girl.* It ran like a nasty little GIF in her mind.

Going from an earth-shattering kiss to his girl wasn't a huge leap, and she didn't fault him for that. But that leap meant he was out of the box, and that was dangerous. Because out of the box was when people got hurt. But it was also when people fell in love. Caroline, Hannah, Janie, and Olivia had all made that leap to trust someone with their heart, and it had paid off. It was exactly what Leah wanted in theory. So why did the reality fill her with panic?

Kade pulled up to the curb in an old Buick that appeared to be held together by patches of rust and hopped out. His messy blond hair blew in the wind as he pulled his messenger bag from the passenger's seat. He slammed the door and walked toward her. She hadn't seen his work, but everyone in town had bragged about his talent with a paintbrush.

"Afternoon. You must be Leah." He extended his paint-stained hand. His boyish grin made him look younger than his twenty years.

Leah stood and shook his hand. "Yes. It's nice to meet you. How did I not know we had an amazing painter right here in our small town?"

He shrugged as he pulled the bag higher on his shoulder. "It was a secret talent until recently."

"What changed?"

"Someone believed in me." He sat down on Otis and pulled his bag up on his lap. "I brought a few preliminary drawings based on what you said on the phone."

He pulled out a black portfolio and flipped it open to a pencil drawing of the storefront. Only it wasn't the run-down storefront in front of them. It was beautiful. The structure was the same, but he'd incorporated the new display window and masked the brick in brightly colored flowers. The texture still shone through, but the drawing hid the years of paint and damage. Leah held it up to get an idea of how things would lay out.

"I took the idea from the Bright Walls down in Jackson," Kade said. "Have you been there?"

"No, but if they're anything like this, I'm going to make the trip."

"Wow. That's amazing." Janie spoke from behind Leah.

Leah turned to face her. "Where did you come from?"

"I was at the diner. Just running home for a second. Kade, I might have to hire you to do the diner and bakery next." She tapped Leah's shoulder. "He paints even better than he draws. Ellie had a huge painting of his above her bed, of Times Square at night."

Kade stood and shifted his weight from one foot to the other. "How's Ellie doing in New York?"

Things started to click into place. This was Kade. The Kade who had started dating Ellie, Janie and Olivia's sister, after the Christmas dance six months ago. The Kade who Ellie had been heartbroken to leave when she went to NYU a month ago.

Janie pulled her phone from her pocket and flipped through it before she held it out. "Her apartment is small, but that's New York."

The photo was of Ellie standing with her arms stretched out in a room smaller than the original size of the WIFI.

Kade nodded. "Tell her I said hi."

Janie's features softened. "Do you two not talk at all anymore?"

"She thought it best—*we* thought it best—to not drag things out." Kade pulled out another sketch from his bag, keeping his eyes fixed on it.

Ugh. That look on his face was why falling in love was so terrifying. Because love led to that.

"I've got to get going." Janie's voice seemed to snap both Kade and Leah back from their wandering thoughts.

Kade met Janie's gaze again. "You know what? Don't tell her I said anything."

Janie nodded and offered him a sad smile as her hand landed on his shoulder. "I'm serious about talking to you about painting the front of the diner. I'll talk to Thomas and call you."

After Janie walked away, Leah pulled the check that she'd already prepared from her clipboard. "I love it. Here's the deposit."

"Wow." He read over the numbers. "You haven't even seen the second option yet."

"Second option?"

Kade held out the other drawing he'd been holding. "For this one I included the hanging sign we talked about with the name."

They would use her grandfather's sign, so this sign wouldn't be necessary, but she should look at the drawing since he'd put the effort into it. She took it and scanned it over. "Why does the sign say *Made in Michigan* rather than *WIFI*?"

"Uh . . . isn't that the name?"

"Where did you hear that?"

Kade's eyes darted around. "My dad, who's on the board, said that you guys had renamed it at the board meeting a couple weeks ago."

Leah's gaze drifted from one drawing to the other, then back. A cold sensation traveled down her limbs as Jon's Mustang pulled up to the curb.

Jon got out and walked up to her. He dropped a quick kiss on her cheek. "Didn't expect to see you here."

Leah stood and shoved Kade's drawing into his hands. "Did you change the name weeks ago without telling me?"

Kade pulled his bag back onto his shoulder and walked backward toward his car. "I'll let you two talk. Let me know when you want me to start painting."

By the time Kade's car pulled away, Jon had gone three shades paler. "I was going to tell you. But—"

"But you thought if I fell for you first, it would be easier? Was anything you said true?"

That seemed to break him out of his frozen pose. "Everything I said was true. This isn't about us. The board wouldn't support the plan any other way. And when you started coming to that conclusion on your own after talking to *Colby*, I figured—"

"You could get away with it without even telling me that you switched it behind my back."

"It wasn't behind your back. I had to make a split-second decision, and you weren't there. You skipped the meeting, and you said you trusted that I could get it done. This is what I had to do to get it done."

Leah waved the drawing in his face. "I didn't flake on the meeting. My sister was having a baby."

"I didn't say you flaked. I said you weren't there when the decision had to be made. And I did try to tell you several times, but I got pulled away to deal with Abby and then you had that date with Colby."

"This is my fault?"

"No. I should've made the time to tell you. But I didn't want to have this conversation. Not when things were finally going well between us."

"Us?" She met his gaze. "There's no 'us.'"

"Don't do that, Leah. Don't use this as an excuse to push me away. That was a business decision. It wasn't personal."

"It was personal to me." Her voice hitched, and she hated that it made her look weak. "And I can't be with someone I don't trust."

Jon looked away a moment then looked back as he shoved his hands in his pockets. "Don't fool yourself, Leah. You never trusted me. You've been looking for a way out from the moment we ended that kiss, and you know it. Looks like you found one."

She swallowed back any argument that she could come up with. She wasn't sure how he knew, but he was right. Still, it seemed she had a good reason not to trust him with her heart. He'd always put the business first. "I want the name changed back."

Jon's shoulders sagged as he shook his head. "No. It's the right decision, even if you want to lie to yourself about that too." He turned away and walked toward Donny's.

This was why she didn't trust people with her heart. Because when she did, it always ended up broken.

———

Madison grabbed the groceries from the passenger seat and climbed out of the car. Had she learned nothing in the last twenty years? First she'd nearly told Leah about the baby, and then she dumped all her baggage on Colby about her dad. What was she thinking letting people get so close?

Heritage wasn't a place she planned on settling. She'd lived under the scrutiny of small-town eyes her whole life, and she didn't want that for her child.

She propped the groceries on her hip and worked the key into the lock, but the door swung open. Her heart slammed in her chest. She'd locked it when she left. She'd even double-checked. Small towns weren't known for their crime, but it wasn't un-heard of. What if . . .

Before she could complete the thought, the faint strums of a guitar wafted through the house from the back room. Madison abandoned her keys and groceries on the table and followed the gentle notes being fingerpicked on a guitar.

Colby sat with his back to her. The wall in front of him was two-thirds painted, and the roller lay in the pan by his foot. A bucket was upside down next to him, holding a piece of paper and a pencil. She opened her mouth to speak, but his rich tenor voice stopped her.

> "When my world turns dark
> And the wind blows strong;
> When peace feels far
> And the days are long;
> When the stones leave scars
> And I'm left without a song,
>
> You.
> I will look to you.
> You;
> I will wait for you.
>
> Because
> You make giants fall
> And seas divide,
> You crumble walls
> And make dead men rise.
>
> As you breathed life into them,
> Breathe life into me.
> As you stood in the fire with them,
> Stand in the fire with me."

The last notes didn't flow with the others, so he paused his strumming and tried again, but that didn't quite ring true either.

"As you stood in the fire with them,
Stand in the fire with me."

The notes were out of Madison's mouth before she could consider the wisdom of singing them.

Colby spun to face her. His eyes creased at the corners as a wide grin spread across his face. He plucked at the guitar again, then ended the song the way she had. He made a few notes on the paper next to him, then patted the bucket as an invitation.

Sitting down and singing with him would be a dumb idea. That was what she'd been telling herself all day. Then why were her feet moving that very direction? Because she was a glutton for punishment.

She picked up the paper and pencil and took a seat. He started the notes again from the top and nodded toward the paper.

When he started on the second verse, she joined in, adding some harmony. When the last notes faded, Madison closed her eyes. There was something about the words that rattled her. It was like Colby had peered into her very soul and heard her. And no doubt if she opened her eyes right now, she'd find him staring at her, wanting more, but right now she couldn't offer more.

"I was stuck on that song, and I thought painting might help me work out the rough spots." He stood and leaned his guitar against the wall. "Guess I was right. Painting and you. You sounded amazing. Would you ever consider joining the worship team?"

"No." Madison stood and walked toward the door, but Colby blocked her path.

"Why not?"

"Let's see." She held out three fingers, then pointed to them one at time. "I'm pregnant. The town hates me. The pastor hates me—"

Colby's hands landed softly on her arms. "He does not."

"He would if he knew I was pregnant with no idea who the father is."

Colby flinched at her words, but she was done softening them. This was who she was, and better for him to realize sooner rather than later that he didn't want her messing up his life. "How can you not know who the father is?"

So they were having this conversation. She steeled herself against the memory. "I went to a party at this huge house in Chicago. It lasted a couple days. I don't remember much. I was drunk most of it, high part of it. I have no memory of who I was with or if I was even only with one person. There were probably over five hundred people in and out of the house over the weekend. The pregnancy test turned pink a few weeks later."

Colby's arms circled her, and against her better judgment she sank into them. She hadn't been held with such tenderness—such care—since . . . never. Thomas had cared for her, but never like this. Never with love so gentle it hurt. So beautiful it ripped open all the dark parts.

She took a step back and wiped a tear with the back of her hand. "You tell your pastor Nate all that, and he won't want me in his church, let alone leading worship."

His hands landed softly on her upper arms again. "You're wrong."

The strength in his hands and the confidence in his tone

almost convinced her. She marched around him toward the door. "His wife thinks I'm trash."

"She does not! I'm confident that Olivia doesn't think anyone is trash. If she doesn't like you, then maybe it's because she doesn't know you." He followed her out of the room, but at least he'd stopped touching her.

She grabbed the groceries, carried them to the counter, and began pulling them out of the bag. "That's never stopped most of the town from hating me."

"If you'd let them in"—Colby took the cans from the pile she was forming and added them to the shelf—"let them see the Madison I know, then they couldn't help but lov—like you. I do."

Her breath stalled at what he'd almost said. But had he corrected himself because he didn't feel that way or because he was afraid to let her know he felt that way? She opened the fridge and placed the milk and cheese on the shelf. "I lived here for more than twenty-five years. You don't know this town the way I do."

"Or maybe the town doesn't know you the way I do."

She kept her back to him.

"In all those years, did you ever tell anyone a fraction of what you've told me?"

"I told Thomas some of it." She folded up the grocery bag and put it in the drawer. "But he still picked Janie."

"Did you love Thomas?" There was no emotion in his words, but it seemed as if Colby held his breath as he waited for her answer.

"I thought I did." She shrugged and leaned back against the counter. "But I'm beginning to think that I don't even know what love is. I loved that he made me feel safe and protected.

I loved that someone cared about me for the first time since I was ten. But it wasn't romantic love. I mean, I was attracted to him—he's a good-looking guy—but . . . I don't know how to explain it."

"You enjoyed his company but didn't crave it." Colby reached up and tucked a piece of hair behind her ear.

She didn't trust her voice, so she just nodded.

He took a half step forward, leaving a couple inches between them. "And when he touched you, it was nice, but it wasn't . . ." He ran the back of his finger up the length of her arm.

She swallowed and tried to remember all the reasons she'd been against this when she'd arrived home a few minutes earlier.

". . . like every cell in your body is responding." His finger trailed over her shoulder to her jaw. "Calling you closer."

"That's an adequate description." Madison's voice came out breathy as her lungs refused to work properly.

Colby leaned closer, but she turned her head at the last second. His lips brushed across her cheek, then hovered by her ear. "Go with me to the festival Saturday."

She blinked at him a few times, trying to get her brain to process the words. "What?"

"The Fourth of July festival."

She moved away from his touch. "Around town?"

"Yes."

"Have you not listened to a word I've said?" She attempted to walk past him, but he wrapped his arm around her waist.

"Come on." He tugged her a little closer. "I want everyone to know you and I are . . . friends. And since Hannah roped me into that bachelor auction, you can bid on me."

"No." She pulled away. "The town loves *you*. The town wouldn't love *us*. Even if they believed we were only friends."

Which she was beginning to doubt. "They'd all think that I was just trying to seduce you."

"Hey, now there's an idea." His voice dropped a little deeper.

Madison grabbed a towel and smacked him with it. "Colby, I'm serious."

"I am too." He caught the end of the towel and tugged it closer until she stood right in front of him again. "Okay, not about the seducing. But I'm serious that this town would adore you if you just opened up to them."

She leaned against him and rested her forehead on his wide shoulder. "I can't."

"Madison, you can't keep pushing everyone away."

"I'll be leaving Heritage as soon as the house is ready to sell, so it doesn't matter."

The muscles in his shoulder stiffened as he dropped his arms. "Maybe you should stay."

"No." She met his hard gaze. "I'm not staying, and I'm not telling them about my life. I don't need their judgment or pity. I'm leaving the first chance I get."

Colby just shook his head and sighed as he walked back down the hall.

She wasn't trying to hurt him. But he didn't understand. She'd spent her life building this wall around herself, and behind the wall she was safe. And neither Colby nor anyone else was going to change that.

He really should've told Leah earlier. That was a no-brainer, but so was the name change.

Jon leaned on the rail of the gazebo and pinned the *Bachelor #15* button on his T-shirt as he searched the crowd again for his feisty redheaded partner. She'd finally answered her door last night and heard him out. He'd apologized for making the decision without her, and she'd calmed down. Everything should be fine. Business-wise, that was.

Personally, things were far from fine. She'd refused to let him touch her or talk about them, the kiss, or anything beyond business. Which made it worse than before. Now that he'd had a taste of what they could have, the absence of it was even more painful.

Jon checked his watch. Leah was ten minutes late. He pulled out his phone and sent off a quick text.

> I'm waiting at the gazebo for you.

"I'm right here." Leah's words were laced with a resigned tone, and Jon spun to face her.

She stood at the bottom of the steps with a clipboard in hand. She had her hair pulled up in a messy bun, and she wore a simple black tank top and black shorts. He hadn't seen her look this subdued since she'd walked into his office with her briefcase five weeks ago.

"What's wrong?" He crossed the gazebo and hurried down the steps to her.

"Nothing's wrong." Her brow twisted, and she focused on her clipboard. "Where do you want to start?"

"Leah." He reached for her arm, but she pulled away. "I thought we talked this through. You said you understood."

"I do understand." She took a few steps away but then paced back. "That's what bothers me so much. I know it was the right decision, but it's like losing a piece of my history. It's like losing my grandparents again, and I'm not even fighting it. Because it makes business sense."

Her outfit choice clicked. She wasn't hiding like before. Leah dressed her mood, and today she was grieving. He wanted nothing more than to scoop her up and hold her, but the way she flinched every time he came near ruled that idea out.

Jon dropped onto one of the benches surrounding the gazebo and stretched his legs out, making sure to leave plenty of space at the other end for her. "When I got the call my parents died, it was the worst day of my life. I was supposed to be home. I'd been home for Christmas and Abby was still there, but I had taken off early to spend New Year's with friends in Barcelona."

Leah settled onto the other end of the bench, and it gave him a moment to collect himself before he started blubbering right here in the square, in front of Leah and the whole town.

"When I came home for the funeral, everything made the pain worse. I could smell my mom as I walked through the halls of our house. I could hear her telling me to slow down as I took the stairs three at a time. Basketball had always been my escape, but playing in the gym my dad had built for me and where he'd coached me for hours as a kid hurt. They were everywhere, and I couldn't take it. So as soon as I could, I turned the business over to Uncle Dale and went back to the life they were never a part of."

Leah set her clipboard and purse on the ground, then pulled her knees up and wrapped her arms around them. "What about Abby?"

Jon flinched at the question. It was obvious that he wouldn't have won Brother of the Year at that time. "I visited her at her school in England when I could, but we didn't talk about our parents. We went on with life like there wasn't part of us missing. It's no wonder my shooting percentage went down and

Abby practically flunked out of St. Mary's. I don't think I've had a time I felt like more of a failure than the day I ran into you at the airport."

"Last November?"

"Yup." Jon laced his hands across his chest. That was better than doing something stupid like running his hand across her knee, as he was tempted to do. "My coach had called me in that week to let me know they weren't sure they'd be re-signing me. That meeting was followed by one with Abby's school about how they believed she needed more support at home. The only two things I had left going for me were quickly going down the drain."

"And then I was horrible to you."

"True. You were." He sent her a teasing look. "But it was a breath of fresh air. You didn't look at me with pity in your eyes. You treated me like the Jon you'd always known. The Jon I wanted to be again."

"You wanted to be the jerk in high school again?" The sassy look on her face caused a flicker of hope to rise in him. Maybe he hadn't completely destroyed what they'd started.

He tapped the side of her foot on the bench. "Need I remind you that you're the only one who thought I was a jerk in high school? Everyone else—"

"Wanted to date you or be you. Trust me, I know."

As if on cue, two women in short shorts and Fourth of July tank tops walked by and offered him a finger wave. "Hi, Jon."

Leah moved her feet away from his hands and back to the ground. So much for that small hope.

He offered the women a tight smile and turned toward Leah. "I'm not saying I wanted to be the center of everything. I'm saying that I wanted to be that confident guy I once was.

The one who lived life fully because he had parents who supported him and made him believe he could do anything he put his mind to. The guy my dad had trusted enough to leave his company to."

"Is that why you decided to come back?"

"That and Abby got kicked out of St. Mary's." He leaned forward on his knees and rubbed the back of his neck as the memory of that call flooded his mind. "But when I returned, I soon realized that the house was mine now—well, Abby's and mine. And I couldn't keep my parents' clothes just because giving them away felt as if my guts were being ripped out slowly."

She swallowed and broke eye contact. "What did you do?"

He sat back again and let his gaze travel over the crowd. "I had a free garage sale of sorts. I invited the people of Heritage to come and take what they wanted." He pointed to Margret Bunting, who was running a booth selling jam. She was probably close to ninety and couldn't be more than five feet tall, but she was full of fire. "That was my mom's hat."

"Does it make you sad to see it?"

"No. It makes me remember the day my mom bought it and my father teased her because he said it was bigger than an umbrella. It's a good memory. And I love how it almost completely covers Margret. She's hilarious." A touch of laughter rumbled in his chest as he stretched out his arms on the back of the bench, taking care not to touch Leah. "It's just stuff. And my mom doesn't need me to hold on to her stuff to remember her." He made eye contact with her once again, and this time she didn't look away. "And your grandfather doesn't need you to hold on to that name to remember him."

"I know you're right." The edges of her eyes glistened, and the sight broke him.

He'd do anything to take that hurt from her. He gripped the back of the bench to keep from reaching for her.

"I haven't changed a thing at the farmhouse since my grandmother died. I guess it made it more like I was coming home. Like she was right around the corner in her rocking chair, waiting. I know I need to, but if I do I'll forget. I don't want to forget." Her voice cracked, and Jon couldn't take it anymore.

"You won't." He scooted toward her, wrapped his arm around her shoulders, and gently pulled her to his chest.

"I don't think I'm very good at grieving." She buried her face in his shoulder. After a few minutes she leaned back, and a bit of the weight behind her eyes seemed to be gone. "How are you handling your parents' death so well?"

"I'm not sure that I'd say I am, but I've chosen to focus on the happy memories. The more I do, the more they outnumber the moments of bone-crushing pain. But I'm not sure that pain will ever completely go away." Jon sighed and stared across the square again. "Like I know the day I get married will be one of the best of my life, and yet there will be grief that my parents aren't there."

Leah's wide eyes and red face telegraphed that he should've thought through his last words a little more. He really needed to come up with a different example. "Not that I'm saying I'm thinking marriage now . . . or to anyone specific. I was talking in general . . . about key events of my life."

Great, now she was laughing at him. She stood and motioned toward the booths. "What do you say we go find some inventory?"

"Sounds good." Jon stood and placed his hand on her back as they navigated the crowd.

She picked up her pace until his hand fell away. One thing was clear. They may have mended the rift regarding the name of the store and maybe even their friendship. But they were nowhere near returning to what had started between them last Friday night.

ten

They really needed to find another day in the year when food trucks could line up along the square. Leah pulled off another piece of her funnel cake and popped it into her mouth, letting the sugary sweetness melt on her tongue. Of course, too many days like this and she might not be able to fit through the door of the WIFI—uh, the MIM.

Leah ignored the small twinge of pain that came with the thought of the new name and walked back to where Jon stood. He reached for a piece of her cake, but she slapped his hand.

"Hey." He yanked back his hand, then held up the clipboard. "It looks like we've gotten almost everyone. We just need to stop by Mrs. Nell's booth."

Leah waved away the idea. "I already told her she was a shoo-in."

Jon's brows rose as he shook his head. "Leah, we can't do that. She has to fill out an application and set up a contract like everyone else."

"Contract? Jon, she was our art teacher for most of our schooling. I think we can trust her."

"Everyone needs to follow the same process." He handed

her one of their business cards. "And that process starts with an application for *everyone.*"

"My grandfather—"

"I'm not in business with your grandfather. Times were different then, and in today's world we're not doing business on a handshake and a smile."

"Fine." Leah shoved her plate into his hand, grabbed the card, and made her way to Mrs. Nell's booth. She extended the card. "*Jon* wants you to fill out an application, and then we can set up a contract."

"Of course. I feel much more comfortable with that too. Always better to have things in black and white when it comes to business." Mrs. Nell pocketed the card, then went to help an approaching customer.

When Leah faced Jon, his smirk made her want to throw something at him. And he was eating her funnel cake. She marched over and yanked it from his hand. "I guess we're done then."

She started to walk past him, but he grabbed one of her belt loops and pulled her to a stop. "Oh no you don't. We still have the matter of the auction." He tapped the button on his shirt that held the number fifteen. "You promised to bid on me."

"I'm sure those girls in the tank tops would be happy to oblige."

Jon lifted an eyebrow, and she cringed. But like he'd really thought she hadn't noticed them walking by and flirting during their talk. And then repeatedly at the booths. Could they have been more obvious?

Jon took a step closer, his finger still holding her shorts. "I don't want to spend time with them, and I could be wrong, but I don't think you want me to either. Do you?"

Leah searched for something witty, but her mind remained blank as her heart pounded in her ears. Her skin hummed with his nearness, and she gripped her plate a little tighter.

So instead of a funny, sassy reply, she only managed a small shake of her head.

Amusement played at the corners of Jon's eyes as he leaned a little closer. "I'm glad we got that settled."

Hannah's voice echoed over the speakers, making Leah jump back. "All bachelors report to the gazebo. Ladies, get ready to open your purses. We're raising money for a new clock tower in the southeast corner of the square, so let's not be stingy."

Jon pulled out a wad of cash and placed it in Leah's palm. "That should be plenty."

She glanced down, then fanned the money out. "Seriously, Jon, a thousand dollars?"

"It's for a good cause." He offered a shrug and then nodded at Luke standing next to Hannah. "Besides, I told you, I really want to beat Luke's record of $733.45."

"Why are you so competitive?"

He held up his hands and then pointed at himself. "Professional athlete. I made my living by being competitive. And I kissed this girl the other day, and now she moves away every time I try to get near her. Maybe I need an ego boost."

"I think your ego is just fine." Leah shoved the money into her pocket and wandered over to where the bidders had started to gather.

Gideon, Olivia and Janie's brother, was up first. A few girls jumped at the bid, but it took only one glare from his girlfriend, Danielle, before they backed down. Danielle may have softened her look since Olivia's wedding, but she was still as tough as they come.

After Danielle won the bid at three hundred dollars, Gideon joined her and dropped a kiss on her lips. They were seriously cute and one positive thing that had come out of Leah getting caught in that snowstorm.

Leah's mind flashed back to when Jon had come close to kissing her that night. She'd pulled away then, and it had probably been the smartest thing she'd done. After just one kiss the other night, he already had a hold on her—as evidenced by their little interaction over there.

Jon seemed to think the kiss had changed things, but it hadn't. They were still business partners, and he still had the ability to shatter her heart. Now more than ever. As much as his betrayal with the store name had hurt, if she let him any closer to her heart, she might never recover. Because with beautiful women throwing themselves at Jon all the time, how long until he grew tired of her and moved on—like her dad had?

Leah shook away the thought and glanced at Colby, who was sweating and scanning the crowd. He was probably searching for Madison, who seemed to be a no-show. He was number fourteen, so he'd go right before Jon. If he had been after Jon, then she could have possibly bid on him with her extra money, but with him first . . . Jon would kill her. Although that would serve him right for being so competitive. Maybe she could split the money between the two guys. After all, it was unheard of for someone to go for more than five hundred. Well, except for Hannah's bid on Luke that Jon was determined to beat.

"How much did you bring?" The girl in front of Leah spoke to her friend next to her. Oh, look, it was the tank-top girls. Joy.

The other girl held up a stack of bills. "Three hundred and fifty."

"I brought three hundred. So as long as Jon doesn't go for more than six fifty, we'll be fine." The first girl clapped her hands.

There went that idea. Leah would need at least seven hundred to win Jon, which left only three hundred. That probably wouldn't be enough for Colby.

At least they didn't have more than a thousand. Then again, maybe it'd be better if they did. As much as Leah didn't want to see Jon with them, the idea of a true date with him sent her mind into a whirl. No matter how much she tried, she couldn't keep her brain in line with her hormones.

Leah inched away from the girls and nearly collided with Margret Bunting. Leah reached her hand out to make sure the woman was steady. She must have left the giant hat at her booth. "I'm sorry. I about ran you over."

The woman's wrinkled hand landed on hers. "Easy to do. People keep getting taller and taller these days. I could be shrinking, but we won't talk about that."

Leah couldn't hold back a laugh when the woman winked at her. "Maybe it would be safer to watch from your booth."

"I'm not here to watch, missy. I'm here to bid. And I have my sights set on that one." She pointed to the end of the line where Jon stood.

"Jon Kensington?"

"Yes. He's cute, and look at those muscly arms."

Leah opened her mouth to respond, but nothing came out.

"I need my furniture moved around, and he looks like he could do it all by himself. And I don't think I'd mind watching him move it either." She offered Leah a wink.

Leah pressed her lips together to keep from laughing again. She glanced back at Jon, who was watching her with a raised brow as another contestant went for two hundred dollars. This was a perfect solution. Maybe she *could* save Colby. She leaned closer to Margret. "How much do you have?"

"I saved five hundred dollars." She waved five bills so crisp she'd probably picked them up from the bank that morning.

"I think you might need a little more." Leah pulled the cash Jon had given her from her pocket and started to pass over several hundred dollars but paused as Jon's words echoed in her head. *"I really want to beat Luke's record of $733.45."* She held out two hundred dollars. No reason to let his ego get too big. "Seven hundred should be plenty. Start with that bid and you won't have any problems."

The older woman's eyes twinkled as she took the money. "Do you want to come over and watch him move the furniture with me?"

Leah about choked as the idea filled her face with warmth. "I'm good. You enjoy, and make sure he moves as much heavy furniture as you want for that price."

When Mayor Jameson announced Colby's name, he stepped forward. He shoved his hands in his back pockets as he shifted from one foot to the other.

It was a win-win. Someone else could save Jon, and Leah could save Colby. She held up the cash. "Eight hundred dollars."

The crowd gasped, and Jon's jaw dropped. The only one who didn't seem in shock was Colby, and he looked relieved.

Mayor Jameson's voice boomed through the microphone. "That's a new record, folks. Eight hundred dollars to Leah Williams. Unless there are any other bids, Leah, come claim your prize."

Leah made her way to the front and dropped the cash in Hannah's hand, then rushed over and hooked Colby's arm with hers. He leaned in. "Thank you. But eight hundred?"

She shrugged and led him to the side just before a tiny voice from the crowd yelled, "And the next one's mine. Seven hundred." Margret rushed forward, waving the bills in the air. Everyone just stared at the woman as she dropped the bills in Hannah's hand and pointed a finger at Jon. "Those muscles are mine."

Even the tank-top girls seemed too shocked to be mad.

The mayor glanced around and turned toward Hannah with a shrug. "That's the end of this year's auction, folks."

Jon's gaze shot to Leah, and she bit her lip to keep from smiling. Didn't work. He shook his head and sent her a look that she had little trouble deciphering. She was in trouble, but it had been worth it on so many levels.

Colby strummed a few chords on his guitar, then shifted his position on the edge of his bed and made a few notes in his notebook. His room at Nate's didn't leave much space to play, with the queen-size bed, antique dresser, and small chair by the door, but he was thankful for every inch. He'd written three pages of notes in the past couple hours, and he wasn't near done.

He'd been so frustrated when he left Madison's on Tuesday night, but the more time he'd given it, the more he could see that he'd pushed too hard. Deep hurt took time to heal, and he needed to be there to walk through it with her, not try to drag her through the journey.

He hadn't been surprised when she hadn't shown up for the auction today, just disappointed. Disappointed and slightly terrified at ending up on a date with a stranger. He'd never been so relieved when Leah's voice shouted out that bid. He wasn't quite sure why she'd started so high, but at least it saved his sorry hide.

Since Madison knew that Leah and Colby were only friends, he wouldn't have to worry about causing more drama there. Because as much as Madison wanted him to believe that she wasn't affected by him, the way her eyes softened when they looked at him betrayed the lie, not to mention the way she'd leaned into his touch.

But he needed to slow down and take it at her speed. Which was why he'd taken a few days off from painting. The way he felt right now, he might try to kiss her again, and she'd made it clear she wasn't there yet. He'd focus on the *yet*.

He plucked out a few more chords and read from the notes he'd written earlier.

> "This is me.
> I stand before you
> with my clay feet . . ."

Nate leaned in the doorway. "Sounds good. Glad to see you writing again."

"Feels good." Colby ran his hand over the neck of the guitar, letting the familiar roughness of the strings settle in. "I'm finally inspired."

Nate crossed his arms over his chest. "A girl will do that to you."

Colby shrugged, but no doubt his face gave him away. He always had been a terrible poker player.

"Well, we're happy for you." Nate slapped Colby on the shoulder. "Leah's awesome. She—"

Colby jerked back. "Not Leah."

"What?" Nate froze, his hand still in midpat.

Colby shook his head and held up his hands. "Leah and I are only friends. She's interested in . . . someone else."

"Are you sure?" Nate shoved his hands in his pockets and leaned against the wall. "I mean, she did spend—"

"Very sure." Colby stuck his pick in his mouth as he settled his guitar back in its case.

"Then who . . ." Nate dropped onto the chair by the door as his brows shot up. "Oh."

So maybe Madison had some legitimacy in her concern about people in this town.

"Don't say it like that." Colby pulled the pick from his mouth and slid it through the strings.

"Sorry." Nate rested his hands on his knees and seemed to be thinking through what to say. Never a good sign. Finally he made eye contact with Colby. "It's just that Madison is . . ."

"Amazing."

"I'm sure she is." Nate nodded. "Honestly, I don't know Madison well. I do know that Thomas confided in me before they broke up that she was putting a lot of pressure on him regarding the physical side of their relationship. You can see why that has me concerned."

Colby cringed at the thought, but it wasn't like he had no idea. She'd admitted she hadn't been in a healthy place when dating Thomas. "She's changed. Did you know she sneaks into the back of church some Sundays, then sneaks out during the final song?"

"No."

"She has a big wall around herself." Colby latched his guitar case and set it aside. "I want her to join the worship team."

Nate rubbed the back of his neck.

181

Colby pushed to a stand. "Seriously, Nate? I can't believe—"

Nate held up his hand. "Hey, I didn't say no."

"You didn't say yes."

"Can you give me a minute to process this?"

Colby dropped back onto the edge of the bed. He needed to calm down, but getting a glimpse of what Madison had to deal with made him want to punch the wall, and he knew Nate wasn't the worst of it. What would he say if he found out she was pregnant?

The thought punched him in the gut. Even if Nate said yes, he wouldn't have all the information. Colby had promised he wouldn't share her secret, but he also knew that Madison would use Nate's ignorance of the baby as a reason to say no to singing. And Nate would keep her secret.

Colby leaned his elbows on his knees as he rubbed his hands over the hair that was starting to curl in the back. "I guess before you decide, you should have all the information."

Nate lifted his eyebrows, waiting.

"She's pregnant."

"Whose is it?"

"Not my story to tell. You of all people should get that." He offered Nate a hard stare. "And you should understand past regrets and the courage it takes to choose a new life."

"I do." Nate nodded, but his expression didn't give his thoughts away. "Just be careful."

"She's not—"

Nate held up his hand again. "Hear me out. Opening your heart up to someone is always a risk. But when there's a child involved . . ." He closed his eyes for a second, then drew a slow breath. "If I know you like I think I do, you've already started opening your heart up to the child as well. And the love for a child never goes away, no matter what happens between you and the mom. That child will always have a piece of you."

With the pain etched on Nate's face, there was little doubt that his mind had gone to his own son, Chase, who wasn't a part of his life.

Colby rubbed the back of his neck. What could he say? Nate was right. He'd already imagined what the baby might look like. He'd imagined holding her. Rocking her to sleep. "Do you regret loving Chase?"

"Never. Got a new photo yesterday." Nate pulled out his phone and passed it to Colby. "But that doesn't mean it doesn't hurt every day that I don't get to be a dad to him."

"You think I should walk away from Madison?"

"I didn't say that." Nate pinned him with a gaze, then took the phone back. "I do think you need to make sure you're considering all the costs. If she's a mom, 'fun for now' doesn't cut it."

"I'm not looking for 'fun for now.' I think I'm in love with her." The words were out before Colby could stop them. He hadn't even admitted as much to Madison. But the more they tumbled over in his mind, the more he knew he couldn't deny them.

"Wow." Nate sat back and leaned his head against the wall, then he pressed his thumb and forefinger into his eyes. "Sorry. Give me a minute, because I missed something between 'she's nice' and 'I'm in love with her.' And you're sure there's nothing going on between you and Leah?"

"We're friends. Actually, she's the one friend I've been able to talk to about Madison—"

"Dude." Nate dropped his hand and stared at Colby. "You can talk to me."

"You say that, and I know you want to mean it. But you have

no idea the looks that pass between you and Olivia every time her name comes up." Colby stood and moved his guitar to the corner of the room. "One of Madison's big hang-ups is that she says the town will never get past who she was. And I keep telling her that she's wrong. That if anyone understands letting go of their past, it's Pastor Nate. But maybe she's right." He walked out of the bedroom and made his way to the kitchen. He pulled a mug from the cupboard and poured the leftover coffee from the pot. It would be bitter and cold, but at the moment he didn't care.

"You're right." Nate's voice filled the small kitchen. "I haven't taken the time to get to know Madison since she's come back, and truthfully, I didn't take the time to get to know her before she left. I'm sorry."

Colby took a gulp of the coffee. The black sludge was worse than he'd expected, but he swallowed it anyway. His face must have shown his disgust because Nate walked over, pitched the coffee down the sink, and pulled the bag of fresh grounds from the cupboard.

"When I became a pastor, I thought certain things would become easier. I mean, like you said, look at my past. Extending grace should be easy for me, right? But I'm still a sinner in need of the same grace." Nate dropped the old filter in the trash and replaced it with a new one. "Madison hurt my sister-in-law pretty bad. My wife is pretty protective of her family, and I'm pretty protective of my wife." He added the coffee and water to the machine, then leaned back on the counter as it started to brew. "But I also care about my friend. I care about everyone in this town, and I promise I'll do better."

"And the worship team?"

"If you want her on the worship team, I trust you. I look

forward to getting to know her." Nate kicked at the floor. "And I'll talk to Olivia."

"Don't—"

"I won't mention the pregnancy. I'll just remind her of the grace she extended to me—and the grace she pretty much demanded that the town extend to me."

"That, I would've liked to see."

"So, you love Madison. Wow." Nate shook his head. "Does she love you?"

Colby shrugged. "She acts like it at times but keeps pushing me away, so I don't know what to think."

"I did the same thing. I wanted Olivia pretty much from the minute I met her my first Sunday. But I pushed her away for almost two years before I let myself love her."

"Why?"

"I'd just found out about Chase, and I thought my baggage was too much for her. I believed I was protecting her because I wanted her to have the best life, and I didn't see how that could possibly be with me."

"What changed your mind?"

"God. But also, Olivia didn't give up. She fought for me and was patient. She saw that what stood between us was less about her and me and more about me and God." Nate pulled another mug from the cupboard as the coffee began to sputter. "I guess that's my advice for you. Fight for Madison. And wait."

"How do I know when to fight and when to wait?"

Nate shrugged. "That, my friend, only comes with prayer. Lots and lots of prayer."

Jon navigated another long row of crowded booths, glancing back to make sure Leah was still with him. Ludington's West Shore Art Festival was ten times the size of the one in Heritage yesterday, and the last thing he needed was to lose her in the crowd.

They had already made a connection with an artist who worked with stained glass and another who did wall sculptures with nails. They'd given out almost all the paperwork they'd brought with them, and if even half the artists applied, they wouldn't have a problem filling their inventory.

The only thing that hadn't been going well . . . Leah. If Hannah hadn't interrupted them yesterday, he would have kissed her. He'd planned on picking that moment back up after the auction, but then she had spent his money on Colby and walked off with *him*.

He couldn't decide if he wanted to demand that she pay back the eight hundred dollars or pull her behind one of the large oak trees and kiss her senseless. And since he guessed she wouldn't agree to either right now, he continued walking.

Leah eyed the items for sale as she passed, always keeping a few feet between them. If he paused to let her catch up, she paused to inspect something until he moved on. They'd been doing this little dance that kept them seven feet apart all day, and he was about at the end of his sanity.

He'd been hoping they could clear this all up on the drive over, but once Abby found out where they were headed, she'd begged to come. At least it meant he knew where she was.

When he came to the end of the next aisle, Jon crossed his arms over his chest, determined to wait Leah out. After all, they only had one row to go before they had to find Abby, who had wandered to the beachfront to read and soak in the sun.

Speaking of which . . . He pulled out his phone and shot off a text to Abby.

> We'll be done in 15–20.

I'm on the beach. Right of the break wall.

Did you hear? Otis is missing. He disappeared last night after the festival. All of Heritage is going crazy.

> Please tell me you didn't have something to do with it.

I wish. Talk about the prank of the century.

Leah glanced up at him, her phone in her hand and her eyes wide. "Did you hear about Otis?"

Jon pocketed his phone. "Abby says he's missing but doesn't know anything more."

"Janie said the diner is packed with people talking about it." Her eyes remained wide as she put away her phone.

"So now you'll talk to me because Otis has gone missing?" He lifted an eyebrow. "Because there are a few other things we need to talk about."

"Are you still mad about yesterday?" Her teeth pinched her bottom lip.

"You mean the part about where you spent my money on another guy?"

"Colby said he'd pay you back, if that's what you're worried about." She waved it away and started to walk past him.

He caught her by the shoulder, holding her gently in place. "I'm not worried about the money."

Her smile melted away as her gaze traveled to his face. "Then what are you worried about?"

He was worried about the fact that she was willing to shell out that much cash for a guy she claimed was only a friend. But it wasn't like he could say all that and not sound jealous.

Instead he released her shoulder and shrugged. "I just wanted to know why you did it."

She followed him down the last aisle but this time kept in step with him. "If you had seen Margret's face, you wouldn't be asking that question. She wanted to win you so badly. I had to help her."

"I'm still not sure what she meant by the muscle comment, but I can't say that I'm not a little nervous." He rubbed the back of his neck.

"She wants you to move her furniture." Leah clapped her hands. "I gave her two hundred to make sure she won the bid over the tank-top twins. She was so thrilled she offered to let me come watch your muscles at work."

Jon paused, his hand still on his neck. "What did you tell her?"

She turned back to him and waggled her eyebrows. "Well . . ."

Was it terrible that he hoped she'd said yes?

She walked backward a few steps. "I told her no."

Of course. Because she was determined to play this dance of yes, no, maybe, until Jon lost his mind.

"Don't look so disappointed. She's adorable."

"She is. But ninety is a bit of an age gap for me. You could've at least given her three hundred so I would've broken the record and not Colby."

She laughed out loud now, clearly aware of what she'd done. "I thought your ego needed a little humbling."

"Trust me, Leah. Hanging around you the past few weeks has been plenty humbling to my ego." He paused to look at some watercolor paintings that filled a booth. Some were of Michigan lighthouses: Big Sable, Little Sable, Big Red, and a few he didn't recognize. He lifted a painting of the Grand Hotel from a box, revealing another one from Mackinac Island behind it. They were good. And a perfect fit for the MIM.

The woman who seemed to be in charge of the booth was assisting another customer, but a teenage girl approached. She tucked a stray piece of hair behind her ear as she blushed and smiled up at Jon. "Can I help you?"

"We"—he angled his shoulders to include Leah, who stood a few feet away, rolling her eyes—"are opening a store in Heritage, just south of here. We are seeking out artists who would like to sell their art in our store."

"My mom painted these." She motioned to the woman who was still in a deep conversation with the customer. "Do you want me to get her?"

"No. But can you give her this letter? It explains everything. Have her follow the instructions if she's interested in selling some of her work with us."

The girl took the letter and nodded. "Can I help you with anything else?"

"We're good." Leah walked up, grabbed his hand, and pulled him away. "Like I said, I don't think your ego is suffering."

He twisted his hand to capture her wrist and tugged her over to a large oak tree. "Because I want sixteen-year-olds to think I'm cute? Seriously, Leah, give me some credit."

"The tank-top twins weren't sixteen."

Jon ran his hand over his face as she leaned back against the tree. He placed his hand on the tree next to her head and leaned closer until there was only a breath between them. "I don't want those women from yesterday or my secretary who flirts with me at the office, nor do I want the girls who threw themselves at the team after the games. There is *one* girl I want. I thought I made that pretty clear."

Leah's wide green eyes stared back at him, not giving any of her thoughts away.

"But it seems that this girl isn't nearly as affected by me as I am by her."

"That's not true." She swallowed hard and then closed her eyes as a soft breeze blew a few curls across her forehead. "Ever since that kiss . . . even before it . . . trust me, I'm affected."

"Then what, Leah? What is it?"

"I'm afraid." Her voice came out choked.

"Of me?" He leaned back a fraction of an inch, but her fingers grabbed the hem of his shirt.

"No. My dad lied over and over. Truth was whatever suited him in the moment. I watched him break my mom's heart again and again until she was a mere shell of herself." Leah's voice cracked as a tear rolled down her cheek.

"He didn't just break your mom's heart, did he?" Jon wiped the tear away with his thumb before dropping his hand.

"I was closer to my dad than Caroline or David. I think I understood his wandering spirit more than they did. He traveled with work a lot, and I begged him to take me to Paris on one of his trips. He promised me he'd take me for my fourteenth birthday." She met his eyes. "He left us a month before my birthday, and I never saw him again."

"Which is why you're against going to Paris."

"You remember that?" She cringed. "I suppose it isn't fair to blame an entire city for my father being the worst, but I still get so mad when I think about it. Even up until a couple days before he left, he had said it was still the plan. But he would have known by that point that he wasn't coming back."

"And when I wasn't up-front about the name change—"

"I know you aren't my father. But yeah." Another tear escaped, and she wiped it away with the back of her hand. "And when I see what his leaving did to my mother, I can't help but believe that all love ends the same way."

"Thank you for telling me."

"I want to trust you. With the business, with my heart." Her voice was now rough and raw. "But I can't make myself take that leap."

"You will."

"How do you know that?" Another tear slid down her face.

"Because my colorful Leah takes risks in every other area of her life. Someday she will in this area too. And if I'm the one you choose to take that leap with"—Jon reached out and caught another tear before it dripped off her chin—"then I promise to catch you. Until then . . . friends."

"Friends." Leah nodded and shoved her hands into her pockets. "And business partners. Maybe I can start by trusting you more with the business."

"Sounds good. Now we better go find Abby." Before he did something crazy like pull her into his arms, which wouldn't really support his whole "I'll wait" speech.

It only took them about ten minutes to locate his sister. She was bumping a volleyball around with some other teens in the sand. She abandoned the group and ran toward them as soon as she spotted them. "My new friends were getting ready to go tubing down Big Sable River. It's about six miles from here in the state park. It dumps into Lake Michigan, but most people get out before that. Can I go?"

"No." First of all, he wasn't about to let her go off with people he didn't know and she didn't know before an hour ago. Second of all, he didn't want to wait around for the next three hours with Leah, pretending like it was easy being just friends. "Grab your stuff—"

Leah's hand landed on his arm. "Why don't we go along?"

Go along? As in spend the day together in their bathing suits? Did she not understand the strength it took for him to pull off this "just friends" bit?

When Abby's eyes widened with a touch of disgust, Leah rushed on. "At a distance on the river."

So not just on the river. Practically alone on the river. Getting better every minute.

Abby's face lit up. "Yes. Please, Jon."

"Okay. Sure." Why was he agreeing again? Maybe it was the hope in Abby's eyes that he hadn't seen in a while, but more likely it had to do with Leah's hand still on his arm.

Leah let go of him. "Oh, but I'll need to buy a suit. And we'll need to buy tubes."

Abby rushed back to talk to her friends, and Jon took a minute to glance at Leah. She was the one who wanted to stay only friends—and now this?

Abby returned, kicking up sand with every step, her arms full of her stuff. "They said there's a place near there that sells both."

It didn't take long for them to find the shop. They hurried in, and Jon grabbed the first pair of shorts that would work and then picked out three tubes. He found the girls and motioned to the register. "Ready to go?"

They both stared at him, then returned to sifting through the rack of suits. Abby held up a suit that appeared to be little more than a bunch of strings. No way would he buy that for her. He was about to say as much when she spoke.

"I told Leah she should get this. She has the perfect figure to pull it off. But she won't listen to me. What do you think, Jon?"

He blinked at the suit, doing his darnedest not to picture Leah in it. His face warmed, and he turned back to the counter, setting the tubes and trunks there. He glanced at the man and held out his card. "All of this and whatever they decide on." Then he made a beeline for the door. "I'm going to go get a Coke next door."

His sister's laughter followed him out as the door jangled shut, but he didn't care. He had to clear his head and get his mind back in the friend zone. He'd told Leah she could trust him not to push her, and he wouldn't. Only first he needed that Coke. And maybe a bucket of ice water.

eleven

She had to admit, moving her sewing room to the living room was a huge step up, even if relocating every piece of her grandmother's furniture had been accompanied by a twinge of guilt. Not that she had moved it all very far. She'd slid the settee and coffee table against one wall and the carved armchair and end tables against the other. But the added space left room for her sewing table, mannequin, and one rolling rack. Jon should be proud—not that he'd seen it.

It had been a month since their conversation by the tree in Ludington, and Jon had been true to his word about not pushing her. Leah didn't know if she wanted to thank him or kick him. She'd asked for space and he'd given her the Grand Canyon.

Leah pulled a pin from the cushion on her wrist and carefully attached the long sleeve to the shirt she was making. Her first male design was one seam from being complete, but she should've estimated better on the size. It was at least a size bigger than David ever wore. Where was her head?

She carried the garment over to the sewing machine and placed it under the needle as routine and habit took over. She loosened her grip on the fabric, letting the material be pulled through as the needle stitched in and out. Why couldn't relationships be this easy? Line two people up and life sews them together. Maybe that was the way for some people, but she seemed to be constantly fighting the machine.

At least the interior construction of the store was nearly done, and the display racks were set to be delivered in a couple weeks. That was cutting it close, but they were still on track for the store to open by Labor Day.

She let up on the pedal and pulled the garment free before cutting away the final threads.

A knock echoed through the room, and Leah glanced at the clock. Who would drop by this late? She stood as she turned the shirt right side out, then hung it on the mannequin as she walked by.

She peeked through the peephole, and her heart did that stupid little flip thing at the sight of Jon. She took a second to mask any emotion that might be lingering on her face and opened the door. "Jon? What are you doing here?"

He held up a folder, and based on the way he stood he was in full business mode. "Sorry it's so late, but we need to get this out to the artists. I was hoping to catch you at the MIM earlier, but I just got away from the office."

"Of course." Leah opened the door wider.

Jon's gaze traveled over her before it flicked to the wall behind her. "I can come another time if you'd rather."

"No, it's fine." Leah left the door open, walked to the kitchen table, and took a seat. She tucked one of her wayward curls behind her ear as she mentally kicked herself for ditching the blouse and dress pants that she'd been wearing earlier. The athletic shorts and ratty old T-shirt that she'd taken from the lost and found back in high school didn't really convey the "yes, I can run a business" look. Unlike Jon, who still seemed to look professional in his dark jeans and light blue polo. Man, he looked good.

Jon cleared his throat as he pulled out the chair on the opposite side of the table and slid the open folder to her. "It's the final consignment contract that each artist will sign. Take a minute to look it over. If it looks good, then just approve it. But if you want changes, now is the time." He pushed away from the table, shoved his hands in his pockets, and wandered around. "I can't believe Otis is still missing."

"I know. I put up one of the reward signs on the new door after they installed it." She flipped the page, but the words were a blur.

Jon stopped at the mannequin. "I didn't know you made shirts for men."

"It's my first." Leah flipped another page, but it was useless. She'd have to either trust Jon and approve it or read it later. Her mind was just not in it.

"Mind if I try it on?" He must have been confident about her answer, because he had the buttons of his polo undone when she glanced up.

"Okay, but it may not fit. If I were to make you a shirt, I'd need to take measurements first."

A smirk tugged at his lips as he opened his mouth to say something, but he seemed to think better of it and nodded as he pulled off the blue shirt.

Leah darted her gaze back to the paper. She'd seen him with his shirt off before. The Fourth of July tubing adventure had put to rest any lingering questions about whether he'd stayed in shape after leaving professional ball. She spent most of the day trying not to stare at him, and he seemed to have spent most of the time trying not to notice.

By the time they had followed Abby's friends to their exit point, both Jon and Leah had practically run to the car. They hadn't spoken most of the way home, and since then they had been fully business.

"Wow, this fits amazing. You can make all my shirts."

Leah glanced up as he fastened the last button. He stretched out his arms, then crossed them in front of himself. He was right. It was a perfect fit. And the blue-gray color made his eyes pop. Well, that answered the question of where her head had been.

"How much do you want for it?" He studied his reflection in a mirror her grandma had hung by the door.

She dropped the file on the table. "You'd wear one of my shirts? In public?"

"Of course." His brow pinched in a frown. "Why would you even ask that?"

"Oh, I don't know. Maybe because you made fun of everything I made in high school?" She stood, picked up her camera, and motioned for him to stand by the white wall. "As long as you're trying it on, can I get a photo for the website?"

He obliged, taking a casual pose as if he'd been modeling his whole life. "I never made fun of your creations. I loved—"

"Ha." She held up the camera and clicked a few shots, then shifted to a new angle. "'Nice dress, Leah.'" She dropped her voice to mimic his mocking tone. "'Wow, that skirt was so colorful I couldn't miss you in the bleachers at my game.' Need I go on?"

"You have a gift for turning my words around." He shifted his weight to his other foot, and that worked great too. Could the guy take a bad picture?

Leah snapped a few more shots, then examined the photos. "That will do."

He reached for the shirt's top button, and his frown was immediately back in place. "Did it ever occur to you that I actually liked that pink-flowered dress? That I was actually disappointed you never wore it again?"

Leah averted her eyes when he reached the third button. "I wore it. Just not around you. I thought you were making fun of it." She set the camera aside and walked back to the table, but he closed the distance between them and turned her around.

"Leah, look at me. I need to make one thing very clear."

She swallowed and lifted her eyes to his face to keep from staring at the gap in the shirt that now ran the full length of his chest, inches away.

He reached for her, but his hand paused in the air. He cleared his throat and dropped his arm to his side. "I liked your dress. I thought your skirt was awesome. I thought *you* were awesome. I don't know why you're determined to not believe that I could possibly like what you create—like who you are. But it has to stop. You're talented."

She must not have looked convinced, because he paced away, then back, his fists clenching. "Honestly, I want to wring the neck of whoever put that look of doubt on your face. Whoever made you believe it wasn't so. Because they're wrong. And if it was me?" His hand landed gently on her shoulder. "I'm sorry."

Leah's breath stopped at the intensity in his eyes. His words offered a soothing balm to all the cruel words she'd heard from people over the years. *Freak. Color-blind. Spaz.* When her breathing finally started again, it was shallow and definitely not providing enough oxygen.

Jon finally dropped his hand and shrugged out of the shirt.

He hung it on the mannequin again and scooped up his blue polo. "Did you know I beat the high school record for points scored and tied the record for steals the night you wore that colorful skirt? I think knowing you were watching me made me play a little harder."

When she didn't comment, he slipped the blue shirt back on but didn't button it. "You're always determined to think the worst of me."

The hurt in his eyes shredded her, but she had no answer.

Jon pointed at the file. "Can you drop that off at the office in the morning?"

"Sure." Her voice was barely there, but he must have heard, because he walked out her door and didn't look back.

If installing a faucet didn't get Colby off her mind, then nothing would. Madison laid out all the pieces on the table so they matched the diagram. She'd shut the water off and removed the old faucet easily enough, but assembling a new one was a step or two more complicated. Why couldn't these things come with the washers already in place?

She leaned over the sink and examined the holes. When she turned back to the diagram, she bumped the counter with her stomach. She could still hide it under large T-shirts and yoga pants, but most of her wardrobe was no longer an option.

She was twenty-two weeks, which meant she had eighteen weeks to go. How could December 4 seem to be taking forever and coming too quickly at the same time? The other day she'd found a pink plush bear on the table. She had no doubt it was from Colby, but he hadn't said anything.

They'd barely said two words to each other since before the

festival. She hated that she'd hurt him, but it was for the best. Their lives didn't mix. He seemed to be finally getting that. Although she'd expected him to finish the painting in record time and not look back, he kept showing up to fix something, replace something, or touch up the painting he'd finished over a week ago. Then yesterday he'd started ripping out the old carpet.

She couldn't afford all the hours he'd been putting in. Good thing he'd turned down his first paycheck from her weeks ago. He just showed up and worked—and occasionally sang. Those days were the hardest, because his voice made her want to melt into him and forget why it was a bad idea. Forget that Heritage was only a pause in her life and not the destination.

He had a career to rebuild, and she wasn't the one to help him with that. Public life was not conducive to her keeping her secrets.

Madison fit the faucet pieces together and then aligned them over the hole in the sink. She wedged herself under the sink and tightened the bolts from the bottom. There. She struggled to sit up, but her stomach muscles weren't what they used to be. She rolled to the side a bit and grabbed one of the water lines. After a little plumber's tape—

A knock echoed in the house before the front door opened. "Maddie?"

She paused at Colby's voice. Just perfect. "In here."

"What are you—are you okay? Did you fall?" He rushed over and placed his hand on her leg, which stuck out from under the sink.

She moved her leg away from his hand as she secured the compression fitting of the hot water. "Yes. I fell under the sink with a wrench in my hand, so I thought I'd install the faucet as long as I was down here."

"Okay. Sarcasm loud and clear." He stood, giving her some much-needed space. "What are you doing?"

"I just said. I'm installing the new faucet." She waved the wrench at him, then tightened the bolt. She knew he didn't deserve her irritation, but if she didn't stay irritated, she wouldn't be able to keep this wall up.

"I could've done it."

"But so can I." Madison leaned out and pointed to the table. "Can you hand me the other water line?"

He handed it to her. "I never pegged you as a plumber."

"YouTube is a great teacher." She tightened down the last compression fitting, then turned the water back on. No obvious leaks. So far so good. She climbed out and worked her way to a stand. "Did you need something?"

"I know you said no before, but hear me out. The person who usually sings with me on Sunday mornings—"

"No." She set the wrench aside and turned her back to him.

"I said hear me out. Stand in this week. It'll be like a trial. Nate already agreed."

"Do you think Nate would've said yes if he knew about this?" She angled back toward him and tapped her belly.

"I told him." He cringed and had the decency to look ashamed.

"You had no right."

"I didn't give him any details, and he won't tell anyone. Pastors are good at confidence and all that." When her lips pressed together, he rushed on. "I'm sorry. I should've talked to you first, but when he agreed last month that I could add you to the team, I wanted him to have all the information because I knew you'd say this."

"Last month?" That added information should have made her angrier. Instead it drained the fight right out of her. Pastor

Nate had known for a month. He'd known when he greeted her Sunday with a smile and a handshake, and the Sunday before that. Maybe she'd underestimated him.

"Please. I need a fill-in, so I thought—hoped—that you might agree for one week."

If she'd underestimated Nate, then there was a chance she'd underestimated others as well. "I don't have anything nice enough to wear up front. None of my dress clothes fit anymore."

"No one cares what you wear. You can wear that."

Madison rolled her eyes. "I'm not wearing yoga pants and an oversized T-shirt."

"Then buy a new outfit."

She turned on the faucet to test the water. She let it run until it was hot and then flipped it to cold. "You have all the answers, don't you?"

"About time you figured that out." The teasing in his tone made her want to laugh, but she wasn't done being upset.

She squeezed the spray setting on the faucet, but it wasn't angled down right and shot Colby in the face. She shut off the water and pressed her lips together to hold in a giggle as she handed him a towel that was by the sink. "Sorry."

He dabbed at his face. "I'm pretty sure you did that on purpose."

"Honest, I didn't." She lifted her chin. "But I might if you keep pushing me on this."

A slow smile tugged at the corner of Colby's mouth as a glint settled in his eyes.

"Oh no you don't." She grabbed for the sprayer, but Colby got there first.

He pointed it at her with one hand on the water control.

"Don't you dare." She held up her hands.

He smirked as he held his position.

"Colby?" When he still didn't put it down, she grabbed for his hand as he turned the water on. It was only for a second, but it was enough to give her a big wet spot on her black T-shirt.

Colby stared wide-eyed at her belly.

She glanced down, and sure enough, the water had plastered her T-shirt to her small but round baby bump. "Yes, I wasn't lying. I'm actually pregnant."

That seemed to snap him out of it. "I know. I mean, I just hadn't seen . . . I mean, wow. Can you feel her move?"

"Sometimes. She's actually kicking right now after all that excitement."

When his eyes widened again, she knew mentioning that fact had been a mistake, because now he'd want to touch her belly. And the more she thought about that, the more she wanted him to. Which wouldn't help in her efforts to keep him at a distance. Then again, was this plan really working for either of them?

She held out her hand. "Do you want to feel it?"

His gaze met hers, and his blue eyes had grown darker. "Are you sure?"

She nodded, not trusting her voice. She led his hand to where the baby was tapping out an irregular rhythm.

"That's amazing."

That was one word for it. But now Madison was thinking less about the kicking and more about how his large, warm hand rested on her belly. Her breathing slowed.

She'd had many physical relationships in the past, but nothing like this. She didn't want to just be closer physically to this man. It was as if her heart called out in a way only he could answer. She wanted him to know her. The good parts, the ugly parts, even the parts she'd never told anyone about.

She wanted him to hold this baby with the same tenderness he touched her with now.

With one hand still on her stomach, Colby reached up with the other and ran his finger along her cheek to her ear. "You're so beautiful."

His fingers trailed down to her shoulder, then back up to her chin. When his thumb brushed her bottom lip, that was it. All the reasons that Madison had been reciting to herself the past month melted from her mind as her eyes closed and she leaned into his touch.

She trailed her fingers up his arms and stopped on his shoulders. She opened her eyes to find Colby inches away. His eyes were so dark they were almost navy, and he seemed to be holding his self-control by a thread.

He ran his thumb one more time over her bottom lip as he lifted his brow in question. It only took the slightest nod from her for him to close the distance. His lips brushed across hers briefly, then again. But it wasn't enough. She released a groan of frustration as her fingers dug into his shoulders.

That seemed to be all the encouragement Colby needed. He deepened the kiss as his hand on her jaw slid behind her neck and the one on her belly traveled to her back.

And in that moment, she was unbroken, whole. This man knew her deepest, darkest secrets, and yet he wanted her anyway. Loved her anyway. And not for what he could get. She had no doubt if she pushed him away right now, he'd still love her and show up tomorrow. And the next day.

But the last thing on Madison's mind was pushing Colby away. She wanted him closer. So much closer. She pressed herself into him and was rewarded by a deep moan.

Without warning, he yanked bank and circled to the other

side of the table. He bent over slightly as he gripped the back of a chair, his eyes still dark and unfocused. "You're overestimating my self-control."

Madison blinked at him a few times as the heat rose in her cheeks. Right, because guys like Colby didn't go there on the first date . . . or second. Goodness, guys like him probably didn't go there until after marriage. And as a person of faith, she probably wasn't supposed to want to take things there either. No wonder everyone was worried about Colby. She was . . .

Colby circled the table again and pulled her back into his arms, but with much more control as he kept a few inches between them. "I don't know where your mind went, but don't go there. You're beautiful and everything I want. And believe me, I *want* more. I don't think any less of you for that desire. Honestly, it makes me . . ." He seemed to shake his thought away, then swallowed and pressed his forehead into hers. "I love you. Fully. Just as you are."

"But I'm—"

"Perfect and beautiful."

"I'm *not* perfect."

"Of course not. And neither am I. I just mean there's nothing you could do to make me love you more, and nothing you've done could make me love you less."

They stood like that for several minutes, neither one moving.

Finally he stepped back but didn't let go of her hand. "Be my girlfriend."

She leaned away. "You're asking too much. This is why no one wants us together. I'm—"

"Exactly who I want." He pulled her closer again.

She shook her head. "If you want to rebuild your reputation in the media, then a pregnant girlfriend isn't the place to start."

He rested his forehead against hers again. "Everywhere is a place to start. You can keep saying no, but I won't give up. I'll fight for you."

"Why?"

"Because you, Maddie, are worth fighting for."

There was no way he'd let a girl throw off his game. Jon dribbled the basketball twice and pushed past Luke to the hoop. He put up an easy layup, but it rolled off the rim. Seriously? He slammed his fist into his palm, sending shocks of pain up his arm. He was hoping the feel of the ball and the squeak of his shoes on the wood floor would settle his nerves like they had so many times in the past. But even being back in his home court couldn't erase the image of Leah's face before he'd walked out of her house.

Luke drove past him and took the easy layup. "Wow, what has you so distracted today? Not that I'm complaining. I mean, normally I don't stand a chance in a game of one-on-one."

"It's nothing. Sixteen–eighteen." Jon squeezed his fingers, which still tingled from the punch, and rotated his neck.

He should've never stopped by Leah's house. When Leah had opened the door in those shorts and a T-shirt that he was pretty sure he'd misplaced in high school, he'd almost reneged on his promise not to push her. He'd only tried on the shirt she'd made for a distraction, and that hadn't helped. He'd probably have thrown caution to the wind and kissed her again if her words hadn't slapped him so hard. Was he really such a jerk in her mind?

He grabbed the ball and bounced it hard on the court as the door that led to the main house opened and Abby walked in. She took him in as she walked toward the bench on the side.

"Looks like the game's going well for you, Luke. Jon's not a good loser."

Jon propped the ball under his arm. "Do you need something, or did you come to heckle me?"

"I left my sweatshirt in here the other night." When he stared at her, she added, "When my friends from Ludington came down. The ones we went tubing with."

"Right." He bounced the ball again. "I remember you telling me that."

"They couldn't believe we had our own basketball court." She swung the black sweatshirt over her shoulder.

"Glad they had fun. Hey, did you ever find your red jacket?"

Her eyes widened for a split second, but she waved him off. "Yeah, it's around here somewhere. I think Luke's waiting."

"He's just putting off the fact I'm about ten seconds from beating him."

Abby pushed the door open. "I wish I had time to stay and watch that."

When the door slammed shut, Jon tossed the ball up and caught it. "Sorry. With how busy I've been at the MIM and her schedule, I feel like I never see her anymore."

"But she seems to be doing better."

"Yup. She got Bs in her summer classes last month, so now she has officially graduated." Jon walked to the top of the key and waited for Luke. "And she told me she wasn't hanging around Gabe Howell anymore. I guess that's an improvement."

Jon dribbled the ball a few times, then checked it. He went for a three, but Luke got his hand on the ball and stole it. He cleared it and went left, but it was a fake. By the time Jon's brain caught up to that fact, Luke had sunk another three-pointer to win the game.

Jon eyed the basket, then walked over to the bench. He grabbed his water and downed half the bottle.

Luke grabbed his own bottle and took a swig. "If it's not Abby that has you off your game, that leaves your uncle or Leah."

"That pretty much sums it up." Jon finished off the bottle and reached for another.

Luke sat on the bench and leaned back. "I don't know what's going on with the business, but never forget you own that company, not him. Don't let him push you around."

"My uncle? Push me around?" Jon let out a humorless laugh but waved away the thought. "I can handle him. He's angry I've missed the past few board meetings, but he'll get over it."

"So, the real problem is Leah."

"I never said—"

"Whatever, dude." Luke ran a towel over his head. "You've had a thing for that girl since high school. Don't tell me that working with her day in and day out has been easy."

Jon didn't bother denying it as he leaned back and stretched his arms across the back of the bench. "Was I that big of a jerk in high school?"

"No, that would've been Derek." Luke shoved the towel in his bag. "Why?"

"Because as much as I liked Leah in high school, the girl doesn't seem to have one positive memory of me. If I complimented her back then, she took it as the opposite." Jon leaned forward on his knees.

"Hannah and I had a lot of miscommunication in high school. We were young, hormonal, and twice as quick to speak as we were to listen."

"How did you work things out?"

"We grew up."

"I don't know. If we couldn't get it to work before, maybe that's a sign."

"Or you weren't ready." Luke stood and looped his duffel bag over his shoulder. "Just because it wasn't right before doesn't mean it couldn't be right now."

"No, but her telling me that she doesn't trust me is a pretty good reason." Jon stood and gathered the trash.

"Then maybe you should show her that she can."

"How can I do that?"

"That's for you to figure out." Luke's phone chimed, and he pulled it from his bag as Jon's phone pinged.

Jon picked up his phone from the bench and glanced at the text.

Chet
Come to my house. In the barn. Bring Luke.

Jon stared at the message, then glanced at Luke. He was staring at his own phone, then held it up.

"Let me guess," Jon said. "From Chet? 'Bring Jon.'" His mind flashed back to the call he'd gotten from Luke a few years ago when he'd been in Europe. Chet had fallen when he'd had a stroke. The guy had recovered but had delivered a scare to them all. "Do you think he had another stroke?"

Luke's eyes widened as he dug his keys out of his bag.

"You can get your stuff later." Jon followed Luke out the door as they both ran for Luke's truck.

They made the ten-minute drive in seven minutes, and as soon as Luke pulled to a stop in front of Chet's shack of a barn, they both jumped out and rushed to the large sliding door that stood half open.

Luke leaned against the barn door, shaking his head. "What in the world, Chet?"

It took a second for Jon's eyes to adjust to the dim light, but at the sight of Chet standing with a wrench in his hand and a toothy grin on his face, some of the tension released in his shoulders. Then his gaze drifted behind Chet. On the floor of the barn lay a large brass shell filled with a complicated set of brass gears.

Jon tilted his head until recognition slammed into him.

Otis.

Chet had stolen Otis and murdered him.

twelve

Jon had been staring at these reports for an hour, but he couldn't get his mind off the image of Otis laying belly-up in Chet's barn. Chet had gone on to confess that he was, in fact, the one who moved Otis. He had been moving him with Jon's father since 1985, but since George had died, the responsibility had gotten to be too much.

Jon had been dumbstruck at first. Logically, he knew Otis didn't move by himself, but it was like he'd found out there was no Santa Claus, Easter Bunny, and Tooth Fairy all rolled into one. Because as much as everyone in town said they wanted to know, there was a magic in not knowing. A magic that stretched from the oldest resident to the youngest visitor. It was a club of Heritage mystery, and he and Luke had just been kicked out.

Of course, after the initial emotions, he'd flooded Chet with questions. How? Why? Who started it? And how did Chet end up as the one holding the reins?

Chet had only touched on the how when Luke got called to a fire. Chet said he wanted to explain it all at once, so he'd wait for a better day. But Jon had hung around for some time, inspecting the inside of the beast. So many gears. And by the look of the antique blueprints Chet had laid out, incredibly old gears.

Which was why Chet had removed Otis from the square a month ago. He'd been cleaning, assessing, and ordering replacements for the gears that were too worn or not running smoothly anymore.

There was a slight knock at the door before Marcy opened it and walked toward Jon's desk. She set a file in front of him, then another. "Here are the notes your uncle would like you to look over before the meeting tomorrow. And a file Leah Williams dropped off. Anything else before I go?"

"Thanks, I'm good." He picked up the file from Leah as the door clicked shut.

They had taken to passing pertinent information back and forth in this folder to keep each other informed on the MIM's progress while still avoiding direct contact. He glanced through her list of completed tasks before setting it aside. Soon Leah wouldn't need his input at all.

Maybe it was time to step back from the MIM and focus more on Heritage Fruits. There was little doubt that his divided attention was causing some grumbling among the board—namely, his uncle. He didn't blame him though. Jon had missed the past three board meetings because of meetings with inspectors for the MIM building, but those were nonnegotiable, and his uncle had refused to move the time of the board meetings. Now he had to play catch-up so he didn't show up tomorrow looking like the incompetent owner they all feared he was.

Jon tossed the file Leah had left aside and picked up the minutes from the past two meetings. Talk about captivating reading. He downed the last of his Coke and grabbed another from the mini fridge by his desk as he lifted the first page of notes. Looked like he might be in for another long night.

At least Abby had babysitting plans tonight. She seemed to have turned a corner. No doubt the new friends from that youth group she'd gone down the river with had something to do with it. They seemed like good kids. One of them had paid a bit too much attention to her for Jon's liking, but Leah said Jon needed to back off.

He ran a hand over the paper as he skimmed it over. His movement froze as the word *layoff* jumped off the page. He paused his skimming and read the section carefully, then re-read it.

How could his uncle think he would approve the layoff of twenty employees? But there it was in black and white. Twenty layoffs to take effect . . . tomorrow? He slammed his hand down on the desk and shoved the paper away. He might have seen this coming and been able to do something about it if he hadn't been working sixty hours a week to get the MIM ready to open.

Luke's words filled his mind. *"Never forget you own that company, not him. Don't let him push you around."* Maybe it was time to remind his uncle whose company it was.

Jon marched out of his office toward Dale's door. He ignored Marcy as she shouted that his uncle was on an important call and pushed his way into the room. He held the layoff memo in the air. "What. Is. This?"

His uncle's gaze hardened. "I'll call you back," he spoke into the phone before he dropped it into its cradle. He leaned back in the chair, his expression bored. "Is there a problem, Jon?"

"You bet there's a problem." Jon whipped the paper onto the desk. "We're not laying off twenty factory workers."

"Profit margins aren't what they used to be. We've been running the numbers and discussing this at the past three meetings. Why didn't you bring it up then?" His uncle's lip curled. "Oh, that's right. You missed them because you wanted to play store with your girlfriend."

"She's not my girlfriend, and leave Leah out of this. This isn't about the MIM—"

"Oh, but it is." Uncle Dale leaned forward on his desk. "When you decided to forgo the multimillion-dollar contract to bring a business into that space, we had to come up with the money from somewhere."

"How does slowing production at a factory that's making money save money?"

"Do you even understand the business world, Jon?" Uncle Dale shook his head and leaned back again. He rubbed his temple as if this conversation was a waste of his time. "I told your father you didn't have what it took, but since he didn't change his will in time, the company that was supposed to be mine fell to you."

The words hit him in the chest. Uncle Dale had hinted before that the company should be his, but he'd never stated it so plainly. Everything in Jon wanted to deny his uncle's words. This was *his* company. His by birthright. But somehow deep down, the possibility that his father had meant to leave the company to Uncle Dale always poked at his confidence. After all, that made more sense. His uncle had a master's in business and decades of experience, and what did Jon have? A barely achieved bachelor's degree and the experience of a professional ballplayer.

"If you don't want to lay people off, then we have to cut funds other places." His uncle shrugged as he handed Jon a detailed printout of the budget. "There's one area that we considered, but we figured you would reject that idea as well. Check the third page. Line item KF."

Jon flipped the sheets and found the line item and the hefty sum of money next to it. "What is it?"

"The Kensington Foundation. Your dad had more generosity than sense."

The foundation. The one that funded Quinn Ranch and a couple other nonprofits. Jon stared at his uncle in disbelief.

"Don't look at me like that. The money has to come from somewhere. You want to make the hard decisions? Fine. You can decide. Twenty layoffs or the foundation. I have a call to finish." His uncle dismissed him as he picked up the phone.

Jon made his way back to his office, stopping by Marcy's desk as he went. "Can you get me the file for the Kensington Foundation?"

She lifted it from a side table. "Mr. Kensington had me pull it for you a week ago."

He was playing into his uncle's hands. But what option was left?

He took the folder and spent the next few hours combing through numbers and files. But no matter how he shifted things, there just wasn't enough money to go around.

If he saved Quinn Ranch, he would be sending another twenty people of Heritage into unemployment, including Mrs. Nell's husband. And if he saved the jobs, Grant and Caroline's dream would fold and the ten kids who were staying at the ranch would have to return to unhealthy situations.

Jon rested his elbows on his desk and buried his face in his hands. How had his dad been able to make it all work? Maybe it was the downturn in the economy. Or maybe Uncle Dale wasn't the savvy businessman Jon thought. Either way, Jon needed to get more answers, and not the ones his uncle was feeding him. Maybe it was time for him to hire his own auditor.

He flipped open the foundation's folder again. If he used this money to save the jobs, it would drain the foundation, but the next checks to the ranch and other nonprofits weren't due to be sent out for two weeks. He wasn't sure how he could find the money in two weeks, but it bought him a little time. There was no way he could lay off twenty families.

He trudged back to Marcy's desk and dropped the file in front of her. "Can you please get me the paperwork needed to move the money out of this account?"

Next he needed to hire an auditor, because he needed to figure out where the company was bleeding, or there might not be a company for him to run even if he did get the board on his side.

Worship had gone even better than Colby had expected Sunday. The way Madison's voice had harmonized with his had been amazing. And that loose dress she'd chosen hid the evidence of any baby. Not that he cared about that. But he knew Madison had been concerned.

Colby pulled his guitar from his car and walked toward Madison's front door. The grass needed trimming soon. Maybe he'd borrow Nate's mower and get to that this week.

Her car wasn't in the drive, so he pushed the front door open without a knock. He still needed to touch up the painting in the bathroom. Only today, painting wasn't what was on his mind.

He set down his guitar case in the kitchen and then ran back to his car for the camera and tripod. He was lifting them from his trunk when Madison's car pulled in the driveway.

"Just in time." He tucked the camera under his arm and slammed the trunk.

"In time for what? Those don't look like painting clothes." She climbed out of her car and followed him toward the house.

He motioned to the camera and then opened the door. "I want to record a video of us singing my new song, 'Clay Feet.'"

"I don't know." Madison's nose wrinkled into a frown as she dropped her purse on the table. "It was one thing to sing up front in a dinky town, but I'm not ready for social media yet."

"Come on." He set the equipment on the table next to her purse and looped his arms around her waist. "I sent a preview to my manager, Roy, and he thinks it's time for me to make a presence again."

"Then you sing." She moved out of his arms and picked up the camera. "And I'll record you."

"But my songs were always best with harmony parts. That's why Dawson and I did so well together. My voice is okay on its own. But with Dawson it was . . . better." His voice was rough at the end, and he hated that his old friend could still cause so much emotion in him.

"How many people will see this?"

"It's just for my fans. Which are pretty few these days."

She stared at him before she walked toward her room. "Give me a minute to put on a better top and reapply my lipstick."

Ten minutes later they were seated in front of the old brick fireplace, Colby on a chair with the guitar on his knee and Madison on a stool. She'd picked out a flowing top, and with her seated on the stool, her belly was completely hidden. He had no doubt that had been her intention. She'd also thrown her hair up in a loose bun that made her aqua-blue eyes pop.

He swallowed and focused on the camera. All he wanted to

do was pull her into his arms, but he didn't trust he could stop at a simple kiss. He'd almost not had the strength to pull away from their last kiss. But he was so glad he had, because Madison deserved better than how guys had treated her in the past.

The look that had crossed her face had confirmed that. If ever he was tempted to take things too far with Madison, all he had to do was remember that look. The look that said she thought she was trash. Whoever had led her to believe that was true, he'd like to . . . well, something that wouldn't help his social media image.

Madison was a gift. And the only way he could show her that was by proving through his actions that her value wasn't in her body.

"I'm going to set it recording and edit it later." Colby arranged the shot and then pressed Record. "Now, forget about the camera and sing with me."

"Oh, forget about the blinking red light over there." She made a face at him. "Well, if that's all it takes."

"That's all it takes." He winked at her as he picked up the guitar and started plucking out the first notes.

Their first attempt was a little sharp. Probably because Madison's back was so tense that it might as well have been pressed against a board. He needed to get her to forget about the camera.

He set the guitar aside and leaned back in the chair. "Did I ever tell you how I met Dawson?"

"No."

"We played together in the worship band of our youth group. I played the guitar, he played bass, and we both did vocals." For the first time in a long time, the early memories of Dawson didn't burn through him. "We were . . . well, fine, I guess. Better than the average high school worship band. But one day our youth pastor, Steve, sat us down and asked us why we sang. We really had no answer beyond that we were good at it and the girls liked it."

That brought a small chuckle from Madison, and Colby reached out and hooked her finger with his. "He told us that we could squeeze what we could out of our talent, or we could let God take over and see what He could do through it."

Madison let her finger trail along his but didn't comment.

"I don't think either of us really understood at the time. But as we grew, I could see what Steve had been saying. The more I let go and trusted God with my gift, the more we saw God move. In the concerts. In our career."

Madison's hand stopped. "What happened with you two?"

Colby rubbed the back of his neck. "Just because you surrender to God, it doesn't mean life will always be roses. We hit a rough patch and got into a little debt. I booked us a few extra concerts to try to make up the difference, but it wasn't enough. Then Dawson came up with the money. I was so relieved I hadn't thought to question where it came from. He told me God provided and I believed him. Turns out the money was what we had raised for the hunger-relief fund."

Colby dropped Madison's hand as he squeezed his hands into fists a few times. "When our accountant reported the fraud after he did our taxes, I went to Dawson about it, sure it was a mistake. Dawson said it was no big deal and he planned to pay the money back."

"Did he go to jail?"

Colby shook his head. "Fines and community service. He did testify that I had no knowledge of it. But it still tanked my career."

"Do you still talk to him?"

"Nope." Colby leaned forward on his knees. "I tried, but he cut me out of his life in one move and never looked back. He just walked away. I think he believed that doing so was protecting me, but he had no right to make that choice—not after fifteen years of friendship."

Madison reached for his hand. "So now you have the chance to start again."

Colby shrugged as he brushed a kiss across the back of her knuckles. "Maybe. I don't know. But I do believe that God gave me this song. I want to lay that gift out and see what He will do next. And I feel like I'm supposed to sing this song with you."

Madison squeezed his hand, then let go. "Then let's sing."

He lifted the guitar and fingerpicked the first notes again. This time when Madison opened her mouth, it was as if all else had faded into the background. There was no camera, no manager to please, no career to save. It was just the two of them, their voices weaving together in a perfect harmony that spoke from the heart.

This was what he was called to do.

If Leah messed up one more thing, Jon was going to want out of this partnership. They had just over three weeks until opening day, and there was still so much to do. The rugs had arrived, but the floor upstairs wasn't done. The wall displays had come, but the painting wasn't finished so they couldn't be hung. She just needed to get one item off her list.

Leah started jotting down an account number as the door swung open, bringing a soft breeze into the room. They were finally getting some cooler weather. Not typical for the middle of August, but she'd take it.

She finished writing the number, then glanced up. "Vangie." She rushed toward the car seat hanging on Caroline's arm and released the buckle. Sliding her hand under her niece's head, she lifted her from the contraption. She ran her hand over the curl of red hair on top of the baby's round head. "You definitely ended up with the Williams red hair, and I think your eyes are greener every time I see you. I can't believe you're two months already."

"I see how it is. As soon as I have a baby, I'm no longer important." Caroline set the diaper bag on the counter and the carrier on the floor as she took in the room. "Wow, you guys have done so much with this place." She trailed her fingers along the freshly polished staircase railing that led to the second floor. "I love the soft green you've painted the walls. With the light streaming in through the front windows, it gives the room a light, airy feel."

"That's what I was going for, but the back wall is still not done, and if we don't get a move on it, we won't open on time."

Caroline turned away from the oak display tables. "You'll get there."

"That's what Jon keeps saying, but we are behind schedule. I'd hoped to get the racks for hanging clothes put up today, but they sent the wrong ones."

"That was the company's mistake. Things like this happened back when it was the WIFI too. It'll be okay."

"But the signage mistake last week was my fault, and it cost us a couple grand. Then there was the delayed inspection that was also my fault. It almost put us back two weeks in opening. Jon had to beg, plead, and nearly bribe them to reschedule sooner. I'm beginning to regret doing this, and I'm betting Jon is too."

"Breathe." Caroline's hand landed on Leah's arm. "It's hard to run a business. If anyone gets that, it's Jon. He's not going to walk away because you guys hit a few bumps."

"But these aren't small bumps." Leah hugged Vangie a bit closer as her niece began to fuss. "Is she okay? Are the paint fumes killing her brain cells? Maybe you should go. Maybe I should go. I mean, Jon—"

"Leah."

Leah froze a moment, then bounced Vangie. "I'm not sure I can do this."

"The business? Or be in love with Jon?"

"I'm not—"

"You have mentioned him three times since I walked in that door."

"We were talking about the business. He's a part of that."

"Why are you so against loving him?"

Tears filled Leah's eyes as Vangie began to fuss again.

"How did I not see it?" Caroline dug through the diaper bag before pulling out a pacifier. "Dad messed us up good, didn't he? But you have to stop waiting for everyone to walk away from you. And you have to stop making an exit plan every time you fear they might." When Leah didn't comment, Caroline shoved the pacifier in her daughter's mouth. "Jon is not going to promise one thing and walk away the next day. He isn't going to abandon this business, and he isn't going to abandon you."

"You don't know that."

"You're right. I don't. But I do know Jon, and Jon is *not* Dad." She ran her finger down her daughter's face. "Watching Grant with Vangie has taught me so much of what a father's love is supposed to look like. Our dad was as selfish as they come. Be honest, does that describe Jon?"

No. Leah's mind traveled over the past few months. He'd been the example of selflessness, over and over.

Vangie's face twisted in a pout, and Leah turned her around and cradled her on her shoulder.

"Take it from someone who let the love of her life walk out that door right there because of all the baggage Dad left behind. By the grace of God, Grant came back, but don't be dumb enough to let Jon walk away. Dad stole so much from us. Don't let him steal your happily ever after."

"I can't give someone that much power over my heart. Over me."

"Grant has the power to break my heart." Caroline claimed the fussing Vangie from Leah's arms. "And this girl. This sweet baby has the power to destroy me. If something happened to her, it'd shred me. Everything you choose to love comes with the risk of heartbreak. Even this business. If it folds, will you be sorry you ever tried?"

Would she? The past two months had been more fulfilling than any before in her life. She loved working on this store, and she loved . . . working with Jon. Arguing with Jon. Solving problems with Jon. And laughing with Jon.

She blinked hard to force back the tears. "I'm so scared."

"If you weren't scared—at least a little—I'd worry. The fact that you're terrified he could break your heart tells me you're already in love with him." Caroline shifted Vangie to the other shoulder and started bouncing her. "Walling yourself off doesn't make you safer. Just lonelier."

The door swung open as Grant walked in. He offered Leah a

quick hug before dropping a kiss on his wife's cheek and lifting Vangie from her arms. "What are three of my favorite ladies talking about?"

Caroline wrapped her arm around his waist. "How amazing you are and that you're worth it."

"Great, because I *am* amazing and *so* worth it." He grunted as Caroline pinched his side.

Leah had once given Caroline an earful for letting the best thing that had ever happened to her walk away, and here Caroline stood doing the same. But telling someone else to bare her soul and doing it herself felt vastly different. The idea of opening herself fully to Jon was akin to what it'd feel like if someone asked her to jump off a cliff.

But what had Jon said? *"If I'm the one you choose to take that leap with, then I promise to catch you."*

Maybe it was time to take the leap. Because as scary as it seemed, life alone on the ledge was no fun either.

Leah grabbed her keys. "I need to go somewhere."

Her sister's eyes darted to hers, and whether it was a girl thing or a twin thing, Caroline's face lit up as if she'd guessed. She offered a little clap. "Yes, you do."

As soon as Caroline and Grant were out the door, Leah called Jon. When he didn't answer, she sent off a text. When he didn't respond after ten minutes, she checked the location app. Maybe that was a little stalkerish, especially since this wasn't business related, but she doubted her determination to jump would last too much longer.

His icon appeared on Chapel Road. That was Chet's house. He was probably working on the roof again. She sent off another text and hurried to her car. It was time to jump, and there was no turning back.

thirteen

Jon never would have guessed he'd be spending his day cleaning the guts of Otis, but since he'd returned from Europe, curveballs seemed to keep coming at him. At least it was better than digging for money that wasn't there. He'd hired a private auditor, but it would be another week or two before he had any answers.

The only place he could find enough money to save the foundation was his trust fund. But the last thing he wanted to do was mix his personal funds with the business. If they couldn't stop the company from bleeding, it would end up destroying him not just professionally but personally as well. Still, he hadn't given up, and he wouldn't give up until he had a solution.

He entered the barn balancing three mugs of coffee in his hands. "Grab it while it's hot."

Luke grabbed two of the mugs and handed one to Chet. "Your phone went off a few times while you were inside."

"Thanks." Jon took a long draw from his mug and then checked his messages. A missed call from Leah and two texts.

His brow raised at the first.

Where are you? I need to talk.

He nearly choked on his coffee at the second text.

I think you're at Chet's. I'm headed that way.

He'd barely finished reading the text when the sound of an approaching car filled the air.

Chet looked up from where he worked at fitting two gears together. "I wonder who that is."

"Leah." Jon set down his coffee and rushed through the wide door. He pulled it shut as far as he could, but a plastic crate and a bucket blocked it. He hurried over to the car and intercepted Leah as soon as she climbed out. He rested his hand on her door and blocked her view of the barn. "Hey, Leah. What brings you here?"

"I needed to talk to you. And I—" She eyed his arm and the awkward way he stood. Her brow wrinkled. "What are you doing?"

"Nothing." He tried to make his stance more casual while still blocking her view. "Just visiting Chet."

She attempted to look past him, but he blocked her way again. "Jon, you're acting weird."

She angled to get around him, but his long legs covered the distance first, thwarting her efforts. "No I'm not."

Leah crossed her arms over her chest. "What are you hiding?"

"Boy, Jon, you're going to have to get better than that at dodging questions if you're going to keep this tradition." Chet walked out of the barn with Luke on his heels. "I was telling Luke that your dad and I decided that even though we made a promise not to tell anyone, it was important for your mom to know. Can't have the wives thinking their husbands are sneaking out at night for nefarious reasons."

"I'm sorry, what?" Leah's gaze bounced back and forth between the men.

"I told him to bring Hannah next time." He waved at Luke, who was getting in his truck.

Luke waved back. "I have to get going. Leah, can you make sure this guy gets home?"

"Sure." Her brow wrinkled again, as if she was still trying to puzzle the whole situation out.

When Luke's truck pulled away, Chet pointed his thumb back toward the barn door. "Now is as good a time as any to show her Otis."

"Otis is here?" Leah rushed to the barn door and froze. No doubt that was much how Jon had looked a week ago. "Why do you have Otis?" Leah's voice was calm, but her rigid posture said she was anything but.

Chet stopped next to her and patted her shoulder. "Welcome to the secrets of Otis. Known only by the movers and their wives."

That wasn't how he would've chosen to start. Jon hurried forward before this got any worse. "Leah's not my—"

"Pardon me." Chet's grin spread across his face. "And fiancées."

Kill me now. Jon rubbed his hand over his forehead. Why had he chosen that moment to go get coffee? He could've gotten the text and met Leah at the end of the driveway, but no. Instead he was trapped in this mini twilight zone.

"Jon and I aren't engaged." Leah finally spoke, her voice shaky as her gaze darted between the men. "We aren't even dating."

"Really?" Chet's face twisted, doubling his wrinkles. "Well,

Jon talks about you enough, I just figured . . . No worries, but after this you'll be forced to marry him."

"What?" Jon and Leah said in unison.

"Just kidding." Chet chuckled as he passed her, then walked into the barn. "Kind of."

When Leah sent Jon a worried look, he shook his head. Leah hadn't sought him out in over a month, and Chet was going to send her running after ten minutes.

Chet wandered back over to the gears he was working on. He picked up a rag, made eye contact with Jon, and then nodded in Leah's direction.

Yes, he knew how to handle a girl. *Thanks, Chet.*

Leah was standing by Otis, staring at the inner workings. "Wow. It's so . . ."

"Weird, I know." Jon stopped at her side. "Like somewhere between your biggest questions of life answered and finding out fairy tales aren't real."

Leah's lip curled, and she nodded. "So how's it work?"

Jon pointed to a barely visible button under Otis's right cheek. "Press that."

She did and then shrugged. "It didn't do anything."

"It released a lever that was locking this door." He pressed against the brass, and a one-inch circle door popped open.

Leah bent over to look through the hole. "What will that do?"

"This is where you slip in the key." Jon grabbed a long metal rod with a star shape at the end. "I put it in here and it'll fit into that spot right there. Not as easy as it looks."

"Just takes practice." Chet's gruff voice came from across the room.

"Got it. Now I turn it, and boom." Jon spun the metal rod,

and slowly a single wheel lifted. "Normally there are four wheels, but we're fixing a few of the gears."

"Then you would roll him around town?" Leah directed the question to Chet. "And no one would see you?"

"Small towns are pretty sleepy in the middle of the night. If I heard anyone coming, I retracted the wheels and went home."

Jon lowered the wheel and set the rod aside.

"That's amazing." Leah walked over and picked up one of the gears Chet was working on. "Who taught you to move it?"

"My parents, who learned from my mom's father, who was the youngest son of a wealthy watchmaker in Detroit." He held out one of the gears to her. "You can see the influence of watchmaking in this design. It's like a watch—just bigger."

Jon picked up one of the original gears as well and ran his thumb over the old metal.

Leah set her cog down. "Your grandfather made it, or his father?"

"His father. My great-grandfather." Chet paused his movements and leveled a stare at Jon. "Why don't you tell her, Jon? You've got to get this story straight so you don't forget."

Jon shoved his hands in his back pockets. "The watchmaker had two sons, Earl and Charles. The younger one was Earl, Chet's grandfather, and the older one, Charles, had lung issues." He glanced at Chet for confirmation.

Chet nodded and reached for another gear. "Probably asthma or tuberculosis. Nothing is in the family Bible but a note about breathing problems."

"Right." Jon walked over to Otis and ran his hand along the smooth metal. "They built the Manor to move Charles away from the factories in Detroit, but even here he couldn't go outside to play much."

"Well, that's sad." Leah stared at Otis, then squatted down and looked him in the eye. "Where does Otis come in?"

"Charles loved to read, and one of his favorite books was about the African savanna. He begged his father to take him on a safari. But there was no way."

Leah stood, her nose wrinkling. "Please tell me this story gets happier."

"Not really." Jon shrugged. "Instead of a trip, his father promised to make him a brass menagerie of African animals."

"Oh, that's so cute. There were other animals?"

Jon held up his finger. "No, Charles didn't like that idea because he said they wouldn't be real. Real animals moved."

"Oh." Leah ran her fingers along the gears. "So his watchmaker dad designed and built an animal that moved."

"Bingo."

"How sweet." Leah tapped the upside-down nose. "I bet Charles loved it."

"He sure did." Chet picked up a gear and held it to the light. "I think this one will have to be replaced."

Jon took the gear and added it to a growing pile of cogs. "Charles would wake up every morning and run to the different windows of the Manor to find Otis in his new spot. Which is why—"

"Otis always stays in sight of the Manor—well, where it used to be." Leah gave a little clap. "Oh, this is a good story. Did his dad create any more animals?"

"No," Chet said. "Charles died before his dad could manufacture a second one, although my grandfather remembers seeing rough drawings of a lion once."

Jon cringed. Chet might have told that first part more gently.

Leah's eyes widened. "Charles died?"

"Yes, when he was twelve. But his father continued to move Otis around in memory of his son."

"Oh my word. I think I'm going to cry." Leah covered her face.

"No crying." Chet tossed another gear on the table. "My grandfather said that his dad didn't move him around because he was sad. He moved him around because it reminded him to find joy every day like Charles had. When my grandfather realized Otis brought others joy too, he picked up the tradition when his dad got too old. Then he passed it to his oldest children, my mom and George's mom, and they passed it to their oldest children, George and me. No crying."

Chet's words must have worked, because a soft smile filled her face as she walked over to him. "When did you take it over?"

"George and I took it over in the eighties. Now I'm passing it to this guy and Luke. Our kids. Sort of. I almost didn't ask Luke, him not being my kid and all. But I learned a couple years ago that closing myself off from others is no way to live." A slight blush filled Chet's face as his grin stretched wide, but he kept his focus on the gears. "And he named his kid after me."

"Joseph Chet. I heard that somewhere." Jon couldn't resist teasing the guy. Chet had only mentioned it a half dozen times while they'd all worked on Otis together.

He turned to say something to Leah but paused at the intensity in her gaze, which was directed at him. She glanced away, but it had been there.

Jon's mind traveled over the past twenty minutes to figure out what he'd missed but came up empty. Maybe it had been Chet's comments. Or the reality of knowing the truth about Otis.

He could've spared her all that had he gotten to his phone.

But how was he supposed to know she'd show up here? She hadn't sought him out in forever. "Why did you come find me?"

Leah stared at Jon as the question ran on repeat in her head. How was she supposed to answer that? Somehow in the face of Caroline living her life with her husband and baby, it seemed easy to spill her heart to Jon. But now, here, with Chet a few feet away, it wasn't the right time.

She broke eye contact and stared at Otis—belly up, all secrets revealed. Something in her recoiled. How could she open herself up like that to Jon's scrutiny?

"Leah?" His voice was softer now. Not so much romantic, just concerned. "Is everything okay?"

No, everything wasn't okay. Her traitorous heart had betrayed her and she'd fallen in love, and she didn't know what to do about it. Because as much as her heart ached for him, the edge of the cliff was too much as the what-ifs rolled through her mind. What if he left her like her dad had? What if he died like her mom had? What if she failed him like she'd failed Caroline in the WIFI and David in Costa Rica?

Leah rushed out of the barn toward her car. The clouds that had been gathering when she arrived had grown angry and dark. A distant roll of thunder seemed to echo the yelling in her mind. She'd been a fool to come here. A fool to think she could change.

Jon's long legs overtook her, and he moved between her and her car, blocking her path. "Talk to me. Is it Vangie? Caroline? Something happen at the MIM?"

The concern in his eyes twisted and tugged at the last bit of strength she had. Leah buried her face in her hands as the tears began to flow.

Jon wrapped his arms loosely around her shoulders. "I don't know what it is, but we can figure it out. Talk to me."

She gripped the front of his shirt. "But don't you get it? You're the problem."

His arms dropped away, but she held on to his shirt.

"Leah, if this is about what Chet said back there—"

"No, I know Chet." She shook her head as the wind picked up, blowing her hair across her face. "He was just being Chet."

"Then what?"

"It's you."

Hurt hooded his soft brown eyes. Man, she was doing this all wrong. This was why she didn't fall in love. Beyond it being terrifying, she was really bad at it.

He started to untangle his shirt from her hands, but she gripped it tighter. "You don't get it. I'm so crazy in love with you that it hurts. Physically hurts."

The sadness vanished from his eyes as a small smile began to spread across his face. "You're crazy in love with me? Next time, could you lead with that?"

Leah finally let go of him. She pressed her hands to her sternum as she closed her eyes, willing the pain to go away. "I'm so bad at this. And frankly, being in love is horrible."

"Horrible?" His eyebrow lifted as his hands gently captured her shoulders.

"Yes. It's like someone's ripped out part of my chest. I thought love was all rainbows and butterflies."

"No, infatuation is all rainbows and butterflies—and if you're fifteen." His fingers trailed down her arms until he found her hands. "Love is letting someone in and trusting them even though they have the potential to break your heart."

She met his gaze, and for the first time she could hide nothing. As if every thought, every emotion, every fear, and every longing was on display for him to see. She was like Otis—exposed—and there was nowhere to hide. But for the first time she didn't want to.

Jon pulled one of her hands from her chest, placed a soft kiss on the palm, then placed it over his heart, covering it with his own. "You took a part of my heart years ago. And the closer we've become, the more I have become yours. If you feel even a fraction of what I feel? Then I consider myself the luckiest guy alive."

"But I could break it." Her voice hitched. The reality of getting her heart broken suddenly didn't sound as bad as breaking the heart of this man before her.

"I know." He reached up and captured a tear she hadn't even realized had escaped. "You did break it a little in Ludington, but not fully. I've had to give you some distance to keep from going crazy, but not enough for me to give up hope."

"I'm sorry." She rested her head against his chest, listening to the steady rhythm of his heart that belonged to her. She soaked in the strength Jon was offering and rested in the knowledge she wasn't alone in this.

Maybe that was the answer. Jumping alone was terrifying, but Jon wasn't asking her to do that. He was there to figure this out with her. To love *with* her.

Leah drew a few slow breaths and lifted her head, but whatever she'd been about to say melted from her mind as his hand trailed along her jaw and down her neck.

And just like that, the space between them charged to life as every spot where his skin touched hers hummed and burned.

Not a painful burn but a hungry flame that moved through her, as if her very cells reached for more contact. More touching. More of Jon.

She longed to close the distance, and yet she was frozen in this perfect moment—this electric connection of first awareness. Him being assured she was his. Her being confident he was hers.

His gaze darted to her lips, then back to her eyes. He leaned in, but she flinched as a fat raindrop landed on her forehead.

Jon brushed away the wetness and grabbed her hand. "Looks like we're out of time. Should we go inside?"

He started to take a step back, but Leah grabbed the front of his shirt again. "Hey, didn't you know girls long to be kissed in the rain?"

She'd tried to make her tone playful and sassy, but it came out needy. Because she did need him. Closer. Now. And the fact that she hadn't hidden the longing that flowed through every inch of her was reflected in the way Jon's eyes darkened with want.

He flicked a glance at the sky, then hesitated as the rain picked up. "I think guys want to be kissed anywhere, rain or not. But I want you to be sure."

"Jonathan George Kensington the Third, if you make me ask twice—"

His mouth came down on her with force. His lips were soft and warm. He deepened the kiss as he wrapped one arm around her back and laced the other through her hair. His height shielded her from most of the rain but not all of it.

He kissed her along her jaw, then worked his way back to her mouth again. His movements were confident, as if he'd been imagining this kiss—longing for this kiss—for the past four weeks, maybe longer.

Maybe he had been. Because like he'd said, she had a piece of his heart. And somehow in this moment, in this kiss, those pieces were all coming together. Knitting the two of them together. There was no way she could walk away from this without leaving part of herself behind.

After a while he slowed the kiss, taking his time to kiss the drips of rain that ran down her face. His thumb traced her damp lips. Her breathing—which had yet to return to normal—paused at the touch.

She'd never grow tired of that sensation.

His mouth had just found hers again when the sky opened with a fury. A shiver stole over her as the water ran down her face and dripped off her curls. Jon pulled her closer, as if also reluctant to let go of this kiss that now tasted of summer rain.

"You crazy kids get in the house before you catch your death. Kiss later." Chet's voice carried through the storm as he rushed toward the house.

They both laughed as they broke the kiss. Jon took off toward the house, holding tight to her hand. She didn't know if it was to make sure she didn't slip or to make sure she didn't run away. Either way, it assured her that he had her.

A thread of fear poked at her from the back of her mind, but she refused to listen. Today she was ready to jump. She'd deal with tomorrow when it came.

───

This was exactly why she'd said the video was a bad idea. Madison skimmed comment after comment on the video as she inched forward in the grocery store line. Her gaze kept returning to the 100K+ on the counter. Her heart sped up as her brain contemplated that number. She couldn't even visualize a hundred thousand people, let alone comprehend that more than that many had watched her and Colby's video.

"That's $12.47," a chipper girl said from the register.

Madison glanced up. She hadn't even realized she was at the front of the line. She pocketed her phone and pulled out a twenty as the girl dropped the prenatal vitamins in a sack, but Madison held out her hand. "I can take them. No need to waste a bag for one thing."

The girl passed them to Madison, took the twenty, handed back the change, and offered a friendly "Have a nice day" before attending to the next customer.

Madison walked out to her car and hurried home. She released a small sigh when she spotted Colby's car in the drive. She rushed inside and found him rinsing a paintbrush in the sink.

"Have you seen this?" She waved her phone in his face. "Over one hundred thousand hits. You said it'd be a simple video. Something for your manager to get a feel for the song. Seen by a few fans. One hundred thousand isn't a few fans."

"Relax. They love it." Colby shrugged as he let the water carry more paint away. "They love you, actually."

"No, they think you love me." Madison leaned against the counter as she scrolled through the comments and paused on one. "Musicfan101: 'Who's this new girl? Please tell us that she's more than a singing partner.' Crazy4cats25 responds with, 'No joke. Would be sad to see Colby off the market, but these two are totes adorbs. I totally ship them.'"

Colby paused his rinsing and peeked over his shoulder. "I'm not even sure what that means."

"Totally adorable and she wants us in a relationship." Madison kept scrolling.

"How do you even know that?"

"Not the point." She shoved the phone in his face again. "There are about a hundred comments here speculating about whether we're in a relationship or not."

"Why is that a bad thing?"

Why wasn't he more upset about this? "They don't know us. How could they have an opinion after a three-minute song?"

"It was three minutes and twenty-two seconds." He set the brush aside, reached for a rag, and wiped his hands. "Those twenty-two seconds make a difference."

"You're going to joke about this?" She scrolled down and stopped on a comment she'd read earlier. "You really don't care that people like Fred831 went so far as to speculate that you're in love with me but afraid to tell me?"

"Really?" Colby picked up her phone and stared at the comment. Finally, some recognition of the problem. But then he shrugged again and handed the phone back. "Fred831 is pretty insightful."

Madison had started scrolling through more of the comments but froze, her finger still hovering over the screen. "What?"

"What?" Colby's brows shot up all innocent as he slid his hands in his back pockets.

"Colby."

"Maddie." His face softened as he moved closer. "I am in love with you."

"No—"

"Yes. And I'd tell the world that you're my girlfriend if you'd let me."

"That's not a good idea." She retreated, but he followed her step for step.

"So you keep telling me. But I want you." He lifted the phone from her hands and set it aside. Then he rested his hands on her waist, his thumbs rubbing both sides of her bump. "And I want her. I don't care who knows."

"But I'm—"

"Perfect and beautiful?" He tucked a piece of her hair behind her ear, lingering on her skin.

The sensation tore her apart and put her back together at the same time. "I'm not perfect, Colby."

"I don't mean it like that. I know you aren't perfect, and I know I'm not. But you see yourself as broken and less than other women, and that isn't true. You're perfect for me. And I'm so thankful that you're in my life. I love you and every broken piece about you and the fact you're letting God heal that broken-ness." His fingers trailed up and down her arms and paused on her shoulders. "And I hope you can grow to love every broken piece about me."

"I already do." The words tumbled out before she could talk herself out of saying them. She wasn't sure when it had happened, and if it had happened all at once or had been slowly building the past two months, but somehow she'd fallen fully, without condition, in love with Colby Marc.

His gaze became intense as his hands paused halfway down her arms. "What did you say?"

"I love you. So much it scares m—"

His lips pressed into hers as his hands captured her face. The kiss was hard at first, but then it softened as he seemed to take time cherishing her lips, her cheek, her jaw.

Madison had been kissing guys long before she should've been, but never in all her years had she experienced a kiss like this. It was as if Colby was intentional with every touch, every contact. As if his sole goal was to make her feel beautiful and adored.

She'd never trusted love before, because in her experience, guys only gave to get. But in Colby's arms she could see how wrong that definition of love was. Love was about giving and honoring.

After a moment Colby dropped a kiss on her nose and pressed his forehead to hers. "You know there's nothing I'd rather do than continue this kiss, but for the sake of my self-control, what do you say we head to Donny's?"

"Donny's?" As in public. As in the whole town knowing that they were together. "Are you sure?"

"Aren't you?"

"Sure about you? Yes. But people may make assumptions when they see this." She patted her rounding belly.

"I love you. And this little girl." He ran a hand across her stomach and was rewarded with a kick. "Did you feel that?"

"Uh, yeah." Madison rubbed the spot on her stomach. "She has to kick through me to get to you."

Colby leaned down and kissed the side of her belly. "No one better mess with my girls."

His girls. Her father had often called her his girl when he apologized for another bruise. But coming out of Colby's mouth, the words didn't burn through her like they used to. Instead they tilted Madison's life. Not in a fall-over, unstable sort of tilt but rather one that shifted her life into the right position for the first time. She was no longer defined by her past or her father's choices. She was Colby's girl. And so was her daughter.

Colby pulled out his phone and held it out for a selfie of them with his cheek pressed against hers. "I think it's time to answer the fans."

Madison couldn't keep the huge smile from filling her face

as he snapped about twenty photos. Then with a few taps at the phone, he waved it in the air.

"We are social media official." He held out his hand. "Now are you ready to make it Heritage official?" When she hesitated, he glanced down at what he was wearing. "Unless you think I'm not really dressed to go out."

He was giving her an out if she wanted it, but no, he was right. It was time. She gave him a slow once-over, then leaned closer. "Are you kidding? Girls can't resist a guy in jeans and a white T-shirt. And personally, I love barefoot, but Donny's might require shoes."

A smirk tugged at his face. "You can't resist jeans and a white T-shirt? I'll remember that." He slipped on his shoes, then laced their fingers together as they exited the house.

The rain yesterday had brought a cold front, which gave her the option to wear a sweatshirt to hide her bump. But another week or two and she'd need to break out the full-on maternity clothes.

There were definitely a few stares as they entered the diner, but nothing condemning. In fact, they were all more curious than anything. Maybe this wouldn't be so bad.

"Can we join you?" Nate's voice came from behind them.

Madison spun around to face him and Olivia. She released her grip on Colby's hand, but he held on and offered a reassuring squeeze. "We'd love it."

Olivia gave a smile that seemed genuine. "Great."

As soon as they slid into the booth, Nate and Colby carried the conversation, with Olivia commenting on occasion. Then she focused on Madison. "I really enjoyed your singing. You two blend together well."

Madison shot a side glance at Colby and looked back at Olivia. "Thank you."

"Did you know," Olivia went on as if there was no awkwardness, "that Janie and I didn't get along well in middle school?"

"I don't remember that. You two always seemed to be—"

"Close sisters. I know, we were practically inseparable in elementary school and high school. But in junior high, Caroline and Leah came to live in Heritage." Olivia unrolled her silverware and placed her napkin in her lap. "I started spending more time with them and Janie started spending more time with Hannah. I think there was a lot of jealousy involved. Anyway, we called them names, they called us names. It wasn't pretty."

"How do I not remember this?" Madison picked at the edge of the paper that held her napkin closed but didn't open it.

"We kept most of the fighting to outside of school. Well, one day we had a food fight right over there." Olivia pointed to the corner booth. "Aunt Lucy—well, she's Hannah's aunt, but she had us all call her Aunt Lucy. Anyway, she'd had it. She called our parents and said she'd send us home when we'd cleaned up."

"How long did it take you?"

"A while, but even after the mess was cleaned up, she wouldn't let us leave. She made us sit there until we'd cleaned up the mess of our friendships. She knew that if we started talking and listening, then we'd realize that none of us wanted to be enemies. We just didn't know how to start over."

Ah. And there was the hidden message of Olivia's trip down memory lane. Three pairs of eyes watched to see if Madison would take the olive branch.

She finally met Olivia's gaze. "What if it isn't possible to start over?"

"But what if it is? Maybe we need to just sit down and get to know each other, listen to each other's stories, and let go of the past."

"And then we become friends? Sounds simple. Too simple."

Colby's hand squeezed her leg under the table. She wasn't trying to rebuff Olivia's attempt at friendship. But there was a good chance that Olivia wouldn't want friendship once they shared their stories.

"You may not want to know my stories," Madison said.

Olivia leaned forward as her eyes glistened. "I'm so sorry for all I've done to make you believe that, because I think everyone's story is worth knowing."

Madison reached for Colby's hand. "So do I."

"Good." Olivia offered a nod, then cleared some space on the table as the food arrived.

Maybe this transition wouldn't be easy, but maybe it would be worth it.

fourteen

Jon took a side glance at Leah in the passenger seat of his Mustang, then picked up an edge of her flowing, colorful skirt and ran the silky material between his fingers. "If I tell you I like your skirt, are you going to think I'm making fun of you again?"

She ran her hands down her legs. "No. I actually made it this week. I used the one from high school as a model since I knew you liked it. I modernized it a bit and added a few inches of length."

"Well, that's a shame—adding length, that is." He shot her a wink, and she swatted his arm. But his teasing seemed to have worked, because her shoulders relaxed and some of the tightness in his chest did as well.

"Did you hear about the upcoming alumni game? We're playing the high school team as a fundraiser. I guess they do it every year, but they think the alumni can win this year with me back."

"You seem a little too happy about beating teenagers."

"No, I'm excited because you'll finally have a chance to wear my jersey."

"Oh no." Leah shook her head, sending her curls swaying. "I told you. Girlfriend or not, this girl doesn't do jerseys."

"Fine, then you at least better wear my old T-shirt again."

"I don't have your T-shirt."

"The one you were wearing when I tried this on." He smoothed his hand down the front of his shirt. "I'm serious about you making all my shirts from now on."

"You can't afford me." She leaned over and pulled at a loose thread. "And that shirt I was wearing was not yours. I got it out of the lost and found in high school."

He held up his hand, then pointed to himself. "I lost it."

"Well, I found it. So it's mine now." She laughed and poked him in the side. "There's no way you're getting it back."

"Really. We'll see about that." He didn't want it back. Not only was it too cute on her, but there was no way it would fit him anymore. But it was good to see her smile.

It had been a busy week at the store, and he'd been so buried with the audit at Heritage Fruits that he hadn't been around much to help. He still hadn't found the money to put the company on solid financial footing, but the initial overview of the auditor had found a large part of the bleed. With his uncle's changes last fall, the workers had been cut but production had remained the same. The workers were overtaxed and making mistakes—costly mistakes. Like the shipment that had made it through quality control with the wrong expiration dates on all the fruit. It had been sent back, and the company had to cover the cost. Jon would take this all to the board after the auditor gave him the full report.

They needed to rehire workers, but that wasn't an option yet. They had to rebuild one step at a time, though he didn't see how he could save the foundation in time. He was still waiting to hear from Marcy on one idea.

But tonight wasn't about business. Tonight was about him and Leah.

He turned into his wide circle drive and parked his Mustang by the front steps.

"Why are we at your place?" Leah asked. "I thought we were going out."

"No, I said a date." Jon got out, rushed around to her door, and pulled it open. "Your dinner awaits, milady."

She took his hand, but her brow knit into a frown as he led her up to the door. "I know you don't cook."

"Cook? No." He led her up the stone steps, through the marble foyer, and to the family area in the back, then opened the door to his rec room. Abby had been true to her word. The room was lit by about two dozen candles, and the side bar was filled with pizza and pop.

Leah stood in the middle of the room and seemed to be taking it all in. She stared at his floor-to-ceiling bookshelves that covered two walls.

He wrapped his arms around her from behind. "If I remember right, you said you were a stay-in-and-order-pizza type of girl."

She spun in his arms and pulled herself up for a quick kiss. "I love it."

He pointed toward the fifty-four-inch TV that was mounted in the center of one of the bookcases. "And after dinner, something you and I have both been waiting for . . . a rematch in Mario Kart."

Leah rushed over to where he had the Wii set up. "Where did you find another one that still worked?"

"The internet is an amazing place. And . . ." He lifted a cheesy six-inch trophy with a car on top. "For the winner."

She walked back to him and circled his waist with her arms. "Thank you."

"I do want to take you to fancy restaurants and romantic walks along the Lake Michigan shore. But I didn't want our first date to be something generic that would be a great first date for anyone. I wanted it to reflect us."

"I was wrong, Mr. Kensington. You're extremely romantic."

He leaned over and brushed his lips against hers. The memory of their previous kiss hadn't done her lips justice. Heat ran over his skin as her finger reached up and trailed along his jaw.

Abby burst through the door. "Did I leave my phone in here?"

Leah took a quick step back. "I haven't seen it."

This was exactly why he'd made sure Abby was going to be home. Because finishing the kiss they'd shared at Chet's now was probably not the best way to start their relationship. He needed her to realize that she was safe with him. That together they were stronger than they were alone. Her dad may have left her mother a shell of herself, but Jon wanted Leah to become the best version of herself.

He searched the room for the phone and spotted it next to the pizza. He picked it up as it buzzed to life, the name *Gabe* flashing across the screen.

Abby reached for it, but he didn't let go. "I thought you said you weren't spending time with Gabe anymore."

"I'm not."

"Really." He stared at the name again, then pointed the phone at her. "Does he know that?"

"It's a different Gabe." She reached for the phone again.

He held it higher. "You just happen to have met two friends with the name Gabe?"

She crossed her arms over her chest. "It's a common name. I'd think you'd get that, *Jon*."

He narrowed his eyes on her. "Then tell me about this Gabe if he isn't Ruffian Gabe."

"Ruffian Gabe? What are you, eighty? And I don't have to tell you anything. If you had spent any time here over the past month rather than working, then you'd know who Gabe is."

The words were like a slap. He'd been busy at work, but there was a lot to be done. She hadn't screamed at their father when he'd had to put in long hours. "You're still seventeen—"

"For two weeks. Two. Then I'll be eighteen. I'll have full access to my trust fund, and I can do what I want." She dropped her hands on her hips and sent him a glare she'd perfected over the past year. "You're not my father—"

"Okay. Time-out." Leah held up her hands between them and pulled the phone from Jon's hands. "You're both being ridiculous." She singled out Jon. "She's right. You can't control everything. If she says it isn't the same Gabe, you have to trust her." She placed the phone in Abby's palm. "You're right. You don't have to tell us anything. But we're here for you. And we hope that if you need something, you'll let us help you."

"'We'? Are you two married now?"

Leah flinched at *married* but seemed to attempt covering it with a shrug. "Well, I know your brother is here for you and I'm here for you, so that means we are here for you."

"Thanks." Abby rolled her eyes as she shoved her phone in her pocket and then spun toward the door and marched out. That girl's mood swings were going to give him whiplash.

Leah started filling her plate at the pizza bar. "She's right, you know. You have to start giving her more freedom if you want to keep that relationship. Like it or not, she gets to make her own choices come September third. You can't hold money over her head like most parents. She'll be as wealthy as you, and you need to build that trust so you can still speak into her life."

"I know." Jon wrapped his arms around her again. "That's why I need you in my life, and now that I have you, I'm not going anywhere."

"Eat up and I'll show you who's boss in Mario Kart. It will be an important test to see if this relationship will last."

"Game on." Jon grabbed a plate and filled it.

Leah may have been teasing about testing him, but he sensed that she still wasn't all in. The fear behind her eyes was ever present, and if her reaction to the word *married* was any indication, he needed to take this slow. The demons she fought wouldn't be defeated overnight, but he'd prove that his love wasn't going anywhere, one day at a time. One battle at a time.

Game on was right. This game was one he had no intention of losing.

His phone chimed, announcing a text. He pulled it up and read it over.

Marcy
The account we looked at was a dead end. Dale said to move forward with officially closing the foundation and send the letters you signed to the recipients.

He winced and shot off a quick reply.

No. Wait on that.

He'd only signed the letters because his uncle wanted every *T* crossed before he'd agree to delay the layoffs. But Jon had no plans to mail them. Not until he had overturned every rock he could to save the foundation. He wasn't giving up yet.

He'd once won a game with a Hail Mary half-court shot with two seconds on the clock. Everyone had called it the miracle shot. Maybe he could pull off another miracle.

He had to, because if he didn't come up with this money soon, Leah's fear wouldn't matter. She'd never trust him again.

If working with Jon had been distracting before, this was downright torture. Leah eyed him as he stood on the extended ladder with his arms stretched over his head. He was changing a burned-out light bulb on the vaulted ceiling of the MIM, but with the way it emphasized the width of his shoulders and arms, she might ask him to replace every one.

Her skin still hummed with Jon's touch, and it had been five days since the date at his house. They'd spent a good share of the evening in their Mario Kart battle, which he'd won by only one race. He had displayed the trophy on the shelf as if it were an Emmy Award.

But he'd made up for it in his good-night kiss. And boy, did that guy know how to say good night. He'd left her with dreams and not just a few moments of wishing they hadn't spent so much of their evening playing Mario Kart.

His speed felt safe. It was more than that he was willing to go slow. It was that he was choosing the slow lane to let her know she was protected, not rushed. She loved that about him—even when she hated it.

"Are you going to spend all day gawking at my brother or show me how to run the cash register?" Abby's teasing tone was back as if the conflict the other day hadn't happened.

"I'm okay with the gawking." Jon's voice carried from the top of the ladder. "If you give me a second, I'll even flex for you."

"Gross." Abby wrinkled her nose. "Can we focus on my training?"

"The cash register. If a customer pays by credit, you press this button, then run their card there." Leah pointed to the card reader. "For cash, you press this button." She tapped at the screen. "Then type in the amount. For a twenty-dollar bill, you press 2-0-0-0. The last two digits are the cents, so don't put 2-0 or it'll think it's twenty cents. Then press Enter."

The drawer popped out.

"Wow. That's a lot of cash." Abby picked up the stack of tens and fingered through them.

"Businesses need cash on hand." Leah took the money back from Abby, placed it in its slot, and closed the drawer.

A knock on the main display window echoed through the room as a guy with bleached-blond hair motioned to Abby to join him outside.

Leah shot a glance at Abby, whose face had shifted into a glare as she stared at the other teens. "Ruffian Gabe?"

Abby rolled her eyes. "You too? Seriously, you guys need a new word."

"What do they want?" Jon was off his ladder and now leaned against the counter.

Abby stiffened and glared at her brother. "I don't know. I haven't talked to them in over a month. Do you want me to go ask?"

Jon's shoulders tensed, but his expression seemed unaffected. "It's up to you. You know how I feel about them, but it's your choice."

Abby's eyes darted to Leah, but Leah just shrugged. This less-overbearing version of her brother was new to both of them.

Abby walked out the door and stood talking to the group by the window. There was a lot of gesturing and she didn't look happy, but she seemed to be standing her ground.

Leah glanced back at Jon, who was white-knuckling the edge of the counter. "Easy, fighter. She seems to be doing fine."

"I know." He pushed off and walked a few feet away, then back. "It's just not easy letting her grow up. But you were right. I have to remember that I'm not her father, and it's time to move away from the role of guardian to brother. Even if it makes me want to level that guy."

Gabe was in Abby's face again, and about the time Leah was going to tell Jon that even big brothers intervened at some point, Abby lifted her hand in a dismissive gesture and walked back into the store, effectively cutting off the conversation.

"What was that about?" Jon made the words sound casual, and Leah almost laughed. He was anything but casual.

"It doesn't matter. It's over." Abby spat the words over her shoulder as she walked back toward the office.

"I'm here if you need me," Jon said as if he were chatting about the day. He could be a good actor when he needed to be. He leaned over the counter to drop a kiss on Leah's lips. "I'd hoped to get the security cameras reinstalled today, but I have to take care of some stuff at the office."

"Go." She motioned to the room. "We still have a couple days until the opening. Inventory is all in. Signage is up. I'll work at steaming my hanging clothes while I wait for Kade to finish for the day. He's set to be done on time, but I don't want to rush him. Oh, and I needed to put out the night-lights that just came in."

"Night-lights? You didn't."

"Oh, but I did."

He rolled his eyes and gave her another quick kiss before heading to the back door, calling for Abby as he went.

Madison walked through the front door as Jon disappeared out the back.

"What brings you by?" Leah leaned on the counter toward her. Memories of doing the same thing at the WIFI flashed in her mind, and a calmness settled into her soul. She was a business owner once again.

Madison held up the computer and a couple thick files. "I'm done."

"Oh." Leah took the offered items and set them on the counter. "Did you want to do more work? I have more for you. But I know you wanted something short term."

Madison shrugged. "I may be sticking around longer than I originally thought, but I still can't do anything long term."

"Right." Leah started winding up the computer cord. "Because you're still planning to sell?"

"It's not just that." Madison winced. "I guess since we're sort of friends now, you should hear this from me." She lifted the edge of her sweatshirt, revealing her stomach. A small but very round stomach.

Leah's hands paused. "Oh. A baby. Congratulations. How far along are you?" Did she sound as awkward as she felt? But that was literally the last thing she'd expected.

"Twenty-four weeks. I've been carrying small, but I can't hide it anymore. Well, when I don't wear sweatshirts." Madison lowered her shirt and leaned back on the counter. "And now you're calculating how long I've been in town and if it could be Colby's."

Leah swallowed. That was exactly what she'd been doing. But she couldn't calculate weeks that fast.

Madison met her gaze, but she didn't look mad, just resigned.

"It's not his. I was about thirteen weeks when I came to town. He's known all along. And this is why I keep telling him that us together isn't a good idea, but he's convinced—"

"That he loves you? I've found arguing with a man in love doesn't get you too far."

"No, it does not."

They shared a laugh, then Leah reached over and patted Madison's hand. "When you're ready, I'll throw you a baby shower."

"Really?" Madison's brow twisted.

"Absolutely. I know Olivia would be happy to come, and I'm guessing others too if you give them a chance."

Madison pressed her lips together as she pushed away from the counter. "I'll think about it."

"Please do. Let me know if you're available for more work."

Madison nodded but didn't move.

"Was there something else?"

"Would you be willing to sell my dad's leather pieces here? I don't know their value . . . I just want them gone." There was so much unsaid in Madison's tone.

"Drop them off. I'll take care of the rest."

"Thank you." Madison's shoulders lifted a little as she walked out.

Just as the door swung shut, Leah's phone rang. She dug it out of her purse and held it up to her ear as she walked toward the utility closet that held the steamer. "Hey, Caroline. I expected you'd call today. Are you wanting to get the details of my date?"

"Any chance you're up for three new houseguests for a while?" There was a definite waver in her sister's voice.

Leah opened the closet door but paused as Caroline's words registered. "What are you talking about?"

"We got a letter. The Kensington Foundation has been liquidated. We'll no longer be receiving a support check for the ranch. We were barely on our feet before, so there's no way we can afford this place without that."

Leah grabbed the steamer, pulled it out of the closet, and kicked the door shut with her foot. She shoved the phone between her shoulder and ear. "This has to be a mistake. I'll call Jon—"

"Jon's signature was on it."

"No. That can't be." He'd promised her that he'd never do that.

"I'm sorry to tell you. But it was."

Leah let go of the steamer and leaned against the wall as cold tendrils spread through her limbs.

He'd lied to her.

Just like when he'd changed the name of the WIFI. What had he said? He'd made the choice that made the most business sense.

He'd told her what she'd wanted to hear, but when push came to shove, he'd picked business over his word. Business over relationship. Business over her.

Colby clicked the last blind in place, then lowered it and raised it again, testing the mechanism. Last room. Last detail before the new floors. He'd put the TV in that corner. A music setup in the far corner. Leave the dining room table where it was but get one big enough for at least six people, maybe eight.

Colby shook his head and carried his tools to the table. When had he started thinking of this place as home? Not just his home, but his and Madison's. That idea pinched a nerve of longing in him that had lain dormant for a long time. There was no denying that he could imagine building a life here—a family with Madison and their daughter.

He'd taken this job to keep his mind off his failing career—not to mention get to know the girl who had fascinated him from the moment she'd peeked at him from above her large round sunglasses. But the job had been so much more—a cocoon that God had used to transform his thoughts and future hopes. Maybe it had been less about the paint and more about time with Madison and time with his own thoughts. But God had sure used it. Colby wasn't the same beaten-down guy that he'd been when Nate had called three short months ago.

Madison approached from the hallway and paused in the middle of the living room. "I can't believe how much those new blinds lighten up the room and make it feel bigger. I guess it isn't the blinds as much as the fact they're now open. But I love it. Once the new floors are installed tomorrow, it'll look like a whole new place."

"Almost too great to sell." Dropping a hint couldn't hurt.

She huffed and started riffling through the mail. "I wouldn't go that far."

The immediate rejection stung. But Madison was not a quick adapter. Easier to start planting the seeds than forcing the issue before she was ready. He'd have to keep his emotions in check until then.

"I was thinking of talking to Hannah about listing it. I was worried about asking her, but after my talks with Leah and Olivia, I'm thinking there's hope Hannah will help me out." She glanced at him, her brow furrowing. "What?"

So much for keeping his emotions in check. "Nothing."

"That look wasn't nothing." She picked up a large manila envelope and pointed it at him. "And when did you start getting mail here?"

"It came?" Colby snatched the envelope and carefully tore

away the edge. "I had it sent here because I wanted it to be a secret until I talked to you."

"Talked to me about what?" Madison's gaze darted from her hands to his face and back again.

Colby pulled a stack of papers out of the envelope and started looking them over. "I got a new contract. And I had them include one for you."

"What? I'm not a singer."

"It's just for one song—'Clay Feet.'" He pulled a section of papers out that were bound by a clip and set it in front of her. "Our song."

Madison's legs seemed to give out, and she landed hard in a chair, her eyes fixed on the contract. Had he done the right thing? He opened his mouth to apologize for overstepping when a smile began to slowly transform her face.

"You want me to be a part of your album?"

"Yes." He squatted down in front of her. "I want you to be a part of my everything."

"What are you saying?" Her eyes widened farther.

In all the ways he'd imagined proposing to Madison, covered in dust and in her kitchen hadn't been among them. He didn't even have a ring, for goodness' sake. But what he did have was zero doubt that this was what he wanted for his future, and he wanted that future to start today.

He dropped onto his knees and picked up her hand. "Madison—"

His familiar ringtone split the air, cutting him off. If he'd planned this, he would've probably silenced his phone too.

He started to ignore it, but Madison peeked at it on the table. She pushed it toward him. "You should take it. It's your manager."

Colby sighed and stood. He snatched up the phone and did his best to keep his irritation from coming through. "Hey, Roy, what's up?"

Roy's voice dripped with tension. "I need you to be straight with me. Is Madison pregnant?"

All warmth drained from Colby. He spun and stared at Madison. "How do you know that?"

"So it's true." A long sigh accompanied the words. Colby could imagine his agent raking his free hand through his hair like he had when he'd told Colby that Dawson was being arrested. "Is it yours?"

"No." He glanced at Madison again. Her face had gone ashen. There was no way she could hear Roy's words, but by Colby's face she must have guessed. He repeated the question Roy hadn't answered. "How did you find out?"

"It's all over social media. Some photo of Madison buying prenatal vitamins. It isn't solid evidence, but it has people talking. And the last thing you need right now is people talking."

"It's not like that."

"You know, Colby, I actually believe it's not. But the label already feels as if they're taking a chance on you. They have rescinded the offer to have Madison sing 'Clay Feet' with you. As far as your contract . . . they're still considering. Anything you could do to stomp this out from your end would help. But I still can't offer a guarantee."

"But this isn't—"

"Fair? Right? Probably. But this is business. I'll call you when I know more."

The call ended, and Colby set the phone back on the table before he did something stupid like smash it against the wall.

He gripped the back of a chair and then finally made eye contact with Madison.

She was no longer pale. In fact, her features didn't convey any emotion, as if she were made of stone. "What did he say?"

"He said there's a photo of you that's causing a bit of speculation on social media."

She pulled up her phone and tapped at it a few minutes before she paused. She drew in a slow breath as her hands shook slightly. Finally she set the phone in the middle of the table and stood. "I told you small towns never forget. This was why I didn't shop at JJ's before, but you said it wouldn't be a big deal. Guess you were wrong."

Colby picked up the phone and stared at the photo. It had been taken at a low angle as if the photographer was trying to hide what they were doing. Madison held a bottle of clearly labeled prenatal vitamins in one hand and was extending a twenty with the other. She was wearing a baggy T-shirt, but if he really stared, he could see the faintest bump in the midst of the fabric. The caption simply read, "Is Colby's girlfriend pregnant? I guess we know what Colby's been doing in his 'time away.'"

He set the phone down and rubbed his temple.

"Can I assume this is recycling?" She held up her part of the contract.

He rushed across the space and gripped her hands. "I won't sing it without you."

"Yes, you will." She carefully removed her hands from his. "It's a good song and the world needs to hear it. What did he say about your contract?"

"It doesn't matter." Colby didn't reach for her again, but only because he didn't want to push her. He didn't back away though.

"It doesn't matter?" Her eyes hardened. "What did he say about your contract?"

"He said I should distance myself from you if I wanted to keep it. But that isn't going to happen."

Madison shook her head. "This is bigger than you or me, Colby. It's your calling. I've seen you lead worship and when you write a new song. You were made for this. We barely know each other."

"Don't say that. I love you. I was a half second away from asking you to marry me before that call came." He pointed at the spot where he'd knelt minutes ago. "And I could tell by your face that you were going to say yes."

"Then I guess it was a good thing Roy called when he did."

Colby lifted one of her hands. "Tell your story. Let people know—"

"No."

He motioned to the phone still displaying the photo. "It is *already* public."

"Not the details. And if I separate myself from you, they'll forget about me. I was defined my whole growing-up years by my father's choices and will not have the same for my daughter. I want a fresh start for her."

"I agree, but a fresh start isn't denying the past. It's letting God redefine it."

"Tell that to your fans. This isn't just best for me, it's best for you too. Even Roy agrees. Your career can't handle this kind of scandal right now."

"We have something special here." He pulled her hand to his mouth, trying to hold her to this moment. To what they had. "Fight for this with me."

Madison pulled her hand away, picked up her phone, and started typing.

"What are you doing?" When she didn't answer, he stepped closer. "Maddie?"

"What needed to be done." She passed him the phone.

Madison247: I guess the cat's out of the bag. I'm pregnant, but no, it isn't Colby's. I know there has been a lot of speculation about our relationship, but Colby and I are only friends. I wish him the best in his career. He was a joy to sing with.

His heart tore a little further with every word. When he finally pulled his gaze from the phone, she stood at the edge of the hall, her arms crossed over her chest. "I guess since you finished the last project, there's no reason to come back."

"Maddie—"

"Have a good life, Colby." She hurried down the hall. Then her hushed footsteps were replaced by the click of her bedroom door.

She'd done it. She'd walked away and severed their relationship in one post. She hadn't even given him a chance.

His phone buzzed with a text, and he glanced at it on the table.

Roy
Perfect move by Madison. It's already trending.
This should help a lot. I'll let you know about
the contract as soon as I talk to the label. But
plan to start recording in Nashville next week.

What had just happened? He'd lost nearly everything he wanted in a matter of minutes. A deep ache flowed through his body. He might still have a contract, but without Madison to sing with—to be with—it all felt pointless.

fifteen

Leah had assumed she would be more prepared to confront Jon after a good night's sleep, but that depended on her actually falling asleep. She rolled over and checked the time again. 12:24. This was going to be a long night.

She should've called him immediately after she'd talked to Caroline, but she had decided it was best to calm down—get her head about her and her emotions under control.

But he'd lied to her. He'd promised that the ranch was protected, but as soon as that wasn't convenient to the business, he'd changed his tune. What else had he lied about? Caroline had said that Jon wasn't like their dad, but now Leah wasn't so sure. And she had no desire to get caught up in that destructive cycle. No doubt he'd have his excuses.

The ring of her phone split the quiet night. She jumped, then grabbed the phone from her nightstand. Unknown number. "Hello?"

"Leah Williams?" A deep voice came over the phone. "This is Officer Hammond. There has been a break-in at the MIM. I need you to come down and—"

"I'm on my way." Leah yanked back her comforter and pulled

on some clothes that she'd draped across a chair. She rushed downstairs and slipped on her pink rubber boots, which still sat by the door from last week's rain, then ran for her car.

She made it to the store in record time and pulled to a stop behind a cop car, its lights flashing. Leah hopped out and had started to cross the street to the MIM when she froze. There was no missing the damage. The large display window had been shattered, and the cash register that was visible from the window had been pried open.

She might be sick. She pressed her hand over her stomach as a hand landed on her lower back.

"Come on. We can face this together." Jon's voice calmed the chaos in her mind, and she hated that fact.

She had so much to say to him, but right now she couldn't seem to see beyond Hannah's shattered vase and Mrs. Nell's broken pottery all over the counter. Whoever had done this seemed to have gone on a rampage of destruction, leaving few displays untouched.

"It'll be okay." With a slight pressure on her back, Jon led her inside. "It may delay the opening, but this is why we have insurance. It—"

"Insurance?" She spun to face him, stepping away from his touch. "Insurance? So as long as it's covered financially, it isn't a big deal? What about the hours that Mrs. Nell put into that pottery?" Leah jabbed a finger at the pile of blue and green shards. She grabbed one of her dresses lying next to Jon's foot. It had been ripped down the front. "What about the hours I spent creating this?"

Jon laid his hand on her shoulder. "The insurance will cover the price the artist would've gotten. They won't lose anything. It'll be like it was sold."

She jerked out of his hold again. "You don't understand. I don't create dresses just for the money. I put a piece of myself into every single one. And I find joy in knowing that that piece of me is bringing joy to someone else. There's no joy in this."

"I know." Jon ran his fingers roughly through his hair, making it stand up on one side. "All I'm saying is that financially—"

"Of course you are." Leah dropped the dress and picked up a piece of shattered glass. This had been a plate of fused glass made by Hannah. She ran a finger over the swirled pattern of yellow and red, then locked eyes with him. "Because with you it always comes back to the money."

His brow wrinkled. "What are you talking about?"

"You shut down your dad's foundation even after promising me that you'd make sure that would never happen. Don't bother denying it. Your signature was on Caroline's letter."

His face paled. "Those weren't supposed to be sent yet."

"Yet? But they were going to be sent, right? Because you did use the funds in the foundation for something else." Leah dropped the piece of glass, but the movement ran the sharp edge along her finger. She pulled her hand back as a dark red line formed and then began to drip on the wood floor.

"Would you be careful?" Jon grabbed the dress she'd thrown down and wrapped it around the cut. "You don't know the whole story."

She yanked her hand back but kept the dress wrapped around her finger. "Then explain."

"This isn't the time or place." Jon's eyes darted to the people in the room who were pretending they weren't eavesdropping. "But it wasn't an easy decision. Unfortunately, as the boss I have to make those tough decisions. But I'm—"

"You've let Dale walk all over you and now you want to pretend you are the boss? Let me ask you this. Was it his idea or yours?"

"*I* made the call. And *I* decided that the money was needed somewhere else. I'm sorry." His shoulders sagged as he came closer until they were inches apart. He ran his hand down her arm as he leaned in. "It was a no-win situation, but the reason the letters were not supposed to go out was because I'm still trying to fix it. Trust me."

She stilled under his touch. She had told him she trusted him. Maybe she needed to trust him with this as well.

"I have spent hours upon hours over the past couple weeks trying to fix this. I still have a few—"

"The past couple weeks?" His words settled in. "How long ago did you do this?" When he didn't answer, her back stiffened. "How long?"

He ran his hands through his hair again. "Two weeks."

"You signed the letters two weeks ago?"

"I had to sign them to move the money."

Two weeks ago. Her hands shook as she retreated another step. Before the kiss in the rain, before the date, before . . . everything. Every memory over the past two weeks became fogged over by this new reality. "Why didn't you tell me?"

"It wasn't MIM business. And I told you, I was trying to fix it—I'm still trying to fix it. You have to trust—"

"Trust? You've been telling me what I wanted to hear. You filtered out all the bad parts that I didn't need to know. That isn't honesty."

Her throat tightened as she surveyed the disaster again before bending to pick up a piece of cracked pottery. This wasn't supposed to happen. It was supposed to go right this time. Their relationship. The business. Her return to Heritage.

The piece of pottery crumbled in her hand as the word *failure* echoed in her mind and a familiar panic filled her chest. Her fingers shook as she dusted the pottery remains from her hands. "This was a mistake."

"What was?" Jon asked.

"Reopening the WIFI and thinking it would end in anything but disaster." She met his gaze. "Going into business with you—a relationship with you—and thinking it would end in anything but heartache. I'm done."

"You're done? With what?"

"This." She motioned to the room. "This business. Us. Everything."

"You don't mean that." Jon lowered his voice to an intimate tone.

"Uh, Miss Williams, Mr. Kensington," Officer Hammond interrupted them, more pottery crunching under his boots. "I'd like to go over a few things with you."

Leah moved farther from Jon and faced Officer Hammond. "He's the owner now. Talk to him."

"Leah, don't do this."

She paused at the pain in Jon's voice, but she forced herself to recall the pain in Caroline's voice. She wasn't just protecting herself, she was protecting her family.

"Write up the papers and I'll sign them." She didn't look back. "Looks like you helped your uncle get what he wanted after all. The business is officially yours."

Jon cleared his throat, all warmth disappearing from his tone. "Of course, because when things don't go perfectly for you, you quit. You quit the WIFI, you quit Costa Rica, and now you're quitting the MIM. Good luck with whatever you try next. Because—news flash—it won't go perfect either."

Leah spun to face him. "I may be a quitter, but you're a disappointment to your father's memory. He would be heartbroken over closing the ranch down."

He flinched at her words, then his eyes hardened.

"If your dad had left the company to Dale, maybe it *would've* been better. At least I wouldn't have put my trust in him."

The emotion melted from Jon's face as he seemed to turn to stone. He settled his hands in his pockets, his head tilting slightly to one side. "Did you really trust me, Leah? Or were you just waiting for me to mess up so you could walk away? Always have to have a back-door option." He stared at the floor before locking eyes with her. "Someday you'll have to go all in with your dreams—with your heart—no strings attached. Ninety-nine percent isn't enough."

Leah marched toward her car before he could see her tears. The shattered glass crunched under her boots. Trust her heart to someone? Not likely. Because trust led to this—heartbreak.

* * *

It took every ounce of strength Jon had not to follow Leah and argue his point one more time. But between Officer Hammond waiting on him and her words *"You're a disappointment to your father's memory"* on repeat in his head, he stood his ground. She wanted the fun parts that came with running a business, but not the tough decisions. Did she think he wanted to close Quinn Ranch? He wasn't heartless. He'd been working his tail off trying to fix the company and save the ranch. But she didn't trust him to do that. She didn't seem to trust him to do anything. And he was done trying to prove he was trustworthy. Because no matter what he gave, it was never enough.

He'd never be enough. Not for Leah. Not for Abby. And not for the company his father had left him.

"Are you ready?" Officer Hammond approached again.

"Sure thing." Jon straightened his shoulders, doing his best to hide the defeat that seemed to be ripping him raw from the inside.

He followed the man to the back door, his eyes scanning the walls as he went. The photo from the first day of construction mocked him. Leah looked so optimistic. He just looked in love and pathetic.

Did he even want to do this without her? No, but after today it was clear he couldn't do it *with* her either.

Officer Hammond held up his notepad and pointed his pen to the busted lock. "They seem to have entered here. My guess is that they went for the cash register first, and when it was empty, they took to vandalism. They threw a large rock from that display through the front window as they escaped. A witness thinks he saw them fleeing the—"

"You think they were originally looking for money?" Jon opened the office door, but the room hadn't been touched. The computer sat undisturbed and the safe wasn't even scratched. "Then why didn't they come in here?"

The officer poked his head in. "Guess they didn't know the office was here. Probably thought it was a maintenance closet." He tapped his pen on the door sign that said Maintenance and lifted an eyebrow at Jon.

"A family joke."

"Well, that joke may have saved you from losing more than you did." The officer led him back out to the main room. "Although I'm not sure why they would've thought the store had much cash anyway since it isn't open yet."

Jon froze midstep as the words sank in. Leah had shown the stocked cash drawer to Abby before she'd talked to Gabe. Of course, Leah would've moved the cash drawer to the safe, but that had been after he and Abby left. Nausea traveled through his body. Why hadn't he gotten the security cameras installed yet? "You said someone saw them?"

"Austin Williams was coming home from some late-night work at his nursery about that time and witnessed three teens run from Teft onto Second Street, where they climbed into an old Camaro. Wasn't too sure of the color because it was parked under the broken streetlight, but he said it was a light color."

Ruffian Gabe.

"Austin didn't think much of it until he drove by the MIM. He's the one who called it in."

"Did he give a description of any of them?"

Officer Hammond flipped a few pages on his notebook. "Two guys and a girl. He didn't see their faces, but the guys were dressed in black, so he didn't have much of a description."

"And the girl?"

"Dark hair and wearing a red coat of some sort."

Jon yanked his phone from his pocket and did a quick location search for Abby, but nothing came up. He refreshed the screen with the same result. *No location found.*

That meant two things. One: she'd switched off her location so he couldn't find her. Two: she hadn't gone to bed early like she'd said. She'd snuck out.

Jon rubbed his hand over his face. "I have two people you should look into from these descriptions. Gabe Howell and Abby Kensington."

When Officer Hammond nodded and turned away, Jon headed to the back room to pull out some plywood he'd stashed there after the remodel. By the time he had pulled out the second sheet, Austin had rounded up Luke and Thomas to help. Together they boarded up the front window, secured the back door, and cleaned the glass from the sidewalk.

Three hours later, Jon didn't even have the energy to take the steps two at a time as he made his way to his front door. He still didn't know what he'd do about Abby. She was days away from being eighteen, and he couldn't help someone who didn't want his help. For now, all he wanted to do was collapse in his bed and deal with it all tomorrow.

He pushed open his front door but paused with one foot in the house. Abby sat on the bottom step of the grand staircase, her head in her hands, her red jacket sitting next to her.

She lifted her head when the door clicked shut, her tear-streaked face crumpling. "I didn't do it. I swear."

Jon walked over, dropped down next to her on the step, and leaned his elbows on his knees. "Do you hate me that much that you need to sabotage my job? I mean—"

"I didn't do it." Abby jumped up and paced the floor. "I know how it looks. But you have to believe me." When he didn't say anything, she rushed on. "At the store when Gabe came up to the window, he saw me looking at the cash. He called me out there because he wanted me to lift it for him. When I refused, he got mad. That's why they broke in."

Jon pointed to the red jacket still sitting next to him. "Austin saw you running away from the scene."

"It wasn't me. I don't know who was with them, but they had her wear my coat. Seriously, if they were all dressed in black, how dumb would I be to dress in red?"

That made sense, but . . . "How did you know they were dressed in black? And why do you have the coat now?"

"After you left, Gabe called me, bragging about what they'd done. I went to his place . . ." She must have read some of Jon's anger in his face, because she paused and glanced away, her shoulders sagging. "I wanted to make it right, but they just laughed at me and threw my coat at me. Said the cops would be looking for it."

Jon ran his hand over his head. "Why should I believe you?"

Abby dropped next to him again and gripped his arm. "Because I'm telling you the truth."

"Like when you told me the truth that your red jacket was 'around here somewhere'?"

She sighed and faced forward, letting her head drop into her hands again. "I left it in Gabe's car, and he wouldn't give it back. I knew you'd make a big deal about it and go all big brother on him, so I lied. I was hoping the game would grow old to him and he'd give it back."

"That didn't seem to work out so well for you."

"I know. I'm sorry."

"Me too." Jon stood and started up the stairs, but her hand landed on his shoe, stopping his progress.

"Do you believe me?"

"I don't know. The better question is, will Officer Hammond believe you when you give him your statement?"

She nodded as she released his foot. Jon continued up to his room before his life could crumble any more in one evening.

Once she got out of this town, things were bound to get better.

Madison carried another bag to her car, dropped it in her trunk, and slammed it shut. She'd hoped to be able to stay until the house sold, but knowing Colby was just three blocks away was too difficult. If she stayed any longer, she'd find herself at Nate's doorstep, begging Colby to take her back. But this was the right decision for his career. For him.

She also knew that Colby would never give up on her. He might back off now, but he'd keep fighting for her until his love wore her down, and she couldn't trust herself to stay strong for that much longer.

She slid into the car and eyed the box on the passenger seat. It was full of stuff Colby had left at the house. It wasn't fair for her to keep it. She'd just leave it on Nate and Olivia's steps and never have to see Colby. After all, she specialized in drive-by drop-offs. The day she'd left Thomas's stuff with Janie floated through her mind. That had been easy enough.

The muscles in her stomach knotted the closer she got to Nate and Olivia's, but she breathed a deep sigh of relief when she didn't see Colby's Civic in the drive. *Thank You, Lord, for small blessings.*

Madison pulled into the drive, slid the box across to her side, and hopped out of the car. She rushed up and set it on the top step, then hurried back to her car.

She had just grabbed the handle when the door creaked open behind her. "Madison?"

She faced Olivia, taking care to keep her emotions from her face. "That's some of Colby's stuff. Can you give it to him?"

Olivia opened the door wider and picked up the box. "Colby left."

"Left?" The words hit her in the chest.

"He moved back to his Nashville apartment. I think he was getting ready to record that new album."

He *had* left. He'd obviously seen the wisdom in her decision, which was what she'd wanted. But why did it have to hurt so bad?

Madison turned back to the car.

"Madison." Olivia's voice stopped her again. "Would you like to come in for some tea?"

Madison paused with her hand on her car. She could get in the car and never look back. Start a new life where no one knew her. That was what she was good at. And that was what she'd wanted since she'd stepped foot in this town three months ago.

But for the first time, living life with people who didn't know her didn't have its usual appeal. When no one knew her, no one cared for her either. No one asked to join her at a diner, no one offered to help paint her house, and no one ever offered to do something crazy like throw a baby shower for her. She'd never known true friendship before, but then she hadn't really known what she was missing.

Tears welled in her eyes, and she pressed her hands over her mouth as a sob stole over her.

After a minute, a gentle hand landed on her back. "Why don't you come inside? You shouldn't be driving right now anyway. Let's have some tea and you can be on the road in an hour."

Madison nodded and followed Olivia into the house. The parsonage was an old Victorian with dark wood floors and matching wide trim. She'd stopped over here once with Thomas. Back then, the mismatched furniture and bare walls had screamed bachelor pad. Olivia hadn't made a ton of changes, but the silk flowers and the wooden sign that spelled WILLIAMS FAMILY in script letters offered that homey touch.

Madison took a seat at the table and did her best to wipe off the mascara that was probably covering half her face.

Olivia pressed a button on an electric teakettle and pulled two blue glass teacups from the cupboard before adding a tea bag to each. "Few problems can't be solved over a long cup of tea. That's what my grandma would always say."

"I don't think tea is going to work this time."

"Well, since Colby didn't look much better than you the day he pulled out—minus the mascara smudges, of course—I'm guessing there's a lot to talk about."

Madison pulled a napkin from the holder at the center of the table and wiped her face again. "I'm sure you've heard about the baby by now."

"So, it's true?" Olivia poured hot water in both mugs, then set one in front of Madison.

"Yes, so now you know why it can't work."

"I know the baby isn't Colby's, but . . ." Olivia's face twisted in confusion. "Does Colby not want the baby?"

"No, he does. He's been . . . amazing. He's known since the day we met. I actually told him as a way to send him running."

Olivia raised an eyebrow as she lifted the cup toward her mouth.

"I know. Now that I know Colby, that would never have worked, but I'd never met a guy like him before. At least not one who looked twice at me. Most of the guys who'd come knocking on my door split at the idea of commitment, let alone the word *baby*."

"I could be reading this wrong, but . . . you want to be with Colby. He wants to be with you and your little one. I don't see the problem."

Madison stirred the hot liquid, then pulled out the tea bag and set it aside. "People on social media didn't seem to agree. His label even threatened to drop him."

"Ugh. This isn't the way Christians should treat one another. But it doesn't have to stand in the way of you and Colby. How does the baby's father fit into all of this?"

Madison's eyes wandered across the table, and she ran her nail along the edge as the familiar ache filled her. But there was no reason to hold back now. She met Olivia's gaze. "I don't know who the father is."

Olivia's eyes widened. "Madison, did someone—"

"No. At least, I don't think so. I was at a party . . ." She picked up her spoon and stirred her tea again. "When I left Heritage, I was hurting. And not because Thomas had chosen Janie. It was something he said to me the night we broke up. He said, 'You're special, Madison. I know not enough people have told you that in life, but you are.' That ripped me apart. Because no one had ever told me I was special before. No one had ever made me feel like I was worth loving before Thomas."

Madison's voice cracked, and she took a moment to compose herself before she continued. "Looking back, I know Thomas wasn't in love with me like he is with Janie. But he loved me like a friend. And I'd never even known the love of a real friend before, only people who wanted something from me. When Thomas left, I hadn't known loneliness like that since my mom died."

"And we were so unkind to you."

"Well, it wasn't like I made it easy for you."

Olivia shrugged but didn't argue.

"I left town and tried to escape that loneliness by attending any party I could get an invite to. It worked about as well as you'd think. The weekend I got pregnant was right after I got the call that my father had died."

"Were you close to your father?"

Madison's head jerked up as a flood of emotions hit her like a sucker punch. How did she answer that? She'd told Colby more than she'd told anyone, and she'd only scratched the surface with him. "You guys really had no idea, did you?" She drew a slow breath and mentally stepped back enough to hit the need-to-know parts. "My dad was a good father before my mom died. After that, he spent more time with a bottle of whiskey than anything else. To say he was an angry drunk was an understatement. But I learned early that makeup hides bruises well."

Madison let out a deep breath. Every time she shared her story, it was accompanied by a little less chest-squeezing, breath-stealing pain.

Tears gathered in the corners of Olivia's eyes. "I had no idea."

"No one did. Somehow I'd always imagined that I would be able to confront my dad as an adult. And that somehow that confrontation would finally give me peace and freedom from him. But with him dying..."

"That was no longer an option." Olivia reached out and squeezed Madison's hand.

"Right. After he died, I felt I would have to carry this burden forever. Now I'm not sure why I thought confronting him would take it away, but I'd carried that belief for so long I couldn't let go." Madison cleared her throat. "So when I found out, I went to a party to find an escape. I drank and took things that I didn't even know what they were. I didn't care, I just didn't want to feel. I don't really remember most of that weekend."

"And then you found out you were pregnant. Oh, Madison, I'm so sorry. So how did you end up at church?"

"I found myself at a place called Hope Pregnancy. I didn't even know what it was. I just knew I was pregnant and hopeless, so it seemed like a good place to start. There I met a woman named Sister Alena. She asked a lot of questions, and even for the short time I considered an abortion, she never looked at me in any way but love. She simply listened. It was then that I realized I didn't know much about faith or God, but I wanted the peace that woman had."

"Was she the one who taught you about God?"

"She helped me to understand that God is my Father, but not a father like I knew. The father I always wished I'd had. Loving. Kind. Accepting. Protecting." Her voice hitched, and she drew a slow breath to push back some of the emotion. "He knows my story. All of it. And He's been with me during every tragic, painful part. But my bad choices don't have to define me. My *dad's* choices don't have to define me. *Jesus* defines me, and He's redefining my story."

Madison finished her tea and set the cup back on the saucer. "We had barely scratched the surface of what it meant to believe when I got a call that I needed to come settle my father's estate. That's how I ended up back here. I had hoped it would be a quick stop, but it turned into a house renovation project. The day I bought my first can of paint I met Colby, and I think you know the rest."

"Madison, you're amazing. I think you might be one of the most courageous people I know."

"No, I—"

"Listen. First you survived an abusive father growing up, which I can't even imagine. But then when you were faced with a pregnancy from a dark situation, you chose to have the baby. I'd like to think I would do the same, but I think no one has any idea how hard that decision is until you're in it."

"At the time, I kept thinking that if I could get rid of it, I could pretend it never happened. My life could go back to the way it was before." Madison ran her hand over her rounding stomach. "But I knew I'd never forget, and I didn't want to go back to who I was before. I just knew that if I was getting a second chance, I wanted to give her a first chance."

"I love your story. I don't love that you've had to go through all that. But I love to see what God has done in your life. Have you ever thought about sharing it publicly?"

"No. I don't want my mistakes to define my daughter."

"They don't have to. Like you said, they no longer define *you*. You don't have to share your story, but there's something freeing about doing so. Don't let your story be something that weighs you down. Let it be what sets you free."

"Colby wanted me to share it too. I just . . ." She stared into her cup and shook her head. "I'm not great with words. Besides, I think it's better after time has passed. I'm not sure people would really believe I've changed. You didn't when I came back."

"And I regret that. I'd like to tell you I'll never make a mistake again or that you won't, but I can't. We're both bound to make more mistakes. But Jesus keeps forgiving us and showing us a better way forward."

"Then how can I get up there and say 'Look at me' when I know I'm bound to fail again?"

"The power in your story isn't that you're done making bad choices. Personally, I think you dismissing Colby was a bad choice. But—"

"I did it for him and his career."

"God doesn't need your help with Colby's career. I mean, He doesn't want you to trash it, but did you even pause to ask what He wanted?"

"God or Colby?"

"Either."

"No."

"Like I said, the power in your story isn't that you're done making bad choices. The power in your story is where you're turning for help now. You said you're learning that God's trustworthy. I'll let you in on a little secret. It isn't only the big-picture items that He's trustworthy with. He even cares what happens with you and Colby. You can trust Him with your relationship. You can trust Him with Colby's career."

"What do you think I should do?"

"I don't think I'm the one you should be asking."

Madison stood and carried her cup to the sink. "Thank you, Olivia."

"Where are you headed?"

Madison walked to the door and stepped out on the porch. Where was she headed? She couldn't ignore that the itch to run still sat close to the surface. But maybe before she did that, she needed to take time to pray. About Colby. About sharing her story. About what was next for her and this baby. "I'm going back to my house. And then . . . I'll let you know."

sixteen

Of all the things Jon didn't have time for right now, putting Otis back together was at the top of the list. He fit the next cog in place and checked the diagram again. They finally had all the replacement pieces, they just had to get them to line up. Jon nudged the gear until it fit snug with the one next to it. Maybe he should've gotten a degree in watchmaking. Seemed a lot more useful than his business degree these days.

He slid a brass spacer on the rod and reached for the final piece. When he didn't spot it, Chet dropped it into his hand. "Where's Leah tonight?"

"Not sure. We aren't together anymore."

"Not together? The way you kissed her, I thought you'd be announcing your marriage plans any day."

"I told her I wouldn't fail her, but I did." Jon slid the gear into position. "I can't be the guy she wants."

"Who does she want?"

"My father."

"Say what?" Chet's mouth twisted into a frown.

"No, not actually my father. She wants someone who can do it all with no mistakes. Well, that isn't me. That was my father, and I can't be him."

"That's the dumbest and smartest thing I think I've heard you say since you've been home."

Jon paused his movements. "What?"

"You think your dad made no mistakes? That's hogwash. He made plenty of mistakes." Chet picked up a bolt and handed it to him. "But you're right. You can't be your father. And I'm glad you finally realized that."

Jon picked up the wrench and tightened the bolt. "So you think my dad made a mistake leaving me the company."

"What? You losing your hearing, boy?" Chet crossed his arms. "I didn't say anything of the sort."

"You just said I couldn't be my dad and—"

"You can't. But your dad didn't leave his company to a clone of himself. He left it to you."

Jon set the wrench down and leaned on Otis's side. "Well, that was a mistake, because I'm making a pretty big mess of everything. The company is bleeding money. The layoffs that Dale made when he took over left too few people to do a quality job. Returns have been happening, orders are down, our reputation for a quality product is shot."

"That was Dale." Chet poked a finger at his chest. "Not you."

"But who put Dale in charge?"

Chet waved his hand as he shrugged off the words. "Your father made mistakes too. And you'll make more. But your father wasn't a good businessman because he never made a mistake." He laid his hand on Jon's shoulder. "Your father was a good businessman because he cared about people and learned from his mistakes. He also surrounded himself with people he could trust. His board, his managers, your mother. I don't care if Dale's your uncle. If you can't trust him—"

"The board isn't on my side either."

"Then get a new board." Cheet's hands lifted into the air. "They're your advisory board, not a governing board. Your father kept them because they were loyal and wise. But if they aren't being loyal to you, then that isn't showing loyalty to him. And wisdom without loyalty isn't helpful."

Jon let his head fall back as he closed his eyes.

"Why do you go to church?"

Jon's head jerked up. "What?"

"I know your parents dragged your butt to church when you were young, but somewhere along the line you had to take ownership of your faith. You had to make the decision to keep going or not. You couldn't just live off the faith your dad left you—you had to make it yours."

"Why are you saying this?"

"Same thing with the company. He pointed you down a path, but you have to make this company yours. You can't live your dad's life any more than you can live out his faith."

"You make it sound so easy."

"Not a bit. Running a company is hard. And you're trying to run two. But you aren't in this alone."

"What if no one wants to help?"

"I guess you pray people will show up." Chet grabbed a rag and wiped his hands. "And while we're on the subject of you doing dumb things, why in the world would you ever tell Leah that you wouldn't fail her?"

"I hadn't planned on—"

"Of course you didn't plan on it. But loving someone isn't never failing them. It's you choosing them and them choosing you day in and day out, even when the failures happen."

"Well, she didn't choose me."

"I'm sorry. Sounds like she needs a good talking-to as well.

Kids these days." He tossed the rag aside. "Speaking of kids that need a good talking-to, what happened with Abby? I heard about the break-in. Was she involved?"

"No. She gave her statement and provided the location where she'd seen Gabe and his friends last. It was some hunting shack on his father's field. When the cops showed up, all three were quick to ask for plea bargains."

"But how's she doing?"

"I haven't talked to her much since. Just one more area I seem to be making mistakes in. Any great advice there?"

"I don't know a lot about girls or teens. But I do know that you may have to let her do some figuring on her own." Chet leaned against the edge of the worktable. "Have you considered letting her help? Responsibility is a great way to grow up."

"I hadn't thought about it. But maybe I should."

"Good. Glad to see you're finally coming around." Chet patted Jon on the shoulder with a solid thump. "I've known you were being an idiot since you came home—letting your uncle walk all over you. But I had to let you come to that conclusion on your own."

"Thanks for that." Jon grabbed the rag Chet had dropped and removed the grease from his hands. Chet was one unique guy, but he couldn't help being thankful he was in his life. "Do you really think I can run that company in a way that would make my dad proud?"

"It's like Otis here." Chet patted the hippo's brass side. "He stopped running smoothly because a few of the gears had weakened the whole system." Chet pressed the hidden button, slipped the long key into place, and twisted it until all four wheels rose with ease. "But after we replaced them, he's ready to move forward. You just need to replace a few broken gears, and Heritage Fruits will be ready to move forward again."

"I could still fail." Jon rubbed his eyes. "Then even more people would be out of jobs."

Chet lowered the wheels again and set the key aside. "Of course you could. Your father could've too. But that isn't your concern. You do your best—be the best Jon you can be—then leave the rest up to God."

The broken gears they'd replaced were now piled in a corner. They had done their job, and the time had come for their replacement. There were definitely a few people at Heritage Fruits who needed replacing—how many, Jon wasn't sure. He could lead and no one would follow. But then at least he'd finally be going in the right direction.

Leah pulled one of her men's shirts from the pile of broken glass at her feet and held it up. This one only had a slight tear in the seam. She tossed it into the box to fix and picked up the next one, which was in shreds. She didn't even bother looking it over before she dropped it in the trash, then checked her watch. She had only been here an hour? Not only did the boarded-up window steal the afternoon sunlight from the room but the boxed-in feel was like being in a coffin.

The dramatic exit the other night hadn't had the lasting effect Leah had hoped for. Even though she had turned the company over to Jon, she still had to make a claim on her items. Not to mention artists had been coming and going all day to record their damage. If she wanted the other artists to get their money, she needed to at least stick it out through the insurance claim.

"So much unnecessary destruction." Mrs. Nell swept some of

her pottery shards into a pile. Most of the other artists had some damage, but Mrs. Nell and Hannah had taken the brunt of it.

"I'm so sorry." Leah picked up the remains of another dress and wadded them into a tight ball. "You trusted Jon and me, and now . . ."

Mrs. Nell paused her sweeping. "I still trust you and Jon."

"Why?" Leah whipped the material into the trash. "We should've installed better security. We could've . . ."

"Could've what?" Mrs. Nell leaned on her broom.

"Something."

"No. You didn't do this."

"How can you not be angrier?" Leah pointed to the broken pieces on the floor. "That's a lot of time and heart. And now they're destroyed."

"Every time I create, it's a gift to my Creator. I create, then let it go. Oh, at first I didn't do that. I created and then worried how people would like my pottery. I worried how much to sell it for and if people thought it wasn't worth that much money. I worried, worried, worried."

"Sounds familiar."

"I came to the point where I let it all go and realized my value isn't in my ability to make pottery. My value is in who I am. And my pottery is an expression of the creativity God has given me."

"You don't care how each piece turns out?"

"I didn't say that. I create each piece as best I can. I pour my heart into it and put a price I feel is reasonable on it. After that, it's out of my hands. I've done all I can, and I have to let it go. Then I aim to make the next piece even better."

"I'm not particularly good at letting go."

"No, instead of letting go, you quit," Mrs. Nell said. When Leah just blinked at her, she continued. "Did you think your argument with Jon would go undiscussed in Heritage? You should know the gossip mill better than that."

"I had to quit." Leah picked up a few undamaged pieces from the next display and carried them to the counter. "I can't work with someone I don't trust."

"It's not that you *can't* trust Jon. It's that you *won't* trust Jon."

"He shut down the foundation that supports Quinn Ranch after he promised me he wouldn't."

"If only business were that simple. Did you know that he used those funds from the foundation to save my husband's job? I, for one, am thankful he made the choice he did. And from what I hear, he's still doing all he can to save the ranch. But being the owner of a business comes with hard decisions. You know that from working here."

Mrs. Nell dumped the pile of pottery into the giant trash bin. "I know you think quitting this business—quitting Jon— is going to shield you from more pain, but it's also shielding you from true success. Imagine it like a gap in the road. Quitting lets you exit early—lets you avoid the chance of falling into the gap—but you also never get to find out if you would've made the jump. And I'll tell you this: you'll never make the jump giving it ninety-nine percent."

The words hit Leah hard in the chest. Ninety-nine percent. That was what Jon had said she'd given him. He wasn't wrong either. It had seemed like a lot at the time, but maybe it wasn't enough.

"Why did you leave Costa Rica?"

Leah's head jerked back up at Mrs. Nell's voice. "What?"

"Why did you leave Costa Rica, or even shut down the WIFI a few years ago?"

"It wasn't . . . I mean, it didn't . . ."

"Did you exit early when things weren't turning out the way you thought?"

Hadn't that been pretty much what Jon had said to her? But this was different. Wasn't it?

David's disappointed voice when she'd called to tell him she wasn't returning echoed back to her. Maybe she'd been wrong in coming home. "You think I should go back to Costa Rica?"

"No." Mrs. Nell brushed some of the pottery dust to the floor and leaned against the table. "Should you have stayed in Costa Rica? I don't know. You've picked up a new dream here, and I think this is one you could be really good at. But you can't toss it aside as soon as you start feeling out of control or when it doesn't look like you imagined. We don't know if the store will be a failure. But don't exit early."

"But this—"

"We lost some inventory." Mrs. Nell brushed more broken pieces to the floor, where they landed with a crash. "But your dream of this store is helping our dreams as artists come true too. For some it's providing the income for supplies to do what we love most. Then there are others like Mrs. Lorencen, who makes soap—she's using the extra income to pay for her kid's piano lessons."

"I didn't realize."

"We believe in your vision. We've gotten in this car with you even though there is a gap in the road. Don't exit early. Let us help you, and together I think we can make the jump."

"And if it fails on the next jump?"

"We'll have enjoyed the adventure while it happened and cheer you on with your next dream. Failure can be a good thing, but you have to learn from it and fail forward. Let the failure push you on to something greater."

"I already told Jon that I was done."

"Talk to him. Jon is a reasonable businessman. And I think he's sweet on you."

Sweet on her? Maybe before, but she'd seen his face just before she'd walked away. He was done with her.

As if reading her thoughts, Mrs. Nell offered a comforting pat on her arm. "People can fail at relationships too. But it doesn't have to be the end. Grow and try again."

"What if I can't fix it?"

"Then you'll learn, grow, and take that into your next relationship. Fail forward, Leah."

Leah lifted another dress. This one was torn in two down the middle. She held it over the trash bin but paused. There was a lot of good material that remained undamaged. She tossed it in the fix box and picked up another. It was time to try again and fail forward. The big question was whether Jon would let her come back. And if he did, what would that look like? She had no idea, but she did know she was done exiting early.

─────

Why had he believed he was ready to get back in the studio? He hadn't stumbled over his words this bad since his first concert in high school.

Colby adjusted his finger placement on the strings again and shifted his position on the stool. Nothing felt right. Even the familiar grip on the neck of his favorite guitar didn't settle his nerves like it had in the past. He leaned into the microphone and made eye contact with the guy running the board on the other side of the glass. "I'll try that again from the top."

After receiving a nod of approval, Colby closed his eyes and plucked the first few notes of the song, trying to settle into the zone. But all that came to mind was Madison's face. The way she smiled. The way she laughed. The way she kissed.

He missed a chord on his guitar and stopped. He let out a huge sigh as he rubbed his forehead. He had to pull himself together. Music was all he had left.

"Hey, Colby." Roy's voice came through his headphones.

Colby lifted his head. His manager stood at the window, leaning into the mic.

"Why don't you take five. Get a drink, walk around, whatever you need."

Whatever he needed? It sounded kind, but that was industry speak for, "You have five minutes to get your act together before we cancel this session and cost the label a ton of money to reschedule." But he didn't see a way around that. Because what he needed was almost six hundred miles straight north. Only she didn't need him.

Madison had walked away without a backward glance. She'd thrown away all they had in minutes, without even giving him an opportunity to try to figure out another option.

It was almost as if it had been easy for her. Maybe he'd been too blinded by his own feelings to see that she wasn't as invested. Or if she had been, then not enough. Not enough to fight for them. The memory of when he'd been about to propose burned through him. How could he have been so wrong about . . . everything?

He slipped his pick between his teeth but left his guitar resting on his knee as he picked up his phone and checked the time. He had another couple missed calls from Nate. He wasn't ghosting his friend, but Nate had been pretty clear that he thought Colby should stay in Heritage. Nate didn't understand that you don't tell your label to wait. Not when your career is dangling by a thread.

His phone lit up again with Nate's name. Well, his career seemed to be tanking all on its own, so he might as well listen to what Nate had to say.

He pulled the pick from his mouth and answered the call. "Hey, Nate."

"You answered."

"Figured you wouldn't quit bugging me until I did." He tried to add a touch of humor to his tone but wasn't sure it worked.

"No man left behind and all that. Right?"

"We were never military, and I'm not sure you can call recording songs in one of the nicest studios in Nashville 'left behind.'" He tucked his pick in the strings, then set his guitar on the stand.

"But you're still miserable."

"I never said—"

"You didn't have to. I can hear it in your voice, and I remember what it felt like last year when I thought things were done with Olivia."

That constant ache in his chest twisted a little more.

When Colby didn't answer, Nate went on. "How's recording going?"

"About as well as you thought it would."

"You're one of the most talented singers in the industry, but you and I both know that trying to force it will never work."

"When it's your job, sometimes that's what it takes."

"Do you know why I said you weren't ready to go back?"

"Because you think I need to heal more?"

"No. It's because you stopped fighting for the vision God gave you for this album. I saw how passionate you were when you were trying to get the label to sign on Madison for 'Clay Feet.' That was your dream. But at the first pushback, you caved."

How could Nate say that? "I tried, but—"

"You didn't try."

"You seem to think I have a lot more power in this career than I do."

"No, Colby, *you* seem to think you have more power in your career than you do. You write songs and you have an amazing voice, but you and I both know that whether this song is your next big hit or it's forgotten within a month is out of your control."

"What are you saying? I shouldn't care?"

"No. But God gave you a vision for that song, and thinking you know better than God—that the label knows better than God—is putting your faith in the wrong place."

"If I tell them I won't do it without her and they refuse, then my career is shot."

"Then God will give you another career . . . another dream." There was a long pause, then Nate continued. "Record with Madison, don't record with Madison—that isn't the issue. I just don't want to see you compromise on the dream that God has placed within you."

Colby rubbed his forehead. Recording wasn't even his biggest problem. "Even if I did get them to consider her again, she walked away from me, remember?"

"She did." There was another long pause. Colby checked to see if they'd been disconnected, then Nate's voice came through again. "Did you watch the livestream of church on Sunday?"

"No. I've been busy."

"Watch it. At least the last fifteen minutes. I think it might be enlightening. I've got to go, but think about what I said. And remember you're always welcome here if you need a place to crash while you're figuring things out."

Nate ended the call, and Colby pulled up the church's recording from Sunday on their website. He tapped Play, then swiped forward to the end. His finger jerked away when Madison's face filled the screen. He backed up to where she'd taken the mic and let the recording play.

"Hello, my name is Madison Westmore, and I'm here to tell you my story. For so long I've feared sharing it. I thought I needed to get my life together and prove that I had truly changed first. But recently I've realized that my story isn't about me or what I've done. It's about what God has done in me, and there's nothing I can do to improve on that. Hiding my story hasn't protected me from gossip like I thought it might. It has only hurt the one man I love very much. And pushing him away will always be one of the biggest regrets of my l—"

Colby paused the video and backed it up a few seconds. "—has only hurt the one man I love very much. And pushing him away will always be one of the biggest regrets of my life."

"Colby, you ready, bud?" Roy's voice came through the overhead speaker.

Colby closed the app and slid his phone in his pocket as he rose from the stool. "No. I need to go."

Roy walked into the studio and came to a stop next to Colby. "Figured you might. Can't promise there will be another opportunity."

"I know." Colby grabbed his guitar and carried it over to where he'd left his case.

"Well then, go get her."

Colby paused with his guitar half in the case. "I thought you said—"

"I said it wasn't good for your career. So as your manager I'm telling you this isn't a good idea. As your friend, I say go for it."

Colby latched his case shut and slapped Roy on the shoulder. "I'm planning on it. And you can tell the label I want to negotiate Madison's contract again. I'm not singing 'Clay Feet' without her. If they won't agree, then . . . I won't record it with them."

"Are you sure?" Roy's voice wasn't judgmental. He just seemed to want to make sure Colby had thought it all through.

"I'm sure. I'm not making this stand because I love Madison, although I do. But I feel strongly about how the song is supposed to be recorded, and if the label can't get behind that, I guess we'll have to go our separate ways."

This might be the end of his career. But he didn't want a career he didn't believe in anyway.

What he did want was Madison, and it was time to go get her.

seventeen

Chet had made it sound so easy, but he wasn't the one who had to stare down these men who had watched him grow up. Jon downed more of his water while members of the board filled the room and took their seats.

Uncle Dale's gaze paused on Jon, who had taken his uncle's regular spot at the head of the table. His eyes hardened, but when Jon made no effort to move, he dropped into another chair and slammed his briefcase on the table. He popped it open and pulled out a stack of papers. "We have a lot to go over today, gentlemen, so we better get started."

"Actually . . ." Jon's voice carried through the room, and everyone paused their movements. "We won't need that agenda today. I have other things we need to talk about."

"Well, since this"—Uncle Dale waved the papers in the air— "is what was agreed upon and sent out, this is what we'll be discussing. If you have other items you'd like brought up at the next meeting, you can get them to Marcy and ask her if there's room to add them."

When his uncle stood and started passing out the papers, Jon rose from his seat. His age was against him, but his size had always been one thing that drew respect. At least it established he wasn't a kid to be talked down to. "But since this is my company, I can change the agenda as I see fit."

The board members' gazes bounced between the two men, but Jon didn't budge. A muscle in his uncle's jaw twitched as his gaze hardened again, but he motioned for Jon to continue.

Jon sat down but didn't sink back in his chair. He tapped his finger on the papers in front of him. "I have an announcement. First, I want to thank Dale for stepping in after my father passed. You've committed a lot of time to this company, which allowed me to finish my basketball contract, and I want you to know it's appreciated."

Uncle Dale nodded, but his gaze remained cold.

"Second, the last six months have been a great opportunity to understand the inner workings of the company. Just under a month ago, when we were faced with the possibility of more layoffs, I hired an outside auditor—"

Uncle Dale sputtered from his seat. "You can't—"

"I *can*, and it's a good thing I did." He lifted a stack of folders and started passing them around. "As you can see in this report, the layoffs a couple years ago led to overtaxing the workers. Our quality has gone down, orders have gone down, and the trickle-down effect has put us in the red. If you flip the page, you will see my plan to get us back in the black. It won't be a quick fix, but I believe it can be done."

"I haven't approved this." Uncle Dale waved his copy in the air.

"You don't have to. I've discussed the details of my father's will with legal, and I'm ready to assume the position my father left me. As of Monday, I'll take the lead."

"You really think you're ready to lead this company?" Uncle

Dale's face reddened as he spoke. "You can barely make it to half the meetings."

"Now that the MIM is up and operational—as soon as repairs are complete—I'll be turning over control to Leah Williams."

"You're just going to hand over that business to your girlfriend, and you want us to believe you're ready to run a multimillion-dollar company?" Uncle Dale exchanged a look with several of the board members.

"She's not my girlfriend." The words scraped across Jon's heart. "But even if she was, she was chosen because she owns fifty-one percent of the MIM and can do the job well. I'll still advise her if she seeks my advice, but other than that I'll turn over full control to her."

"We won't support that." Uncle Dale slapped the folder against the table and stood, sending his chair rolling back.

"I understand. But technically, I don't need your support. Which brings me to the third item to be discussed." Jon settled back in his chair and made eye contact with each board member as he spoke. "My father chose you to be on this advisory board because he respected you. He valued your opinions, and he knew you respected him."

The men nodded but kept their serious expressions.

"I'm happy to extend that invitation to anyone who wants to remain on my board in the advisory role. But if you can't support me as you once supported my father, I ask that you decline the invitation. I won't take it personally, and I'll respect your decision."

"And what position do you intend to offer me?" His uncle, still standing, placed his hands on the table and leaned toward Jon.

"You can stay on and work for me in the same way you worked for my father, or you may also step down."

"You want to demote me?"

"It isn't a demotion. It's the job you have technically always had. I'm simply moving into the role my father held."

The muscle in his uncle's jaw twitched a few times. "Should I assume you want your father's office too?"

"Yes. Abby will be moving into mine. At least, I'll offer it to her, as well as a spot on this board. Technically she owns a large part of the company as well." When his uncle didn't comment, Jon let his gaze travel to each member again. "I'll give you all some time to think about it. Let me know by September fifteenth."

No one spoke as Jon stood and walked from the room. He'd nearly made it to his office when Ed Hoffman's voice came from behind him. "Jon, do you have a moment?"

Jon stopped and faced the man.

Ed extended his hand as a grin stretched across his face. "I'm proud of you. Well done."

"Thank you."

"And now I can confidently retire from the board."

"I'm sorry to hear that." Ed had been one of the few he'd counted on to stay.

"To be honest, I'd announced to your father I was ready to retire a few weeks before he died. We were set to announce it after the first of the year. But with his death, I stayed on at first to make sure the transition went smoothly, then to make sure Dale didn't destroy this company."

Jon inwardly cringed at how close he'd been to letting that happen.

Ed patted him on the shoulder. "After today, I'm finally confident I can walk away knowing you'll do your father proud."

"Thank you, sir."

"Please let me know if there's anything I can do." Ed shook Jon's hand again and moved toward the elevator.

He'd done it. He'd taken back the company.

Jon closed his office door and rested his head back as he sank into his chair. His chair for now, that was. Come Monday he'd be in his dad's office across the way.

The door opened, and Jon lifted his head.

Abby shut the door behind her and took one of the chairs across from him. "What's Uncle Dale's problem? He was ranting from his office like a child throwing a full-blown temper tantrum."

"I told him I was taking over."

"Really?" She leaned forward. "Good for you."

"And you get this office if you want."

"What?" Her face twisted as if he'd asked her if she could fly.

"I know you want to go to college, but you can work here part-time if you'd like—get to know the company. Half of it's yours, after all. When you're twenty-five, I can either bring you on as a partner or offer you a monthly stipend."

She paused with a thoughtful look on her face. "You'd do that even after all the trouble I've caused?"

"You didn't break into the MIM. And you're an adult, and I need to remember that."

Abby drew in a deep breath as she sat on the edge of her seat. "Speaking of that . . ."

"Yes?" He didn't like the look in her eyes, but he had to let Abby be Abby.

She bit her lip. "I decided to take the semester off."

Jon drew a long, slow breath and pulled in all the words firing back and forth in his head. "Okay."

"Okay?" Her eyes went wide.

No kidding. He wanted to tell her to go to college. Get a job. Grow up. But she was on her own now whether he liked it or not.

"I don't like it." He rubbed his temple. "But I can't stop you. What are you going to do?"

"I'm still figuring that out. I thought I might travel."

"What about this office?"

"Can I tell you when I get back?"

He nodded.

"Thank you."

"Just don't come back married."

Abby laughed as she left, but that didn't make him feel any better.

He'd stood up to the board. And he'd let Abby go. Last item on his agenda—telling Leah that the MIM was hers.

Her father's empty workroom didn't bring the sense of vengeance she'd imagined it might a few months ago. Madison stopped where her father's workbench had once stood. The last of his tools had been sold last week, and someone had shown up and taken the shelving that morning. Just a hint of leather lingered in the air, but that would be gone too when she painted and the new carpet arrived.

Life had dealt her father a rough hand, but he chose the bottle over love. Life had dealt her a rough hand as well, but she would choose differently. Even if she didn't have Colby, she would choose love every day for her daughter.

She crossed the room and flipped the light switch, then closed the door, leaving it all behind. Her father didn't define her. God did.

It had been four days since she'd told her story in front of the church. She wasn't sure how, but something about saying it all out loud and telling of how God had met her in her darkest hours had freed her from the last strings of guilt and shame that had still clung to her.

She'd been tempted to text Colby the link. Not to get him back, but he'd always believed she was stronger than she ever thought. Turned out he was right.

She hadn't sent it though, because she respected his decision to leave. He was recording his next album, and she couldn't be happier for him. The last thing she wanted to do was guilt him into returning.

Little Miss offered a resounding kick in her side. She rubbed her hand across it and walked toward the kitchen to get herself some water.

She had just pulled out a glass when the faint notes of a guitar drifted in from the front yard. Was there an event in the square that she'd forgotten about?

She almost dropped the glass when Colby's familiar voice started weaving its way through the notes. She stood frozen for a second before she rushed to the front door and yanked it open. There in the middle of her yard, in a white T-shirt, jeans, and bare feet, Colby played his guitar as he sang "Hey There Delilah," but he'd changed the words to fit her name. When he hit the chorus, she started running toward him, and she reached him before his third "It's what you do to me."

He dropped the neck of the guitar, the strap swinging it to his back. He swooped her up in a big hug, singing the last of the chorus in her ear. When he stopped singing, he slowly placed her on the ground. "Hi."

"How long are you here for?"

He reached up and tucked a strand of her hair behind her ear. "That's up to you."

"How's that up to me?" She leaned back to see him better. "When do you have to go back to record?"

"I told them I wouldn't sing 'Clay Feet' without you. Roy's supposed to call."

"But Colby—"

He placed his fingers gently over her lips. "I know you said I needed to distance myself from you for my career. But guess what? I don't want a career without you in it. If that means I make less money—which I don't think will happen, but no matter if it did—I don't care. I love you."

"I love you too."

Colby opened his mouth as if he was ready for an argument but froze. He blinked, then swallowed and blinked again. "I'm sorry, could you say that one more time?"

"I love you, Colby Marc, and I don't care what anyone says. No matter how crazy our life might be together, I want it. I want you."

"And here I thought I'd have to talk you into this. It's the white T-shirt and jeans, isn't it? You said it was irresistible. I guess you were right."

She loosened her hold. "Would you rather I played a little hard to get? Because I can go back inside and—"

"Oh, no you don't!" Colby pulled her back to him and lowered his lips to hers. She stood on tiptoe and wrapped her arms around his neck, pulling him closer. His lips were warm and as soft as she remembered. He slowed the kiss, taking his time. It wasn't as passionate as some of their other kisses, but it was tender and cherishing. As if he'd been anticipating this kiss as much as she had and needed to memorize every second.

A solid punch on the side of her stomach from Little Miss jolted her back to the present. Right, they were standing in her front yard. And they had caught the attention of a few on-lookers.

Colby leaned back and placed his hand where the foot continued to kick with determination. "She's glad I'm back too."

"I think she missed your singing."

He bent down and placed a kiss on the side of Madison's belly. "Then I'll have to sing to her more. Which brings me to my next question."

"And that is?"

"I want to marry you. You know that's why I came back, right?"

She nodded, not trusting her voice.

"And I'll wait as long as you want to. But I also would love to marry sooner than later so that her birth certificate lists the mother as Madison Marc."

She bit her lip. *Madison Marc.* The name did funny things to her insides. She wanted that more than anything, but she also wanted to make sure they were getting married for the right reasons.

"The only reason you want to get married sooner is for her birth certificate?"

Colby's face reddened slightly as he pressed his forehead against hers. "Okay, there are a lot of reasons I want to get married sooner than later. I was trying to sound more gentleman-like. I know beyond any doubt that I want to spend the rest of my life with you. But if you need time, I—"

"I don't need time. What are you thinking? This weekend?"

Colby's brow lifted as he leaned back. "I was thinking next month, but hey, I'm game."

"Oh." Her cheeks warmed. "Next month would be good—"

"Nope. You can't take it back. You said this weekend."

"Colby." She let her head fall back as her laughter filled the air. "Why don't we look at the calendar and then decide? And find out when Nate's available."

"I think Nate said he's available this weekend."

She poked him in the side, making him jump.

"Seriously though. I'll wait as long as you need. If you'd like something fancy, that could take some planning, and I want you to have the wedding you want."

"I don't need fancy. I just want the whole world to know you're mine."

"That, Maddie, has always been true." He lowered his mouth to hers again.

Madison did her best to memorize this moment. The moment where her future looked bright for the first time. And it wasn't just because of Colby. Her past didn't disqualify her from God's perfect plan for her life, and she was grabbing that truth with both hands.

It had been four days since Mrs. Nell's words had given Leah new conviction. But Jon had dodged every attempt she'd made to contact him. How could she fail forward if he wouldn't give her a chance? Tonight was the long-anticipated alumni basketball game, so that pretty much ruined her chances of seeing him today as well.

Leah shifted in the rolling office chair as she leaned over the laptop. She opened the folder where she kept emails with copies of the receipts. She clicked on the first receipt and pressed print, then opened the next email.

At least the intruders hadn't smashed the printer and she'd

been organized enough to keep all the receipts together. She'd gotten a quote for the window, and all the artists had submitted their damages. All that was left was turning the claim over to the insurance.

The back door that led to the alley opened and shut just before Jon appeared in the office door. He wore a white, long-sleeve shirt with a red tie. His hair had been trimmed and his face freshly shaven. But there was a distance in his eyes that Leah had never seen before, and it ripped away a little piece of her hope.

"Hi, Leah." He laid his briefcase on the edge of the desk and clicked it open.

"I have the information you'll need for the insurance." She held out the file. Her voice came out thin, and she cleared her throat.

He nodded but didn't reach for it. He pulled two files from his case and shut the lid.

"Jon, about the MIM. I—"

He held up his hand as he moved his case to the floor and laid both folders on the desk. "Let me go first. You've done a great job with opening the MIM. I know the break-in was a setback, but I still believe that this is a good thing for the community." He placed his hand on one of the files. "I can see that you no longer need my assistance in this business venture. I've laid out a model that would make you full owner of the MIM."

He couldn't be serious. "I can't afford to buy you out."

He tapped the file again. "It's a slow buyout over the next several years. If the MIM profits are even on the low end of what we projected, it would be doable for you. In the meantime, I'll turn over one hundred percent control to you."

When she didn't say anything, his hand landed on the other

file. "If you still want out, however, these are the papers for my offer for the full buyout of the business."

She flipped open the file and stared at the first page. The amount he was offering was way too generous. "Why are you doing this?"

His brow furrowed. "Doing what?"

"You're pretty much buying me out for what I'd invested, and we haven't made a dime."

"Because, believe it or not, I'm not all about the bottom line. I want you to be happy, Leah. And if that isn't here"—he finally looked up, emotion rimming his eyes—"then go find what you're looking for. But if you think you still want to make a go at this store on your own, then make that happen."

"But what if I do and it goes under?"

"Then you'll lose money and so will I. But you'll still be Leah—creator of amazing clothes." A small smile tugged at his mouth, but when she returned it, it disappeared.

Right. Because what he wasn't offering was an option for them to move forward together. She'd never be Leah, Jon's girl, again. And that reality hurt more than she ever thought it could.

He picked up his briefcase and took a step back. His eyes hid any hint that he'd ever once had an attachment to her. "Drop the signed set to Marcy. I'll take it from there."

To Marcy. Not to him. She was officially only business now. Leah willed the tears back. As soon as she nodded, he hurried out the back door, slamming it in his wake.

The back door opened again, and she froze. Had he come back?

"Leah?" Her sister's face peeked around the door frame.

"Hey." She forced a calmness into her voice. "I didn't know you guys were coming to Heritage today. Where's my niece?"

"Grant has her down for a nap at Nate and Olivia's. I decided to come see how cleanup's going." Caroline glanced out the back door. "I saw Jon leave as I was pulling in."

Leah's fingers shook as she pointed to the folders. "He was dropping off two sets of papers. One to buy me out for way too much money and the other to let me buy him out for too little."

"That's nice of him."

"Yup." Leah pushed away from her desk and exited the office. She couldn't stare at those folders anymore. "I guess it all worked out."

Caroline followed her to the main room. All the debris had been cleaned up, and other than the absent cash register and boarded-up window, there was little evidence left of the break-in.

Leah stopped at the counter, and Caroline leaned on it next to her. "Then why don't you sound happy?"

"I'm happy. He's being very generous." Leah's voice cracked.

At her sister's knowing look, the dam of emotion broke inside Leah, and a sob shook her body. Her back slid down the counter as she sank to the floor. She wrapped her arms around her knees and dropped her head.

Caroline settled next to her and wrapped her arm around her. Leah buried her head in her sister's shoulder, much like she'd done the day their father left. And like the strong, steady Caroline she was, her sister held her.

After a few minutes, Leah leaned her head back against the counter. "How pathetic am I? He's giving me the option to choose whatever I want. How can both sound horrible?"

"Because neither option includes you and Jon together."

"I didn't want to love him. I shouldn't love him. After what he did to your ranch—"

Caroline placed a hand on Leah's arm. "First of all, I should've never gotten you involved. Grant and I have been so thankful for the foundation's support the past three years. But from the beginning we've trusted that God would provide, and He has. If Jon needed to use that money, we have to trust—and you have to trust—that he made the tough decision that needed to be made. And if what you said was right, he didn't lie to you either. He did what I failed to do—he kept you out of it. Imagine the burden he's been carrying. He was trying to spare you from the same burden."

"But don't you want Grant to share his burdens with you?"

"Yes. But that takes time. It doesn't happen overnight. Jon has been shouldering everything alone since his parents died. I imagine it's a hard habit to break."

"It's too late. I think he made it pretty clear with those files that he's done with me."

"Three years ago, you and I sat on this very floor—almost in this very spot—in a pile of postcards while I cried about Grant. You said to me, 'Caroline, you didn't see Grant's face when he left. He was devastated.' Those were the very words that popped into my head as I walked in today, because I imagine Grant's face that day looked a lot like Jon's did when he walked out of here a few minutes ago."

"But that was different. Grant thought you were marrying Mason. All you had to do was clear that up."

"And Jon thinks you don't love him. Maybe you should clear that up."

Leah turned her head away, pulling her knees tighter. "I've failed him over and over, so why would he forgive me? What if he doesn't love me anymore?"

"Love isn't fickle. It doesn't promise Paris one day and abandon you the next. Face it, Dad didn't love us. But Jon has loved you—really loved you—for a long time. That won't change overnight." When Leah didn't comment, Caroline pushed on. "Yes, you messed up. And you're a fool if you think you'll never mess up in your relationship again. Jon will mess up again. Grant and I mess up. We had quite the argument after he found out that I dragged you into the stuff with the foundation. But we worked through it. So offer each other love and forgiveness, and hopefully grow from the experience."

Mrs. Nell's words floated back. *"Failure can be a good thing, but you have to learn from it and fail forward. Let the failure push you on to something greater."*

"But what if you're wrong and he's done?" Leah asked.

"Then at least you'll know for sure. But do you want to take the chance of missing out on something amazing because you didn't take a chance?"

"He's got that game tonight."

"Then you'd better hurry."

Leah pushed to her feet and grabbed her keys.

"Go get him," Caroline yelled at her as she hurried out the back door.

Leah prayed the whole way to Jon's, hoping this wasn't just another mistake. But even if it was, she'd fail forward. But man, failing hurt.

Leah's heart still pounded in her chest as she rushed up the steps of Jon's house ten minutes later and rang the bell. His Mustang was here—he had to be here.

The large door creaked open, and Abby's smiling face appeared. "Leah? I didn't know you were coming today."

"It was unplanned."

"Oh." Abby's eyebrows shot up. "Let me tell him you're here."

She opened the door wider, and Leah stepped into the entryway. She clicked the door shut and waited as Abby disappeared behind a large set of oak doors that Leah had never seen used before.

When Abby returned several minutes later, her look was slightly less welcoming. "He's on a call. He told me to have you wait in the rec room."

Leah's heart pinched as she entered the room where they'd shared their date night. The pizza bar was gone, of course, but so was the Wii and the trophy. Jon had erased that night from his life. Erased *her* from his life.

"Let me go get you some water," Abby offered before she disappeared out the door.

Leah took in the walls of books again. She ran her finger along the spines, looking for a connection between them, but couldn't find one. Some classics, others new releases.

She lifted the book that lay on the end table and opened it to where the bookmark lay. She froze. It was one of her bookmarks—the ones they'd sold in that high school economics class. She ran her hand over the drawing she'd done almost a decade ago, then slid her fingers along the turquoise ribbon on top. How had she not known he'd kept one?

"Isn't that cool?" Abby appeared behind her, holding out a glass of water. "But don't try and take it. He'll freak. Even though he has like a hundred."

"What?" Leah set the book down and took the water.

"That bookmark. He has like a hundred of them, but every time I took one, he freaked out. Sometimes I'd do it just to bug him."

Leah's gaze skimmed the room. Now that she was looking, several of the books had bookmarks sticking out, and all had her telltale blue ribbon. "I made them."

"You did?" Abby's brows shot up again. "When?"

"In high school. I thought they all got thrown away." But they hadn't. Jon must have saved them.

"Well, now it all makes sense. I'm going to see what is taking Jon so long." Abby disappeared out the door.

It did make sense. Jon had always been there. Jon. He'd been loving and giving, but she was always running. Much like she'd always been running from God.

God hadn't forgotten about her. He'd been there with her the whole time. When her dad left. When her mom died. When she'd gone to Costa Rica. When she'd come home to Heritage. He'd been there every step of the way, but she'd just refused to see it.

Leah's legs gave out, and she dropped onto the couch as she remembered the look on Jon's face when she'd told him she was done. The emptiness in his eyes—so much like her mother's. She'd been so worried about Jon being like her dad that she hadn't seen the truth. *She* had become like her father. She had become the prodigal of her own story.

Abby returned in record time. "He said the call is taking longer than he expected, and then he has the alumni game to get to. But he said you could leave the file with me if you wanted. Did you bring a file?"

Right, because she had failed him, failed them. The question was, would she run like she usually did or choose to fail forward? She was confident that her heavenly Father would always welcome her back. But Jon? She wasn't so sure. Going after him and declaring her love could end in epic disaster, because she hadn't just broken things between them, she'd shattered them.

But she loved him with all her heart, and she'd rather crash and burn than exit early and always wonder what God could have done. It was time to put it all out there, 100 percent.

She turned to Abby. "I need your help."

eighteen

Jon tightened the laces on his high-tops and picked up a ball from the rack. The stands were already packed, but they had another ten minutes before game time. A kid walked by with a little too much swagger in his step and *#14*—Jon's old number—on his jersey. Had he ever been that scrawny or cocky? Probably yes to both.

He stretched against the sleeves of his shirt. The high school had offered jerseys, but some of the alumni couldn't squeeze into those, so they'd gone with T-shirts. Maybe next year he'd donate funds to buy some bigger sizes. Then again, his discomfort was probably less about his clothes and more about a certain redhead.

He dribbled the ball a few times, then scanned the crowd out of habit. Leah wasn't there yet. It would probably be better for his game if she didn't show. He'd taken the easy way out at his house, but he just didn't have it in him for another confrontation today. The few minutes at the MIM had taken everything out of him. She hadn't given any hint to which option she'd choose. Not that it mattered. It was a lose-lose situation for him either way.

If she stayed, he'd see her around Heritage day after day, moving on with some other guy. But if she left, he didn't know when he'd see her again—and that sounded pretty miserable as well.

He sank a warm-up jump shot, then caught someone else's rebound and dunked it.

"Show-off." Luke nudged his shoulder and then dribbled past him to the three-point line.

"I have to remind these kids we aren't old yet."

"Speak for yourself."

Jon grabbed another rebound, but when he went up for the shot, he froze. Leah stood just inside the gym doors, her eyes locked on him. She wore a pink jacket zipped up to her chin and a school color–themed skirt beneath. Did she have something on her face?

When she didn't move toward the bleachers, he jogged over to her. "Hey."

"Hi."

Now that he was closer, he could see that the blue marks on her face read *#14*. He took care to school his features. It meant nothing. Half the people here had something written on their faces. "You're going to give that high school kid more of an ego than he already has."

Her brow creased as if he'd pulled her from some far-off thought. "What?"

"Nothing."

A few people squeezed by them on the way to their seats. One guy stopped and held up his hand for Jon. "Hey, man, don't let us down."

"I'll do my best." He high-fived the guy and glanced back at Leah, who hadn't moved. She obviously wanted to say something, but he wasn't sure how to help her. "Which papers did you leave with Abby?"

That seemed to snap her out of it. She lifted her chin a little higher and met his gaze. "Neither."

"Excuse me?" Jon tugged her to the wall. "I've given you whatever you want, Leah. How can it not be enough?"

She swallowed hard. "I want to remain partners."

Jon broke eye contact as he stared across the gym. "I don't think that's a good idea. You don't need my help anymore."

"I am so sorry about what I said. You're an amazing business partner. I do need you. I don't wish Dale had the company. And I'll do better. I'll be more professional. I can even take a business class if you want."

"Leah." Jon stepped closer, but he couldn't keep the pain out of his voice. He reached his hand out but then let it drop. "It isn't that. You do great. But I've realized that I can't work with you that closely and keep my emotional distance. It'll be easier if . . ."

She placed her hand over her heart. "But I don't want you to keep your distance, emotionally or physically—any kind of distance, really."

Jon paced a few feet away, then back, keeping his voice low. "You say that now that the ranch is saved, but—"

"The ranch is saved?" Her eyes widened, and she gripped his arm. "Really?"

"That's what my long call was about. I got a bunch of other companies that respected my father to help set up a new foundation. The Jonathan George Kensington Jr. Memorial Fund."

"That is awesome. I hadn't heard."

"If you didn't know the ranch was saved, Leah, then what is this all about?" He motioned to her painted face.

"It's about the fact that I love you."

That stopped him. Then again, she had said as much before, but it hadn't made a difference. "You tossed me aside at the first sign of trouble. That isn't love."

"I know." Her fingers gripping his forearms. "I'm sorry. So sorry. I see you now. I really see you. I see all the ways you have loved me for so long. I was so afraid of you failing me that I didn't realize I was failing you over and over." When he didn't react, a small sob escaped her, but she continued. "I'd like to say I'll never mess up again, but I know I will." Her hands followed the curve of his arms up to his biceps, stopping at the edge of his T-shirt. "But I can promise I'll never walk away again."

When her finger trailed under the hem of his sleeve, Jon took a quick breath, his lips parting slightly. "I'm not sure I believe you, Leah." He stepped away from her. "What if I fail your expectations again? What if I make you mad? I can't live always wondering if you're going to take off after every fight. No matter how much I love you, I can't love you enough for the both of us."

"That's just it. Since you've been gone, I haven't slept. I'm barely eating. I'm miserable. I was leaving to keep from being left, but heartache isn't less painful just because I'm choosing it. I am never going to choose that again." She closed the distance again but didn't touch him. "I've been so scared that you'd fail my trust that I didn't see I was failing you over and over. But I'm telling you, I'm all in. I'm willing to do anything to show you—"

"That's just it. I'm not sure if there's anything you can do." He glanced up at the scoreboard. A minute before game time. "I gotta go."

She nodded, and he turned away before he could change his mind. He jogged back to where his team was gathering at the bench.

Luke stepped up next to him. "I nearly let Hannah walk away because I was so angry. Don't make that mistake."

"How do I know it would be different this time?"

"Do you not shoot the ball because you might miss?"

The buzzer sounded overhead, announcing the start of the game, and Jon walked to center court. He took his position, then scanned the crowd again, his eyes immediately finding Leah. In. His. Old. Jersey. She must have been wearing it under the jacket. He stood up straight as her words came floating back. *"I don't think I could ever love anyone enough to wear their jersey."*

He wiped his hands down the sides of his shorts to dry his fingers for the tip-off. *It's just a shirt. It doesn't mean anything.* Then again, with Leah it was *never* just a shirt. She spoke her mood and her heart through her clothes—and in that jersey, she was shouting that she was all in.

Maybe it didn't prove that she'd never walk away again, but then, that was true for anyone. Love couldn't offer a guarantee. It was both people showing up day after day. Today Leah had shown up, and he'd be a fool not to take the shot.

"You ready, Jon?" the ref asked.

"No." He hurried over to the bench and tapped Luke's shoulder. "Take the tip-off."

Jon wove through the crowd, which was no small task since everyone had stood up to see what he was doing. He stopped one bleacher down from Leah, putting him almost eye to eye with her. "You were wrong."

"About?"

"You most definitely can make a jersey look sexy." Jon wrapped his arms around her as his mouth found hers. He pulled her closer, pouring the promise of forever in every movement, every touch. Because this kiss wasn't about today. It wasn't even about tomorrow. It was the assurance that he was going to love her, cherish her, and be there to catch her every time she fell. And he trusted her to do the same.

As the whistles and claps started, Jon pulled back but kept his mouth close to her ear. "Please tell me this means you'll marry me." He was done going halfway. It was all in or go home.

"Yes. I will even go with you to Paris for our honeym—"

Then he was kissing her again, bringing another round of cheering from the crowd. Man, what he wouldn't give for a little bit of privacy.

She pulled back slightly. "Did you just propose to me?"

He let out a deep chuckle. "No. If I propose, you'll know."

"If?" She poked him in the side.

"Got to keep you guessing." He took a full step back now. "As much as I would like to continue this conversation, I've got a game to play." He glanced back at the court, but they had paused the game. "I guess small towns don't get much more exciting than this."

Leah pulled a blue-and-yellow pom-pom from her bag. "I'll be here cheering."

He couldn't hold back his laughter as he ran back to the court. His life would never be boring with Leah, that was for certain.

It took more muscle than Jon had imagined, but eventually they got Otis on Chet's truck and covered him with a tarp. It was well past two in the morning when they backed the truck into the square. Chet had shut off his lights as they entered the center of town, but he needn't have bothered. The place was dead.

With a little finesse and a lot of pushing, they rolled Otis down the ramp and onto the sidewalk. Chet had said he'd used pulleys and harnesses to get Otis up and down on his own, and after doing it with two other guys, Jon had a new respect for that man.

Chet lowered Otis with a turn of the key, then pulled it out and placed it in the bed of Luke's truck. "That's it. I'm officially retiring my position of Otis guard. Do me proud, boys."

Luke pulled Chet into a brief hug. "We will."

Chet patted Jon's back. "And you do your father proud."

Jon nodded but didn't try to comment past the lump in his throat. Chet climbed back in his truck, started it up, and disappeared into the darkness.

Luke waved Jon toward his house. "I think the girls are waiting for us."

Jon followed Luke across the street and into his house.

Hannah and Leah stood around the island, sipping from mugs of tea. Jon wrapped his arms around Leah, soaking in this new normal. Leah was his. It seemed like he'd been waiting for this forever, and just when he'd about given up hope, there she was, loving him for who he was. Flaws and all.

Luke dropped a kiss on Hannah's cheek and opened the freezer. "I think this calls for some ice cream." He pulled a few cartons out of the freezer and set them on the table. Hannah grabbed bowls and spoons, but Luke's hand circled her wrist. "Are you sure I can trust you with those spoons?"

She poked him in the side. "Throw a spoon at a guy one time and he'll never let you forget it."

Luke winked at his wife, and Jon hugged Leah a little closer. He was so ready to be married. Have inside jokes. Make her blush after years together. And he wanted that to start today.

He slipped his hand into hers. "Actually, I need to show Leah something. Can we take a rain check on the ice cream?"

Hannah nodded. "Of course. We'll have a lot of opportunities for ice cream nights in the future."

Jon tugged Leah out the door and across the street to where Otis now sat.

Leah sat on the hippo's back and ran her hand over his ear. "I must say, it's good to see him back home, even if this did ruin a bit of the mystery."

"But now we'll get to be a part of the mystery for the next generation." When she nodded, he sat next to her and stretched his legs out. "Do you know why I chose this spot for Otis?"

"It was near Luke's house?"

"You were standing right about here the spring of your freshman year of high school the first time you went from Leah, a girl at our school, to Leah, the girl I had to get to know."

"Really?"

"You were talking with Hannah and Janie. And I was there in Luke's driveway playing one-on-one with him. You were wearing jean shorts with a rainbow ribbon down the side and an orange shirt."

"I do remember that. Those were vintage nineties shorts. You stared at me like I was an alien."

Jon let his head fall back. "No, I looked at you like you had turned my mind to jelly. I almost came over and talked to you, but you rushed away."

"I should've stayed. I'm sorry it took me so long to really see you."

"Probably for the best. We were kids and had a lot of growing up to do. But I'm glad you see me now." He shoved his hand in his pocket until he found what he was looking for. "I've been carrying this around for a while."

"What?" Leah's head jerked toward him.

He stood, turned to face her, and dropped to one knee. He pulled the solitaire diamond ring from his pocket and held it out for her to see. "This was my mom's. I always knew one day I'd give it to my future wife. And I'll admit, every time I imagined that moment, your face was smiling back at me."

Leah's hand flew to her face.

"Leah Williams, will you—"

"Yes, yes!"

He lifted an eyebrow. "I haven't asked you yet. I mean, what if I was going to ask you to mow my lawn?"

"Jonathan George Kensington the Third, if you—"

He stood and pulled her up into his arms, pressing his lips against hers. "Marry me?"

"Yes. Absolutely yes."

———

So much excitement in just a couple days. Leah hung up the phone and rang up the next customer. They'd been open for over a month, but last weekend's Black Friday sale had given them hope that they had found their market. Things had slowed down this weekend, which was good, with Jon away at meetings in Chicago. But he was supposed to be back for Heritage's first annual tree lighting in the square, which was set to start in an hour.

She rang up the customer's last item and then added everything to the bag with the printed receipt.

"Thank you." The older woman's face wrinkled with her smile.

"Thank *you*." Leah waved as the woman pushed out the door. "Come again."

"Oh, I'll be back, and I'll bring my friends."

Leah followed the woman out and flipped the sign to CLOSED. Before she could lock the door, Olivia and Caroline rushed in.

Olivia gripped her arm. "Did you hear?"

"You mean about Lyla Marc? Seven pounds, eight ounces. Born forty-five minutes ago." Leah walked back behind the counter and punched a few buttons to close out the cash register. "I still can't believe Madison worked a full day yesterday."

"I know." Olivia clapped as she squealed. "I can't wait to get my hands on that baby."

"Well, from what Madison says, you'll have to stand in line, because Colby has yet to put her down." Leah leaned on the counter. "She said he's already made up three songs with the name Lyla in them."

"And I heard 'Clay Feet' was number one this week. Talk about an exciting week for the Marcs." Olivia lifted one of Leah's newest dresses from the rack and held it up against herself. "I bet his label is glad they gave in and let him record it with Madison."

"I'm so happy for them." Caroline gazed around the store. "Do you have anything I could buy baby Lyla?"

"There are some quilts and knitted headbands on the second floor." Leah pointed up and to the left, and the two girls walked in that direction.

Caroline paused on the steps and pointed to the old WIFI sign hanging on the back wall. "By the way, I love that, and I think Grandpa and Grandma would have loved it too."

Leah nodded as she swallowed back a lump in her throat.

Jon breezed through the front door. He leaned across the counter to drop a kiss on her lips, then froze, squinting at her shoulder peeking from behind her apron. "What are you wearing?"

She pulled off her apron and turned from side to side, modeling her newest project. She'd taken one of his jerseys from

Valencia Basket and remade it into a winter top. "What can I say, I've missed you since you've been gone. And I am addicted to the jersey now."

"I told you jerseys could be sexy." Jon winked at her and leaned forward to claim that kiss. "And I have dozens of those, so feel free to get creative." He peeked over the counter. "If you tell me that you're also wearing another one of those colorful little skirts again, I might beg you to skip this tree thing."

She pushed his hand away and tried to look stern. "Six months to go, buddy. Don't you forget it. Besides, I told you I remade that into something longer."

"Such a shame." Jon shook his head. "But with this type of welcome, I should leave more often."

"Not a chance. It's time for you to stay put."

"Yes, ma'am."

The door opened again, and Nate walked in, followed by Janie, Thomas, Hannah, Luke holding Joseph, Grant holding Vangie, and Jimmy licking an ice cream cone.

Caroline made her way down the stairs. "Are you all ready to walk over to the square?"

"Austin and Libby are meeting us there," Olivia announced as she followed Caroline.

"I'll close if you're all okay leaving by the back door." When no one objected, Leah walked to the front door and locked it. As she turned back, she glanced around. "Do you realize that three years ago, the five of us girls were all sitting around the old counter in this very store, bemoaning the fact we'd never find love in this town?"

"Technically I was in Europe, bemoaning over Skype." Janie snuggled into Thomas's arms.

Hannah wrapped her arm around Luke and pulled him

closer, then ran her hand over Jimmy's floppy hair. "And now look at us. We've had four weddings—"

"Soon to be five." Leah waved her hand. "And the addition of one child, two babies—"

"Soon to be three." Caroline waved her hand too.

"What?" Everyone turned to stare at her.

"Turns out we have another surprise arriving in July. It wasn't planned."

Before anyone could fully react, Olivia's hand waved in the air as Nate said, "Make that four babies."

Leah couldn't keep the smile from her face as everyone started offering hugs and congratulations. Little had they known back then that God had such great things in store for each of them. They'd just had to wait on His perfect timing.

Acknowledgments

It's amazing to think I have written three full-length novels. I learn so much with every one, and this was no exception. In this book I learned to lean into God and create with Him. What a joy writing this book was—not always easy but a tangible example of God's daily grace in my life. It makes me so excited to write the next one.

And like with the other books, I have so many to thank . . .

My Lord and Savior—As I mentioned above, creating with God has been such a joy. Although I am reminded of my shortcomings often when I write a book, His daily portion of grace and love is always more than enough.

Scott Faris—Not only are you my champion, my love, and my hero, but you even read my stories and offer so much insight to make them stronger. You give up so much to make this dream possible. You're my biggest blessing. And thank you for not giving up on me when I was just as fickle as Leah.

Zachary, Danielle, and Joshua—Thank you for meal help, housecleaning, and even reminding me to drink water. You are such blessings to my life. I couldn't do this without you.

Dave and Joyce Thompson—Thank you again for all you do to support my writing. You guys are such a gift. I wouldn't be the mother, wife, or author I am without your support and lending hand.

Dave and Jan Faris—You are both such a gift. Thank you for all your support and for raising an amazing son. I couldn't do this without him.

Andrea Nell—Your continued friendship means so much to me. I would not be where I am today without you.

Mandy Boerma, Janette Miller, and Lindsay Harrel—Thank you for reading an early version of this story to make it stronger. I dearly appreciate each of you.

My Book Therapy—I am a published writer because of My Book Therapy, and that is not an exaggeration. The teaching, the books, the retreats—they build my career. I thank you.

Susan May Warren, Beth Vogt, Rachel Hauck, Lisa Jordan, Alena Tauriainen, and Melissa Tagg—Thank you for your encouragement, prayers, and support. You are always pushing me further. You are all a gift in my life.

My agent, Wendy Lawton—Thank you for believing in me and my stories. And thank you to the entire Books & Such team. It's a privilege to be a Bookie!

My editor, Vicki Crumpton—Thank you for taking a chance on me and my stories. Thank you for your wisdom, guidance, and care for my stories. You make me a better writer, and I am so grateful!

The Revell team—Being a part of this house is a dream come true. You are all so amazing, and knowing you and working with you is such a gift. Each one of you is a rock star at your job, and my books are blessed by you living out the gifts God gave each of you, so thank you! I am so excited to be a part of the family.

Libby, Hannah, Leah, Danielle, and Ellie—Thanks, girls, for lending your names to the series. It has been fun.

My WiWee girls, my huddle girls, and my AZ Tuesday night writing group—God has blessed me with so many writer friends, and I appreciate each of you more than you know.

Tari Faris has been writing fiction for more than thirteen years, and it has been an exciting journey for the math-loving dyslexic girl. She had read less than a handful of novels by the time she graduated from college, and she thought she would end up in the field of science or math. But God had other plans, and she wouldn't trade this journey for anything. As someone told her once, God's plans may not be easy and they may not always make sense, but they are never boring.

Tari has been married to her husband for nineteen wonderful years, and they have three sweet children. In her free time, she loves drinking coffee with friends, rock hounding with her husband and kids, and distracting herself from housework. Visit her at tarifaris.com to learn more about her upcoming books and to read what happened the day Leah and Jon were on the river.

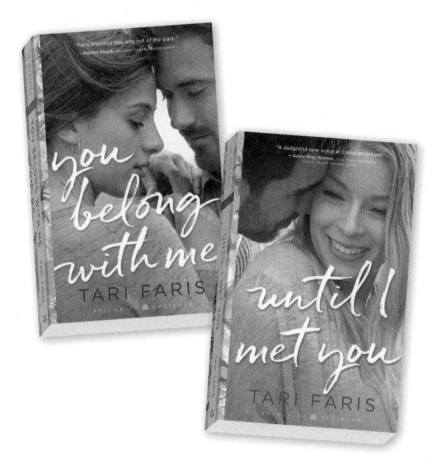

Meet *Tari*

www.tarifaris.com

 Tari.Faris.Author   FarisTari

 TariFarisAuthor   Ⓟ TariFaris

Be the First to Hear about New Books from Revell!

Sign up for announcements about new and upcoming titles at

RevellBooks.com/SignUp

@RevellBooks

Don't miss out on our great reads!

LET'S
TALK
ABOUT
BOOKS

- Share or mention the book on your social media platforms. Use the hashtag **#SinceYouveBeenGone**.

- Write a book review on your blog or on a retailer site.

- Pick up a copy for friends, family, or anyone who you think would enjoy and be challenged by its message!

- Share this message on Twitter, Facebook, or Instagram:
  I loved #SinceYouveBeenGone by @TariFaris // @RevellBooks

- Recommend this book for your church, workplace, book club, or small group.

- Follow Revell on social media and tell us what you like.

 RevellBooks

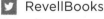 RevellBooks

 RevellBooks

pinterest.com/RevellBooks

219823199884468